C000054582

This is a work of fiction.
actual events, methods, tec\
or dead, is entire
References to office holders or other people in the EU,
the Foreign Office, the Home Office, the National
Criminal Intelligence Service, the Secret Intelligence
Service, the Police or any other body are also fictional
and are not intended to relate to any actual person
who may have been in the post or position mentioned
at any time.

www.jo-calman.com

ISBN 979-8-5520-3802-2

An Inner Circle

by Jo Calman

From the First Circle thus I downward went
Into the Second, which girds narrower space,
But greater woe compelling loud lament.
Minos waits awful there and snarls…
…and he, omniscient as concerning sin,
Sees to what circle it belongs in Hell…

Dante Alighieri – Inferno, Canto V

Chapter 1 – London, January 2003.

A woman was running hard, being chased by someone. Her short blonde hair was a beacon in the fading light, guiding her pursuer. The blonde veered off the path to cut across a grassed area but quickly realised her mistake as she lost her footing on the muddy surface. She fell, but was on her feet again in no time and she surged for the solid tarmac once more. She was fast but her pursuer was gaining on her.

As she started up the incline towards the lights on Chelsea Bridge the chaser's footsteps closed in. She felt a hand grip her shoulder.

"Gotcha!"

The blonde stopped running and bent to catch her breath.

"I'll outrun you one day, Dunn," she gasped.

"In your dreams Kelso!" Mel replied. "Let's jog back to warm down. Good run, Jake. I think you're getting quicker."

Commander Julia Kelso of the Metropolitan Police looked at her friend and they set off at a steady pace across Chelsea Bridge towards Dolphin Square.

In Julia Kelso's apartment at Dolphin Square the friends showered and dressed. Julia made them coffee and they sat and talked.

"So how were the holidays for you, Mel?"

Mel, short for Demelza, Dunn, a senior intelligence analyst at the National Criminal Intelligence Service or NCIS, had met Julia Kelso less than a year before. Since then they had become extremely close friends.

They had almost nothing in common, which probably explained why they liked each other so much.

"Peace and good will to all, naturally, except in my family. Mum and Dad were fine, just pleased to have everyone there for once. Brother Zack brought his new girlfriend - a bit of a wet dishcloth but I think she's set on getting married once his divorce from the last one comes through. She made him all tense and defensive, which really wound up my little sister Morwenna - I really curse Winston Graham and his bloody Poldark books. She was there with two of her kids. Her ex had the other two. There was quite a bit of bitchiness going on. Wenn told me she's had enough of men and she's thinking of going properly gay this year. Anyhow, Christmas was quite nice, but there's always that dead bit between Boxing Day and New Year when no one really knows what to do so they start fighting. I was almost hoping for some kind of major crime wave so I could run back to London and go to work."

"You're a festive soul, Mel Dunn! I don't know why I like you at all!" Jake Kelso said.

"Yes you do. Now, what did you get up to? Do you heathens do Christmas or is it just the anagram that excites you?"

"Anagram?"

"Mahogany or whatever it's called."

"Hogmanay, twit. We *do* have Christmas, but New Year's more fun. I suppose it is a bit pagan, celebrating the birth of a new year and the circle of life and everything. I stayed with Mum and Dad, just the three of us. It was nice. Very grown up and civilised. I'm not sure how Dad kept it up for over a week - he's normally a total rascal. They keep probing to find out why I'm not married. I'm sure Mum wants a grandchild or two before I'm past it."

"What do you tell them?"

"I just change the subject. I can't really tell them about you and Alf, can I?"

Julia Kelso, Mel Dunn and the person formerly known as DCI Alan (Alf) Ferdinand had developed a complex and unusual friendship, a close one in which - among other things - they all went to bed with each other from time to time, but only ever in pairs. Mel and Jake 'did it', in Jake's terminology, every few weeks in what they had both come to regard as the perfect end to a good workout. Mel hadn't seen Alf since they all left France in the autumn, but Jake had travelled to see him once or twice in Portugal where he was currently living. Mel had a detached attitude towards sex - for her it was a purely physical but necessary thing which she did with a small number of trusted friends and which involved a lot of technical skill - while Jake and Alf had genuine and warm feelings for each other. Not that they could do anything overt about it, of course. Jake no longer tried to rationalise or figure it out. Instead, she and Alf just enjoyed the exuberant physicality of Mel Dunn and the close comfort they had with each other. Jake and Alf couldn't say why Mel fitted with their relationship, she just did. And as long as everyone stayed happy about it there was no need to change anything.

"What about Major Evans from the SAS, Action Man? Have you seen him again?" Mel asked.

7

"He's Lieutenant Colonel Evans now. I had dinner with Justin before Christmas," Jake said.

"Was that the third or fourth date?"

"I wouldn't necessarily call them dates, but it was number four."

"So have you shagged him yet?"

"You can take the girl out of Yorkshire but you can't take Yorkshire out of the girl, can you? Since you're asking, yes - just the once after we had dinner. He came here to the restaurant and it just sort of happened when we came up here for a nightcap. I don't think we'll do it again, though."

"Why? Was he rubbish?"

"You're awful nosy! Not rubbish so much, just a bit over organised, like it was a military operation. It was quite nice though, he knows what to do. But that's not the reason I don't think we'll be doing it again. I'm pretty sure he's still sleeping with his ex-wife - he was with her and their kids for Christmas and he let slip they share a room 'so the children don't get confused', even though they're divorced. I don't think Justin shares a room, meaning a bed, with his ex and just goes to sleep. Mostly though it's because he's getting posted to Abuja as Military Attaché in a few weeks. I think that's quite a long way to go for a militaristic bonk."

"I didn't know you had it in you, Kelso, I'm proud of you. Abuja? In Nigeria?"

"Is there another one?"

"I suppose not. So that means you're stuck with just me and Alf the dead detective for your entertainment then. Your mum will be disappointed."

"He's only administratively dead. Now, are you staying over? You're welcome to, but I'm the senior officer on-call from any minute now."

With that Julia's phone rang.

"Here we go," she said.

"I'll leave you to it if it's all the same. Last time we spent the night together while you were on duty it was like trying to have a cuddle in a call centre."

Julia picked up the call as Mel blew her a kiss and left.

"Commander Kelso," she said. The weekend was starting.

On her way to the station Mel's phone pinged. A text message from Jilly, one of her small and select group of sex partners. Jilly and Frank were wondering if Mel wanted to come over on Saturday night?

"Yes please x," Mel sent back.

Chapter 2

Across London late that same Friday afternoon Vesna Nikolić, who they called 'Venus', was running for her life. It was dark but strangely warm for a winter afternoon, and she had escaped. They were chasing her; she could hear running footsteps getting closer, but she would *not* go back, she wouldn't let them take her again. They had brought her to that room early in the morning. They allowed her only the thin off-white coat with a hood, the one they always made her wear. Beneath it she wore nothing at all, just the coat and a pair of old flip flops. In the room it had been worse than ever before.

The Albanian boys were there, Ilir and Pali, the Krasniqis. They were brothers. Large, powerfully built, and very stupid. Their much brighter brother Luan was the one who had caught her and got her into this. Luan wasn't there, he never was, but the slimy Englishman was, the one they called the Director. He made the movies.

When she first arrived in London they sold her as a prostitute. They had made a lot of money because she was a virgin and some men will pay a lot to take a girl's virginity, especially by force. That first time she thought she would be safe. There were two other girls there, from Kosovo like she was, even if they were Albanian. She thought they would help her. Instead they stood and watched as he tore off her clothes, then they pulled her down and held her for him. When he nodded they flipped her over. When it was over and he had gone they comforted her, saying she had been a good girl and that the second time would not be so

10

bad. They washed her and put soothing creams on her torn parts. They gave her a nappy to wear, and a dressing gown. Vesna wanted to kill them.

After that first time she refused to cooperate, no matter how much they beat her. The punters didn't enjoy a surly girl who stayed as rigid and unmoving as a plank of wood and soon no one wanted her, so they made her do the movies instead. With the movies they could physically force her to do things, dreadful things, because there was no punter to please or be worried about, just the 'actors', usually the Krasniqi brothers.

Today she had been chained to a metal frame for hours while the Director filmed it all and gave instructions. After several hours he called 'cut' and told the boys to get ready for the finale. When it was all over they congratulated each other, laughing loudly.

"Cut! It's a wrap!" the Director called, as if it was a proper film. The Krasniqi brothers collapsed onto a sofa, joking about her as they lit cigarettes. They left 'Venus' chained to the frame, beaten, bruised and bleeding. Eventually the Director unlocked the manacles and pulled her upright. She kept her face rigid despite the pain and the humiliation.

"Not bad, Vesna. But you should try to look like you're enjoying it a bit. Not too much though!" He laughed.

Inside Vesna raged. In here she was 'Venus', never Vesna, it was the only advantage she had, to be someone else while these terrible things were happening. The Director had turned his back. He had left the manacles and the long chain draped on the frame. She seized them.

Turning swiftly, she swung the manacles like a hammer, hitting Ilir Krasniqi on the side of his head. He roared and fell to the floor. Pali rose to his feet, swearing loudly in Albanian. She swung the manacles again, aiming between his gaping legs. He collapsed writhing on the floor.

The Director was a small man and she ran at him. She flailed the manacles and he cowered. She grabbed the tatty coat and ran for the door as she pulled it on. The door wasn't double-locked and she opened it. She flew down the long staircase to the outer door of the building and she ran. She had no idea where she was. She saw the van they had brought her in. It was parked in the driveway of the flats. She ran the other way. There was a footbridge over a main road and she climbed the steps up to it. Her bare feet were getting torn by thorns and broken glass but she didn't care. She had to get away. Behind her she heard the street door of the flats crash open. They were coming for her. They couldn't afford to lose her; their brother would make them pay.

Breathless, Vesna reached the level part of the bridge. She was dismayed at the length of it, but she kept running. She felt the blood running down her legs, from her waist and from her ankles, and her feet were slipping on the damp ground. A voice not far behind her was yelling in Albanian and Kosovan.

"Stop running, you stupid whore!" the voice shouted.

She ran on. Halfway across the bridge Vesna knew she wasn't going to make it. She knew what she had to do. She wasn't going back. They were *not* going to have her again!

Vesna pulled herself onto the high parapet of the bridge. She turned to face the person chasing her. It was Ilir, blood still pouring from a wound behind his ear. She let herself smile as she cursed him in Kosovan. He grabbed for her legs. The blood and mud had made her ankles slick and his hands slipped off. She aimed a kick at his head, then she stepped backwards off the bridge into space.

Ilir swore. He turned and ran from the scene, back towards the flats. They had to get out of there. Their brother would be furious. 'Venus' still owed them a lot of money and the revenues from the porn films came in more slowly than from the prostitutes. Their brother would want payment, but that would come later. For now he and Pali and the Director had to clear out the flat and get away before anyone came looking. He heard sirens approaching from Holloway, coming up the hill to where 'Venus' had landed in the main road. Hopefully the police would think it was just another suicide off a bridge that was famous for such things and wouldn't coming looking too closely until they were gone.

Chapter 3

Julia was in her office at Scotland Yard on Saturday morning. She liked the quiet of the building, which, despite its 24/7 operations, was largely deserted at weekends. The duty inspector from the Service Intelligence Bureau sat opposite her sipping the coffee she had just made him.

"What's new, Brian?" she asked.

DI Brian Kearney, one of the inspectors in the SIB, was a long-serving traditional officer, but bright and astute all the same.

"There was an apparent suicide last evening, ma'am. A girl went off the bridge over the Archway Road - sadly quite a few jumpers use it. It's a long drop on to a busy road and not many survive. This girl didn't, that's for sure. She was young, maybe 18 or 19. Thing is she was only wearing a lightweight coat, nothing else at all. No identification, documents, handbag, nothing. Just the coat, and a single cigarette in one pocket."

"What's significant about this, Brian? Sure it's tragic, but why is SIB picking up on it?"

"The post-mortem won't be done until Monday, but the preliminary examination tends to suggest this girl had been subjected to repeated multiple sexual assaults over quite a long period. The pathologist will be able to say more once he's done his worst, but if the initial indicators are correct I don't doubt she's been the victim of serious crime. Homicide are reluctant to get involved and time is ticking. Evidence could be getting lost. I wanted to bring this to your attention in case you wanted to bang some heads together."

"Fair enough, Brian. I know homicide have their hands full, but this sounds like it needs a closer look. But I'm getting a sense that there's something else on your mind. What is it?"

"Frankly, ma'am, I think this girl's been trafficked. I can't back it up, there is no identification or apparent geographical DNA pointers or anything, but it has all the signs. The sexual injuries, the lack of any documentation, no possible matches on missing persons records. It's just a hunch. I think this girl may have been lured to the UK or kidnaped and smuggled in and then put to work as a prostitute. My granddaughter's the same sort of age, and I feel sorry for this one."

Julia looked at the serious officer opposite her. He was a good detective, and a good man.

"I'm with you Brian. Let's ramp this up."

Julia picked up her phone and dialled the homicide command operations room. The duty Chief Inspector was in her office within a few minutes. She poured him a coffee and with a charming smile left him with the clear impression that she expected him to get a team to Archway Road immediately and treat the apparent suicide as a possible rape and murder, and she expected it to be done right now. He scuttled off, coffee untouched, and did exactly what she wanted.

"Anything else, Brian?" she asked.

Kearney went through the rest of the overnight reports suggesting actions and asking her for instructions where needed. As always, a London weekend was the backdrop for multiple tragedies and some comedies that affect ordinary people as well as the criminal classes. The police had to administer help and assistance as much as enforcement, and in a setting as complex and diverse as London there was never a dull moment.

Late that afternoon the homicide Detective Chief Inspector called to give Julia an update on the unidentified girl who had died so suddenly under the Archway Road bridge. Despite some overnight drizzle the team had been able to follow a trail of fading but still discernible bloody foot marks from the middle of the footbridge back towards a large block of flats not far from the footbridge. They had also found other blood stains, including a very smudged palmprint on the bridge parapet. The palmprint was large and probably male, it certainly wasn't the dead girl's. In the block of flats they had identified a stairwell door that had blood on it and they had narrowed their search down to one of three or four flats from where the dead girl may have come. Did they have her authority to enter any or all of them as they saw fit? Julia said yes.

An hour later he called back saying they had identified the probable flat in which the girl may have been raped. There were signs of recent hasty evacuation but there was enough blood and some traces of what could be semen and other bodily fluids to give grounds for a full forensic search.

By Monday morning they were no nearer to identifying the dead girl, but they had enough DNA and other forensic evidence to start drawing up profiles of the rapists and / or killers. Julia said well done.

She went to the mortuary herself on Monday morning to see the body and speak to the pathologist. She looked down on the serene face of the still nameless Vesna Nikolić, which still had a faint smile. Her injuries were appalling. The fall had shattered her spine and flattened the back of her skull, but worse still were the wounds to her genital area, and the bruises and rope marks.

"This girl has been abused repeatedly and violently over a prolonged period. There are signs of healed and partially healed wounds as well as fresh ones. Internally she's suffered multiple assaults with foreign objects and her reproductive organs would be irreparably damaged if she were still alive." The pathologist spoke calmly and quietly, but Julia could see he was seething.

"Any idea where she might have come from, who she was?"

"I can tell you she wasn't, isn't, British by ethnicity. I would say she's lived most of her life outside the UK. Her dental work, such as it is, suggests eastern Europe or the Balkans. The cigarette found in her coat pocket was an Albanian brand - 'Porti Blend' - although the girl wasn't a regular smoker. Her hair colour isn't natural or particularly well done, but in my view it was fully dyed no more than three, possibly four, months ago judging by the root growth, and it's been partially touched up here and there. She wasn't particularly well nourished, which is common these days among inhabitants of some of the Balkan states, especially Kosovo since the war. We can do some tests on bone tissue to try to date periods of poor nutrition. If they coincide with the Yugoslav civil war or the Kosovo conflict I'd say there's a fair chance that's where she is from. I'll let you know. I don't think she's ethnic Albanian, though - a full DNA profile should give us more of an indication of her origins."

"Thank you, professor," said Julia, "the poor girl didn't deserve this."

"No one does, Commander."

"Of course not, you're right." Julia left the autopsy room feeling both angry and incredibly sad at the same time.

Chapter 4

Back in her office Julia asked her assistant Raj to find out who in the Met was an expert on human trafficking. An hour later she was surprised to find out that there was practically no institutional knowledge of the subject, but Raj had found a sergeant at West End Central who had taken a special interest in the eastern European sex-workers who were starting to appear on the London scene. Julia asked Raj to get the officer in to see her.

Police Sergeant Kim Morris appeared in Julia's office just after lunch. She looked tired. She was probably in her mid-forties but was turning prematurely grey. She was wearing an anorak over her police uniform and she smelled vaguely of stale tobacco.

"Afternoon, ma'am. PS Morris. Raj said you wanted to see me."

"Come in and sit down, Sergeant Morris, or shall I call you something a bit less formal?" Julia treated the tired woman to one of her bright smiles.

"It's Kim, ma'am."

"And I'm Julia. How are you doing, Kim?"

"OK. Just off the early shift - a quick changeover from a late one yesterday. Sorry if I seem a bit droopy."

"I'm the on-call this week so I sympathise with your sleep deprivation. I asked Raj to find me an expert on human trafficking. It seems that in the whole of the Metropolitan Police you might be it. For some reason human trafficking is seen as an immigration issue rather than a crime. I'm going to try to fix that, I hope. I'm interested because of a young girl who jumped off the Archway Road bridge on Friday evening. I think she may have been a victim of human trafficking and involved in the sex trade."

"I wouldn't say I'm an expert ma'am, sorry - Julia. There are a lot of young foreign girls showing up on the scene these days, around Soho and the West End. They try to avoid us, the cops, but I've had a few chats with some of them. Mostly they're terrified, of us and of their pimps. A picture I've put together from talking to them is that Girl A is groomed in her home country and enticed to the UK with a fake offer of legitimate work or education. The groomer - I think the groomers are organised crime gang members and can be male or female - says they can arrange to get entry visas and work permits as well as travel to the UK. Girl A hands over her passport, if she has one. If not, the groomer can get her one of those too.

"Girl A is duly shipped over here, and on arrival her passport is taken off her again by the gang members who meet her. She's told that she owes a lot of money to the people who got her to England and she'll have to work it off before she gets her passport back. If she's reluctant she gets beaten up or raped, and one way or another she ends up on the game.

"Usually the only way she gets her passport back is by joining the gang as a willing member. She's never going to work off the 'debt', which increases by the day. Once in a blue moon one of the girls will manage to escape and if she's lucky she'll get into a women's refuge. If she isn't lucky she'll be recaptured by the gang and punished, or caught by us and deported. Once they're too knackered to work the

"I know him vaguely. Bit of a strange bloke, he's on the illegal immigration unit. Why?"

"I want to know more about human trafficking. There was a young girl killed on Friday evening. I think she was trafficked into the sex trade here in London, possibly from the Balkans. I'm told Jerry Keynes is the expert."

"I can go and see him if you like. As it happens I've been reading up on it myself recently. It's a really nasty business, people trafficking."

"Go and see him, Mel. If you think he's the business I'd like to meet him myself."

"OK. How's your week looking?"

"Busy. I'm going out on vice patrol in Soho on Wednesday."

"Will you be wearing your fishnets?"

Julia hung up.

Chapter 5

Jerry Keynes was one of those men who could have been anywhere between 30 and 60 years old. In fact he was in his early forties and had been in the immigration service since leaving school at 18. He was single, lived alone and drank far too much. He was stick thin because he hardly ate anything. Because he was unencumbered by a partner or family he'd had quite a few foreign postings to UK Embassies and High Commissions processing visa applications and liaising with the locals over deportations. He hadn't been too keen on India, but had developed a strange attachment to the chaos of West Africa. He had worked in Lagos and Accra, after which he was rewarded with a two-year stint in Nairobi. An unfortunate booze-fuelled incident at the famous Norfolk Hotel accelerated his return to London, and after serving a year's penance at Heathrow he was posted to the National Criminal Intelligence Service, if only to get him away from the airside bars.

Mel called him. He was free, as usual, and would be happy to chat. They met outside in the weak winter sunshine. Keynes lit a cigarette.

"Hi Jerry. I'm Mel Dunn from intelligence development. I hear you're the guru on people trafficking."

"Am I? That's a worry." He had a boyish smile, but Mel found him a bit creepy.

"Kim Morris from West End Central said you were. She said you were trying to put a study together. I'm an analyst and I was wondering if I

"The traffickers are getting help. High level, or at least influential help. That's why I need to know who I'm talking to. I'm comfortable talking to Sergeant Kim Morris, she's just a worker bee like me. But your 'senior' friend? Not so easy."

"How can you check her out?"

"That's just it. I can't. I need to make a judgement, or get her referenced by someone I can trust."

"Do you trust me, Jerry?"

"I don't know, Mel."

He ground out his cigarette in the wall-mounted ashtray. He looked at her.

"I'd like to, though. I'm starting to go paranoid on my own."

"Give me all the data you've got, Jerry. Phone numbers, emails, names, addresses, car numbers, anything. I might be able to help you make sense of it and see if the traffickers are getting the help you think they are. No promises, but I can give it a go using all my analytical tricks."

"I'll think about it, Mel. Thanks for the offer, but I'll need some time to reflect."

Jerry Keynes walked away. Mel Dunn watched him go, letting out a long breath. Was he just another fruitcake, or was he on to something? After the last two cases with Jake Kelso and Alan Ferdinand she was fed up to the back teeth with corruption and intrigue. Just a few months ago Julia Kelso had been shot at and had to kill someone to save herself. Alf too had taken out some very nasty people, but there had been too much killing. She went back to her office and thought about what she would say to Jake Kelso. She missed Ferdinand, whose advice and counsel she felt

29

an urgent need for. That evening she would use the covert email to contact him and ask him for his thoughts. Mel took a deep breath and decided to stall Jake Kelso for a while.

Chapter 6

Kim Morris called Julia Kelso on Tuesday. She would pick her up outside St James's Park tube at 5pm. It might be a long evening. Julia was waiting as Kim pulled up in an anonymous looking Ford Focus. She was wearing smart jeans and a casual jacket. Kim was less smart and more casual. She still smelt of stale tobacco smoke, as did the car's interior. Julia didn't comment.

"I thought we'd start with a couple of brothels I know of that use foreign girls," Kim started. "One's in north Islington, the other's on the Bethnal Green / Hackney boundary. I think both are Albanian run, but the areas aren't particular Albanian stamping grounds. They're handy for the trade, the punters. On main routes to and from the City and not too far from the stations. They do a lot of early evening business. Soho and the West End street girls get busier a bit later in the evening. I'm not even going to start on the call-girls and 'escorts' working the hotels, that's a whole other story."

"You say that the places you're taking me aren't particular Albanian areas. Why not?" Julia asked.

"Too pricy, plus there are too many established British crims working those places. You've heard of the Adams family, and not like in the movies? Well they run Islington and Holloway, it's their home patch. The Albanians are wary of them, so the operations they have going are quiet and discreet, at least on the outside.

"Albanians are settling in the poorer areas further east and south east. They're still relatively new on the scene so no doubt they'll develop an established community in due course, like every other migrant group has."

Kim Morris drove in a slightly distracted fashion. Julia was guessing she was over-stressed.

"How long have you been doing this, Kim? The vice beat I mean," Julia asked.

"Too long! Feels like for ever. It's not good for the home life I can tell you - too many long late evenings, too much time hanging out in bars with disreputable types, and I don't just mean coppers."

"Who's at home?"

"Am I married you mean? No, I'm not. I've got two kids though, twins. I live down south, in Sutton. It's a slog, but property is still quite cheap. I've had to take on an au pair to look after the kids while I'm out working. Au pair sounds posh but it's not. Flora was one of the lucky ones who got away. We kind of hit it off and she's now my au pair, all official like, with a work permit and everything."

"She was trafficked?"

"Yes. And raped and put on the game. But she's a decent kid. She's one of the reasons I keep doing this job. If I can help rescue a Flora every now and then it kind of makes it worth it."

"Does she ever talk about being trafficked?"

"She doesn't like to. Once in a while if we're chatting over a glass of something she might loosen up a bit, not about the trafficking so much as about home, where she comes from, her old family and her life before. I asked her once, very early on, about how she came to be in London. She started shaking and crying, traumatised like. So I let it drop. When I found

32

Chapter 7

Earlier that evening in her flat in Raynes Park Mel Dunn had been communicating with Alan 'Alf' Ferdinand. She would always think of him as 'Alf' despite his having been through at least two names since he was last Alan Ferdinand. It was a long story.

She went through everything that Jerry Keynes had told her. Her analytical mind had been working overtime and she had been trying to work out what sort of corrupt leverage would be needed to facilitate human trafficking within Europe on the scale it had reached. In talking to Alf, albeit in typed form using the draft email system they had adopted, a system in which one person could type messages which could read by the other person but nothing was ever sent between addresses. Alf asked good questions and challenged some of her assumptions.

Mel's conclusion was a scary one. The scale of human trafficking could not be facilitated by a single corrupt individual, no matter how high up he or she was. There were too many agencies, people, processes and even countries involved. So it was either an awful lot of corrupt people - unlikely as it was inevitable that some of them would have been identified and caught by now - or it was a small group of very well placed individuals working together. Mel was aware of a few arrests of visa clerks and such like, but they were small fry and could never be tied to a group. The idea of a cartel of corruption was one that filled her with dread.

Alf ended the conversation with a message saying he thought Mel should come to see him - he was in

Portugal. It was up to her whether she discussed her thoughts with Kelso first. Alf was advising against Mel sharing her suspicions with Jake just yet on the grounds that she was a senior police officer and certain courses of action would need to be followed. It might be better to let Mel's theories develop a bit first. Mel tended to agree.

"I'll book a flight to Lisbon either tomorrow or Friday and let you know."

"Try to make it tomorrow. I'll meet you at the airport." Alf had responded.

Mel smiled to herself. She'd missed Alf and it would be good to see him again. She didn't relish the prospect of her discreet visit being rumbled by Julia Kelso and she promised herself that she would tell her about it as soon as possible.

On her laptop she found a flight with late availability leaving Gatwick at 8 the following morning, getting to Lisbon just after 9.30 local time. She booked it and sent a message to Alf.

Mel set her alarm for very early, turned her phone off and went to bed. She could shove some overnight things in a bag in the morning. She went to sleep feeling both happy and apprehensive, and had strange and troubling dreams – the recurring ones she had been having since the Murston case. In these dreams Julia Kelso and Alan Ferdinand both died violently over and over again, but they kept coming back for more. The dreams worried Mel Dunn a lot.

At 6 the following morning Mel called the NCIS duty officer and reported sick. She took a train to Clapham and changed for a Gatwick one. After the post 9/11 airport security circus she was drinking a disgusting coffee in the departure lounge well before her flight was called.

******

Alf was waiting for her. She saw him leaning against a pillar looking calm and relaxed. He looked weathered but had put on a bit of weight. Mel tried to stay cool as she approached, sauntering instead of running, which was what she felt like doing. She stood in front of him.

"You're getting fat, Ferdinand," she said, before dropping her bag and throwing her arms around him.

"Just a bit of winter insulation. It'll be gone by the spring. It's good to see you Mel!" Alf was smiling at her.

"Shall we go?" he asked.

"Lead on. Where are you taking me?"

"I'm renting a small place up the coast a ways. I was here in town for a while but people are too inquisitive. Too many foreigners are living here and they all feel like they should be friends with all the others. I live among Portuguese folks who only get friendly after they've known you forty years."

"Are you turning into a grumpy git, Alf?"

"I thought you said I've always been a grumpy git."

"True enough."

They were walking towards the airport car park. Ferdinand paid his parking ticket and led Mel to an elderly and modest Seat hatchback.

"I see you still know how to turn a girl's head, Alf." Mel said as she chucked her bag on to the back seat.

"As long as it works it's fine," he said.

Mel chatted as he drove through the northern outskirts of Lisbon and on to the motorway network that leads up to the Atlantic coast and onward towards Porto.

"Have you talked to Jake about this yet, Mel?"

"No. I listened to your advice and I've kept my thoughts on Jerry Keynes and the trafficking business to myself. I'll need to tell her, though, sooner rather than later. Can we talk about it in a while?"

"Of course," he said.

After about an hour's driving Alf pointed out the picturesque painted village of Obidos off to the left.

"We can visit later and have lunch there if you like. It's really quaint and much more genuine than it looks," he said.

Shortly afterwards he left the motorway and entered a sleepy looking town with a large central park and the obligatory massive church. Alf navigated his way to a small pretty house with its own gated driveway. He opened the gate and drove in, parking under the shade of an old tree, even though it was chilly and overcast.

"Welcome to my humble abode, Miss Dunn."

"I'm honoured, Mister whatever your name is today."

"Make one up, it doesn't matter." He smiled at her. "Coffee?"

"Not if you're making it, but take me to your kitchen."

Mel made coffee and they sat, an awkward moment passing briefly between them.

"Did you tell Jake you were coming to see me?" Alf asked.

"Not yet. She's senior on-call this week and we haven't spoken much since last Friday. Has she been here?"

"Yes, and to the place I had in Lisbon. She told me you and her still sleep together - or 'do it' as she puts it - every now and then."

"It's only for the exercise, Alf, promise."

"If you say so. We spoke about you, and about us. We're serious, I think, Jake and me, but the situation is tricky."

"I can't think why Alf! I mean, just because you're officially dead and your hobbies are shooting people and taking all their money, and she's one of the top-ranking police ladies in the UK and she knows all about it. You'd have to be pretty small minded to make any of those tiny facts an impediment to a serious relationship."

"I'm going to ignore you, Miss Dunn. But before I do tell me everything about this people trafficking stuff.

Mel spent the next hour recounting in detail everything that Jerry Keynes had told her, as well as everything she knew about the case Julia Kelso was interested in.

"So what Jerry is saying," Mel started summing up, "is basically that it ought to be impossible for human traffickers to get people, especially the girls being exploited as sex workers, into the UK and other countries in Europe on the scale and at the speed that it's happening. The odd few here and there can be explained through human error, system failures or low-level bribery, but dozens and possibly hundreds of people being moved quickly by organised crime groups screams corruption, according to Mr Keynes."

"What's Jerry Keynes like?"

"He's strange, Alf. He's a loner, I'd say a bit obsessive-compulsive, OCD. And he's also flaky - he's got a reputation as a drinker and he gets into a lot of arguments. He's not big on people skills either. I do think he knows his stuff, though, even if he is jumping at shadows. That could be his paranoia shining through. If he's right to any extent I reckon it's only his paranoia that's kept him out of harm's way."

"Do you think there's anything in it, Mel?"

"I really don't know, but possibly. You know me, I need data, information. I'm an analyst and I can't just jump to a conclusion without exploring a theory. I've asked Jerry to trust me with everything he has so I can do my stuff and see if there *is* anything in it, or at least a theory to work on. What are you thinking?"

"I think there's a logic to what Jerry's saying, but I wouldn't rely on him as a source or want him to be part of an investigation. You're right - we need to examine anything and everything he's got. And by 'we' I mean you of course."

"I guessed as much."

"You'll have to use all your charming wiles to get him to trust you and give it over."

"I'm not shagging him if that's what you mean! Not for you or anybody."

be a day or two before anything came through so she closed her work down for the day and went home.

Mel was physically tired and her eyes ached. She felt she had overdone the sex over the past week or so, what with her weekend session with Jilly and Frank, Alf in Portugal and then Jake Kelso on Saturday and again on Sunday. Kelso seemed to get very excited when Mel described her sex session with Ferdinand. Mel was exhausted and looking forward to an early and undisturbed night.

Instead of eating and going to bed early Mel made the mistake of opening up the files on the memory stick she'd got from Jerry Keynes and starting to read them on her own computer at home. It was almost midnight when she called a halt. She still hadn't eaten and her throat was dry. She cleaned her teeth and dressed for bed, but in the quiet darkness of her own room sleep evaded her. She was replaying some of the horror stories she had read in Jerry Keynes's files, stories about the girls enticed away from their relatively safe if impoverished homes to be dropped into shark-infested cities far away where they were consumed alive until there was nothing left of them. Mel cried herself to sleep.

Chapter 11

Tuesday morning. Mel was up early after her troubled night and she was at her desk by 8am. She called Jake's office number and asked if she could meet her for a coffee around 11 at their usual Italian place in Victoria.

Jake was already there with the coffees on the table when Mel arrived.

"Christ, you look awful, Mel. What's happened?" she asked.

"I'm OK. Just didn't get much sleep. Jerry Keynes handed over a shed load of stuff yesterday, for my eyes only, and I made the mistake of taking some home with me. It makes for very unhappy reading and I was quite upset, hence no sleep and the way I look this morning."

"I'm sorry Mel," Jake said, "can I do anything?"

"No, it's OK. I'll get over it. I think Jerry might be on to something but I'm waiting for some data to come back before I can say anything further. I've found a few phone numbers that look weird, it's similar to a pattern I've seen before in organised crime where there is a small network controlling a load of larger ones."

"You mean like the Banbury case, Operation Catchpole and all that?" Jake was referring to the first case that she, Mel Dunn and Alan Ferdinand had dealt with.

"That sort of thing. Not identical but with some similarities. I'll need to take all the data into my thinking cupboard when it comes back and I'll let you know. By the way, Jerry was very insistent that he is only sharing his stuff with me - no one else at all, especially you. So please don't drop me in it. He's very strange and a little bit frightening."

"How so?"

"I don't mean scary frightening, I just mean that he has a very short temper and he doesn't care about consequences. He turned up at work yesterday stinking of booze and with a black eye which he says he got in a 'heated debate'. He's a loose cannon, Jake."

"I'm not telling anyone anything for now. Just keep me posted."

The friends parted and Mel walked slowly back across Lambeth Bridge towards her office. She suddenly felt weary and wanted to go home. Not to Raynes Park, but to the moors and windswept beaches of East Yorkshire, to a simpler life. She shrugged it off, deciding that a simpler life would actually bore her senseless inside a week.

There was a large envelope on Mel's desk when she got back to the office: the billing records and call data she had asked for. There was a sticky note attached on the outside from the admin office demanding an operation name to allocate the cost to. Mel threw it in the bin.

It took her the best part of two hours to go through it all. She ended up with a scribbled hand-drawn chart which showed that the numbers she had found were connected with each other, and that they changed regularly. Not just frequently, regularly. In fact every month. What she had was a snapshot over a two month period of a covert communications network which was in contact with organised human traffickers. Mel reckoned that there were four people in the covert network, and possibly a fifth.

Mel put in requests for comprehensive cell-site data for the eight numbers she had identified, which she thought represented two phones for each of the four unknown people. She was hoping that there might be pointers towards other phones used by those people, maybe even currently in use. And of course which might show her who those people were.

Mel then selected several of the phone numbers seemingly used by the traffickers which had been in contact at some stage with one of her eight suspect phones. Some of these were overseas ones, and these she sent down to GCHQ at Cheltenham for any call data they might have. The UK ones she submitted for billing and call data records. She called registry and got an Operation name allocated to her so she could attribute costs and authorities to it. She described it as an analytical research project with no operational priority. It was tidier that way.

******

Jake took a call from Kim Morris. Kim had spoken to Flora, her 'au pair' who had been a victim of trafficking. After some persuasion Flora had agreed to meet with Julia Kelso, who Kim had described as a friend rather than a senior police officer. Could Julia see her way to coming to Kim's place in Sutton for supper, which she called tea, the following evening? She could meet Flora, who would be more relaxed at home. Julia agreed and made a note of the address. Kim called back a few minutes later. She wasn't a vegetarian or anything, was she? Flora would probably cook something Balkan, which meant it would be delicious but have at least two types of meat in it. No, Julia was Scottish and would eat anything as long as it had stopped moving.

Julia had a meeting scheduled with the investigation and prosecution team dealing with Charles Murston (no longer Sir Charles) and his son Charlie. Both had indicated that they would plead very not guilty when their trial came up in February, blaming the whole thing on the mysterious and missing Thomas Donohue, of whom there was no current trace. There was also precious little evidence of his involvement. However, the team did have some intelligence that linked Donohue to the acquisition of an illegal firearm and his name did appear on a contract between someone of that name and Charles Murston. The address shown for Donohue was that of a prestigious law firm in Dublin which was refusing to confirm or deny any knowledge of, or involvement with, any Thomas Donohue.

The team was satisfied that the evidence they had was sufficient to convince even the most gullible of juries that Murston senior and junior were responsible for poisoning hundreds of people, distributing cocaine, and stealing a lot of money. That would do.

Julia listened carefully and when the team left she put in a call to Hugh Cavendish at the Secret Intelligence Service. Hugh was a family friend who had been more than helpful to Julia in both of her recent escapades.

"Hugh, it's Jake. Do you fancy meeting for a drink this evening? At Dolphin Square at 6.30? Great. See you then."

Hugh Cavendish arrived promptly and found Julia in a quiet corner of the bar. He gave her one of his rugby-player bear hugs and a big sloppy kiss.

"Happy New Year Jake. You look wonderful. How's the Rake?"

The Rake was a service nickname for Jake's father, Ralph Kelso, who had been a senior SIS officer and was fondly remembered.

"He's fine. No doubt he's escaped from enforced good behaviour at home and gone back to his rooms in Edinburgh by now. God only knows what he gets up to there, but as long as it doesn't make the newspapers we're all happy. How are you and your lot?"

"We survived the festivities. Off skiing next week, so we'll see if we survive that as well. How's work?"

Julia ordered drinks for them both.

"All pretty good. I just wanted to ask you about that Ukrainian guy, they one you snatched off the street when he was targeting me. What happened to him?"

"Well, he did the strong and silent bit for ages, so we told him we'd take him home. Said we'd arranged a flight back to Kiev via Amsterdam. He'd have to change planes there and it was always possible that someone from the war crimes team might become aware of his presence on Dutch soil and want a word. If not we'd make sure he got to Kiev, where we had it on good authority there were also a lot of officials keen to talk to him about this and that. After that

Pavel, that's his name by the way, had a pretty massive change of heart and started answering all our questions, and then some. He's being very helpful now. He's actually quite a decent chap when you get to know him. He works for us now, down at the Fort. He does odd jobs, a bit of role play with the recruits, even some weapons and hostile interrogation training. He seems as happy as Larry. He lives on site and goes out into town once in a while to let off some steam. I think he's even got himself a girlfriend. Why do you ask?"

"It's about Thomas Donohue. It's time he died, or appeared to. No, wait, I don't want you to do anything nasty to Pavel. But if we had a sample of his DNA, a sample which would match other samples found in the Murston Rolls Royce which he drove quite a lot, and we could attribute that sample to an unidentified body somewhere, we could make it look like the body was that of Thomas Donohue."

"I take it Donohue being dead would make life easier."

"Yes. The Murstons are blaming everything they did on him. We might need to use him, I mean as Declan Walsh or some other name, soon, so it would help if no one was looking for Donohue anymore. Do you think Pavel would help?"

"I have no doubt at all Jake. Donohue spun Murston a yarn about West Africa didn't he?"

"Yes, why?"

"The civil war in Liberia is still going strong. Lots of South Africans are joining in, and a few others. It means there's no shortage of pale body parts washing up on the beaches near Monrovia. It wouldn't be too tricky to identify one of those as Donohue and get a sample of his, or rather Pavel's, DNA to the authorities here. Would you like me to attend to it?"

"Would you, Hugh? It would be helpful, to say the least."

"It's only a bit illegal, but we needn't worry about that. Murston is a total disgrace to everything that matters in this country. Anything to ensure his swift descent to the cells is fair game as far as I'm concerned."

Julia ordered more drinks and they chatted about family and old times for a further hour before Hugh looked at his watch and rose.

"You really must come down to the house one weekend, Jake. The family would love to see you again."

"I'd like that."

"Give my best to the Rake. Good night." Hugh kissed Jake again and left, humming quietly to himself.

private, just Jake's phone and the yellow one. It was where Jake lives, Dolphin Square. I think that suggests Jake knows whoever has the yellow highlighted phone quite well, don't you think?"

Alf was looking serious. He nodded but said nothing.

"The phone highlighted in pink was in the same cell as Jake's on 6th December. Quite a few other phones were there as well, not surprising as it was in the Westminster area in the middle of the afternoon. On the Monday 23rd December there are only four phones in the same cell, the pink one, Jake's and two others. Westminster again, and late afternoon, but a lot of people would have pushed off for Christmas the previous Friday. The final connection on Wednesday 8th January only has Jake's phone and the pink one in the same cell. It's Dolphin Square again."

"Are there any other connected phones? Ones which appear in the same cells as the highlighted ones?" Alf asked.

"I haven't had time to look yet. I was just so shocked to see Jake's phone in the mix."

"I'm going to need you to get as much data as you can back here so we can go through it together. We need to make some sense of this. I can't believe that Jake would be involved in trafficking, so we need to find a reason. I really don't want to have to confront her with this, at least not yet, not until we have an explanation. It'll be best if she doesn't know I'm here just yet. Are you expecting her to come here any time soon?"

"You can never tell with her. She'll always call, though, but sometimes when she's already on the train or at the front door."

"I'll get a hotel then just in case she pitches up, but I want to spend as much time as I can here, working through this with you."

"OK. I'll gather everything I can and bring it home tomorrow. They think I'm going down with some bug at work, so I'll go sick again tomorrow afternoon and we can have a clear day before the weekend."

"I'll go now. I'll get somewhere sorted to stay and get hold of a phone and some transport. I'll call your mobile later to let you know my number and where I'm laying my head. It's good to see you Mel, but I'm sorry about the circumstances. I'll be thinking it all through, I'm sure you will too. There's got to be a plausible reason for these connections."

Alf picked up his bag and let himself out. Once he had gone Mel looked at the phone data once again. She had omitted one thing, something she hadn't told Alf. It was to do with the pink phone on 23rd December. One of the other two phones alongside Jake's and the 'pink' phone was also one she knew. It had also been in the same place as Jake's later in the day, not just in Westminster but at Dolphin Square - for the entire night. It was Justin Evans' phone. It wasn't something she wanted to share with Alf, at least not just now.

Chapter 14

That evening Julia Kelso drove herself to Kim Morris's small semi-detached house in Sutton. It was neat and tidy, and it felt warm and homey. Kim opened the door to let Julia in. There was a moment of awkwardness around the greeting, which Julia broke by kissing Kim on the cheek. She handed over the flowers she had brought, and a bottle of decent but unpretentious red.

Julia was introduced to two scrubbed and polished medium-sized children. Julia judged them to be around 11 or 12 years old. They were Kim's twins, a boy and a girl - Ben and Sarah. The other person there was Flora. Flora was around 20 or 21, small and pretty with close-cropped dark hair. She didn't wear make up and her clothes were as shapeless as she could get away with. She was trying to hide her femininity, and who could blame her? Julia shook her hand and introduced herself.

The children had already eaten and were packed off upstairs by Flora.

"She seems nice, Kim." Julia said.

"She is, now that she's settled in. She was scared stiff of her own shadow at first. She still has nightmares though, I can hear her sometimes in the night. I think having the twins to keep her occupied helps."

"You took a big step in bringing her into your home."

"I know. The few people I told at work think I'm nuts, but there's a vulnerability about Flora. Some of the girls like her that you come across have become

73

quite tough and can cope - Flora hasn't and couldn't. She knows I'm kind to her and don't make any demands, as long as she's good with the kids. I do worry about her sometimes, though. She doesn't go out except for shopping and to do the school run. Even with shopping she'd rather come with me in the car than go on the bus. She hasn't got any friends and as far as I know she's not been in touch with her family back home at all. She doesn't have her own phone. I gave her an old one of mine but she only ever speaks to me on it. She won't use a computer even though we've got one and I'm sure she knows how to. Now, can I get you a drink or something."

"I'll just have water for now, Kim. I'm driving, but I'll have a glass of wine with dinner."

Kim went off to the kitchen and came back with a glass of sparkling water for Julia and a hefty glass of white wine for herself. As they settled down in armchairs Flora reappeared. She got herself a sparkling water as well and sat quietly on the sofa.

"Kim probably told you that we work together, Flora." Julia started.

Flora nodded like a small bird.

"She's told me a bit about you, and I'm pleased to be able to meet you," Julia continued.

"Thank you," Flora said in a virtual whisper, "I have cooked for you. You are Kim's boss, yes?"

"Sort of. What have you cooked? I'm hopeless in the kitchen."

"Kim said you would like some food from Serbia. I have made some *sarma*, this is leaves of cabbage baked with some meat inside. This is to start. Then *ćevapi*, which is very popular in Serbia, like kebab

74

sausage with some flat bread and onions and sour cream. With the *ćevapi* is some *prebranac*, a stew of beans cooked in the oven. And to end some *vanilice*, these are cookies with filling and sugar. In Serbia there is a lot of meat." Flora gave a fleeting smile.

To Julia she seemed no older than the twins, she was just a child. Which made what had happened to her so much worse.

"It sounds delicious," said Julia, who was already making a mental note to get some indigestion pills on the way home.

"Where are you from in Serbia, not that I'd know if you tell me? I've never been there."

"From the eastern side, near to Bulgaria in the hills. I am from a small village which no one has ever heard of. It's much closer to Sofia than to Belgrade. Are you going to ask me what happened to me?"

"Only if you want to tell me, Flora."

"I go to the kitchen now to cook." Flora stood and left the room.

"I think she likes you, Julia," Kim said, "that's more than she usually says in a week."

Flora returned and set the table, which was in a corner of the sitting room. Kim explained that they'd had to lose the dining room to make another bedroom now that the twins were 'of an age'. Flora had the small room upstairs and the kids had a room each up there too. Kim slept in what was the dining room. It was easier to come and go at strange times without waking everybody up.

"Please come to table, *sarma* is ready," Flora announced.

Kim opened the red wine and poured a glass for herself and Julia. She looked at Flora who simply shook her head. The *sarma* was deliciously light and flavoursome. Julia complimented Flora on it. Flora smiled shyly.

Kim and Julia maintained a stream of chatter as they ate. Flora listened carefully but didn't join in. When the *sarma* was finished Flora cleared their plates and went to get the main course. The aroma of grilled seasoned meat and freshly baked flatbread preceded her. Julia found herself looking forward to the next part of the meal.

The *ćevapi* was juicy and moist, its greasiness overtaken by the sour cream dressing. Flora had made rice instead of the usual fried potato accompaniment, for which Julia was grateful. The meat disappeared rapidly. Kim had quite an appetite. When the main course was over Flora again vanished into the kitchen. She came back with a tray of two-tier biscuits with a creamy filling, a pot of Turkish-style coffee and three small glass beakers. Flora served them all. Then without any preamble she started.

"My family is not rich. Our village is poor, there is no school except for the small children. When I was thirteen my parents had saved enough money to send me to a school, but it was in Sofia. It was closer and not so expensive as the nearest schools in Serbia. In Sofia I went to school, but it was hard. I had to learn Bulgarian, which is not the same as Serbian, and I made mistakes in my schoolwork. After one year the school said I would have to go because I could not do well in the examinations. It was just because of the language.

"I could not go home. My parents would have been shamed. So I stayed in Sofia. I got work in a hotel and spent all my spare time studying in my room. One of my friends from the school gave me some old books to use. Bulgarian became easier for me, and I tried to get back into the school. The principal said I could go back, but only if I paid him a lot of money or promised to sleep with him every week for as long as I was there. I didn't have enough money, and I wasn't going to sleep with the principal, who was an ugly smelly old man. So I kept going as before. I wrote home to my family once a month and they thought everything was going well for me in Sofia.

"The hotel I was working in closed down to be repaired. I had no job and very little money. I went to the other hotels, nearly all of them, asking for any work. I didn't care if it was in the kitchen, or making the beds or cleaning the toilets. I knew I could be a receptionist because I was good at language and clever enough. My Bulgarian was by then OK, I knew English, as well as Serbian and some Russian. But I was prepared to do anything so I didn't have to go home as a failure. I went to the casino in the hotel by the government building. I asked for work. They said to come back next week.

"As I was leaving a boy came up to me. I didn't think he was Bulgarian because he spoke to me in English. He said he heard I was looking for work and he might be able to help me. As we talked I realised he was Albanian, but he seemed very nice. He was polite and respectful to me. He said he would call some people and could I come back to the entrance to the casino the next day. I said of course.

"The next day he was there, on his own. He was excited and said he had an uncle in London who had a restaurant, a Balkan restaurant. He needed someone who could speak Serbian and English, and who was also clever and pretty. The job was to greet the diners and take bookings. Was I interested? I said I was, but I had no papers to go to London. The boy, he said his name was Luan, it means 'lion' in Albanian, said it was a problem but he would see what he could do. For now, could he buy me some coffee or an ice cream. I said yes and we went to a place near the big art gallery in Sofia. I had iced coffee, he had some beer. We talked. He was nice. We agreed to meet again in two days time.

"I had nearly run out of money and had to sneak into my room while no one was looking because I had not paid my rent. I stayed in my room for two days, with nothing to eat and only water to drink. Then it was time to go and meet Luan again. I washed and dressed as nicely as I could and put on some lipstick to make myself prettier for him. When I saw Luan my heart nearly burst. Here was a boy who could save my life and make everything better. Luan was very excited. He held my hand and kissed me, and said he had good news. He said if I gave him my identity document for the school he could get me a passport and a visa to go to England. He had spoken to his uncle who agreed to pay the cost and to give me a job in his restaurant, just because Luan said I was a good girl who would do a good job.

"Because I am a simple country girl and an idiot I believed him. Luan bought me some ice cream and said I should come to his apartment to fill in some forms. He lived in a smart apartment on the slope of Vitosha, the mountain near Sofia. It is very expensive there. Luan drove me in his car, a big car. At his apartment he asked me a lot of questions as he filled in papers, all in English. When he finished he held my hands and looked at me. He asked me if I had ever been with a man, because he was in love with me and he wanted to make love with me. I said I had never been with a man, but if he wanted to he could be the first one for me. He said no, he would wait until we were married. He said he wanted to marry a *devica,* this means a virgin in my language. He let me stay in his apartment and sleep on my own in a spare room. He didn't try to sleep with me, he was always very nice. I stayed in the apartment for a few weeks. I cooked and cleaned. Sometimes Luan went away for many days at a time. Sometimes I heard him come in very late at night, sometimes I heard other voices, some girls and some boys, different languages. Once there was a strange girl in the bathroom in the morning, wearing one of Luan's shirts and nothing else. She didn't speak to me.

"Then one day Luan came home in the afternoon. He gave me an envelope. Inside was a Bulgarian passport, not in my name but with a picture that looked like me in it, and with a tourist visa for the United Kingdom issued by the British Embassy in Sofia. He said I was to learn the name in the passport, which was to be mine from now on, and learn the date of birth and all the other details. He said he was going to put me on the express bus to Greece so I could take the ferry boat to Bari in Italy, and from there I could go by train all the way to Paris. In Paris I would get on the train to London. He said it was slower than flying, but with the passport in someone else's name it was safer for me. I agreed.

"The journey to London took me four days. Four days with not much sleep and not much food. Luan had given me some money for the journey in Euros but it wasn't enough. I got through all the border controls with no problems. By the time I got off the train at Waterloo Station I was exhausted and hungry. Luan had told me his brother would meet me at Waterloo Station and take me somewhere I could rest, and when I was refreshed he would take me to meet his uncle.

"When I was through the customs check I saw a man holding up a paper with the name in my passport written on it. I went to him. I asked was he Luan's brother. He said nothing. He just took my arm and made me walk very quickly from the station. Outside there was a van waiting. He opened the back door and pushed me in. There were no seats, just some rags on the floor. He got in after me. I was starting to be scared. He still hadn't said anything. Then he shouted a word in Albanian and the van started to move. I asked him what was happening, and he didn't say anything. He just hit me in my face very hard and I went unconscious.

"When I woke up I had no clothes and was tied to a bed. I called out. The same man came into the room. I tried to cover myself but couldn't move. He just laughed. He threw a bucket of cold water over me and went to hit me again, but he didn't. He just laughed some more and went out. Later a girl came in and gave me some food. She untied one hand so I could eat. She gave me a bucket to use as a toilet and she watched me while I did it. Then she tied my hand up again."

Julia was surprised at how calm Flora was, and how clearly she was giving her account.

"It went on like this for many days, punching, hitting, pretending to punch, the soaking, the shouting," Flora continued, "until I was so scared I did whatever they told me. They stopped tying me up. I got dressed when they told me to. I got undressed when they told me to. I went to the toilet when they told me to. I ate when they told me to. When Ilir, he was the one who had hit me, came in and told me to suck his dick I sucked his dick. When one of the girls came in and told me to lick her pussy I licked her pussy. I just did everything they told me to.

"Then one day Ilir said it was time for me to start to repay them for the trouble they had taken. He took me with two other girls to a house, I don't know where. There I was taken to a man who told me he had paid for a virgin. He was very ugly and smelled bad. He raped me both ways, very rough. The girls helped him by holding me down, although by then I did not fight anyone anymore. When he had finished he didn't say anything, he just put his clothes on, lit a cigarette and left. The girls cleaned me up and said that I lived in this house now. They said I wasn't a virgin anymore so I was just like them, a whore to be rented and used.

"I was there in that house for a very long time. Every day men came, sometimes women too, and they paid money to Ilir to fuck me or hurt me. For me it was living in hell, but it was my life. I told myself it was my fault for not going home to tell my parents I had failed at school.

"One day, when they thought they had total control over me, they sent me to see a 'client'. He was an old man who paid a lot of money for a blow job or a hand job and afterwards to scream and curse at us, but he was sick and couldn't leave his house. So he sent a taxi to get me; Ilir said the old man liked my blow jobs and hand jobs. They gave me some outside clothes to wear and told me to go on my own in the taxi. Ilir would pick me up after two hours. None of the girls had clothes in the house, not proper clothes. Just a dressing gown and disgusting underwear. I hadn't been in an English taxi before, but I worked out that sometimes when it stopped a light would come on, and that meant the doors were unlocked. In the Trafalgar Square - I recognised it because I had seen pictures in a tourist book - the light came on and I opened the door. I ran away into the crowds. The taxi driver didn't care, he had been paid to take me from one place to another and now I had run off. So what?

"I was on the streets for a few days. Once I saw Ilir and his brother Pali. They were looking for me but they didn't see me. And one evening there was an English girl, I know she was a prostitute, who asked me what I was doing. She was kind to me, and I just started crying and crying. She knew Kim and called her, and Kim rescued me. Kim is like my mother now."

Flora's composure finally collapsed. She fled from the table and ran upstairs. After a few minutes she returned. She had washed her face and dried her eyes.

"I am sorry, Yulia. I was upset. I haven't told anyone like this before. I thought it would be easy, but it is not easy."

"You're doing so well, Flora, and thank you. You won't have to tell me again I promise. I'll get the people who did this to you, and you won't have to give evidence against them. I'll get the evidence from somewhere else, but they're going to pay for what they've done to you, and to all the others. I'm glad you found Kim. She is a good person and she'll take care of you. Thank you too for a marvellous dinner, I had no idea Serbian food was so good."

"Serbia is a beautiful place, Yulia, but with some crazy people. One day I hope I can go back, when there is no shame for me anymore. Maybe then you can come and see me, in my country."

"You don't need to be ashamed, Flora. You've done nothing wrong. It's the others. Now, I must go."

As Julia was putting her coat on Kim tugged her arm. She was a bit tipsy.

"I need to say something, before you go. I've fibbed to you, twice. No one from work knows about Flora. And she isn't all legit and above board. She's got no documents. The immigration don't know she's with me. I just had to help her, Julia. Will you keep it to yourself?"

"You're doing the right thing, Kim, just not in the right way. I can see where you're coming from and I'll do my best to protect Flora, and you. Don't talk to anyone about it before you've spoken to me, OK?"

Flora came back from the kitchen. Julia said goodnight to them both, and Kim put a matronly arm around Flora's thin shoulders as she waved Julia off.

Julia used her car phone.

"Mel? I need a lot of gin. Can I come round?"

"Of course, who is this?" Mel teased.

"Fifteen minutes."

"OK."

"I'd best be buggering off then," said Alf.

"Too right," Mel agreed.

Alf had checked into the Cannizaro Hotel on Wimbledon Common earlier but had gone back to Mel's for a drink and to talk. He checked that he hadn't left any traces and departed rapidly. From his now familiar vantage point in a nearby pub he watched Julia Kelso park up in her dark blue BMW convertible and saw her walk briskly towards Mel's flat. His heart almost melted when he saw her. She was very special.

Chapter 15

Julia Kelso left Mel's flat early the next morning, remarkably undamaged by the several large gins she had downed. She had repeated everything that Flora had told her to Mel, and then spent a good twenty minutes saying exactly what she wanted to do with the bastard pimps, rapists and kidnappers who did that to young girls.

As Mel listened her inner fears about Jake and her phone being linked to people involved with traffickers eased. She knew Julia Kelso well enough to see she was truly incensed by Flora's story, and by what she had pieced together about the young girl who had jumped off the Archway Road bridge. Still, she decided not to talk to Jake about the phone connections until she had spoken to Alf.

Mel made her way in to work as she had planned. On the way she called ahead to get subscriber details on the two permanent phones she had identified, the 'yellow' and the 'pink'. The information she had asked for was on her desk when she arrived.

The 'yellow' phone belonged to an Andrew Strathdon with a billing address at an Edinburgh law firm. Mel guessed it could be Jake's ex. The 'pink' phone was registered to the Foreign and Commonwealth Office in London. No user identified. She made a call to get the subscriber details of the other two phones, the ones that hadn't, as far as she knew, been near Julia Kelso. While she was waiting for the reply Mel printed off copies of the phone and cell-site data she had gathered. She placed the copies in a large envelope and sealed it.

The subscriber information she had asked for appeared on her email. One of the other two phones belonged to a Bijan Bukani with the billing address at one of the major high-street banks headquartered in the City of London. The other belonged to a company called Elissa Global with a Clerkenwell address. Mel decided that Alf could start digging.

At lunchtime Mel rushed from her desk to the ladies' loo. She splashed some water on her face and afterwards told the admin clerk that she was feeling really rough and was going home. The clerk was very sympathetic and offered to go with her. Mel thanked her and declined. She would get home alright on her own. On the train she sent a text to Alf's new mobile number saying she was on her way home and could he meet her there.

Alf arrived at the flat shortly after Mel got home. She'd had time to change into jeans and a sweatshirt. She was laying out her array of printouts on the dining table when he buzzed the door.

Alf looked rested and relaxed. Mel felt neither. She quickly went through everything that Jake had said the previous evening.

"I can't believe she's involved, Alf. Her reaction last night was one hundred per cent genuine. I think we should tell her what we've got and get her thoughts."

"I don't think she's involved either, but until we know whose numbers they are I still say we don't tell her. Imagine if she has a close friend who *is* involved. What will she do if we tell her? I'm not saying we hold out on her for long, just until we know who we're dealing with."

"Let's work through this stuff and discuss it again later," Mel said. "I've got subscriber information for all four 'permanent' phones. I'm working on the numbers to see if I can find the current temporary ones. The two we've linked to Jake belong to an Andrew Strathdon and someone at the Foreign Office."

"The Foreign Office?" Alf asked.

"Yes. Don't know who, but it's definitely an FCO phone. Jake told me the other day that she bumped into her ex in Edinburgh. His name is Drew, or Andrew. He's a lawyer. I think Andrew Strathdon could be Jake's ex."

"Ex what?"

"Fiancé. She was going to marry him."

"I didn't know she'd been engaged. When was this and what happened?"

"Jake said it ended about three or four years ago. Seems he asked her to drop an investigation she was running into a dodgy property developer. She blew a fuse and walked out on him. Hadn't seen or spoken to him since, until they met at a party in Edinburgh just before New Year. She said they exchanged polite words and she left."

"But the 'yellow' phone was near her at least two more times. Am I right?"

"Yes. In Edinburgh again on 3rd January and once more in London on 7th January."

"So she could have met with him at least twice more."

"She could have, but she didn't mention it to me. There's always the possibility that she didn't know he was there, that it's a coincidence."

"Or he could be following or stalking her."

"That too. Moving on, the 'pink' phone, the FCO one. It was with Jake's on 23rd December with a lot of others. I'm thinking a drinks party or something. Then it pops up again on 6th and 8th January. Jake hasn't said anything to me about meeting anyone from the FCO, not that she necessarily would. Has she said anything to you?"

"No, nothing."

"Any ideas on how we might find out whose it is?"

"Just one, call it." Alf got his mobile out, made sure that his number was withheld, and did it. The FCO mobile rang for a long time.

"Jasmira Shah's phone," a male voice announced.

"I'm sorry, wrong number," he said and ended the call. "Now we find out who Jasmira Shah is. Isn't Jasmira a female name?"

"It sounds like it. I'll google it." Mel tapped away on her computer.

"Yes, it is. So it's a Ms or Miss or Mrs Shah. It's good that the FCO is old fashioned and they still publish a list of staff, and now it's all online. Jasmira Shah is a serving diplomat, currently in London as deputy head of Human Resources. She's previously worked in Rome, Madrid, Budapest and Vienna, mostly in consular roles but more recently she was a first secretary political in Vienna. I don't think her current job would have been much of a promotion."

"Has Jake said anything about being offered jobs or anything?" Alf asked.

"No. But she and I do know someone who's just been seconded to the FCO. He's an army officer and he's being posted as Military Attaché to Abuja. It's possible the three of them met at a drinks do and he introduced Jake to Shah."

"So, two names to get working on. What about the other two phones?"

"Right. One belongs to someone who works for one of the big banks. Someone by the name of Bijan Bukani. On the internet he's shown as a senior foreign exchange trader, whatever that it. I can't find anything else about him yet, no pictures or anything. The final phone isn't attributed to a name but it belongs to a company called Elissa Global. It's got a registered address in Clerkenwell but I don't think that means much. Companies House doesn't have a lot on it, just two directors with one share each and the same address. Looks like formation agents. Its memorandum of association says it's a media and information company. It's new so there aren't any accounts or anything."

"Plenty to be getting on with. Can you talk to this army guy?"

"I've a feeling he's already gone to Nigeria, but I can try. What are you going to do?"

"I want to get to know some more about Andrew Strathdon. Do you know where he is?"

"Jake said Brussels. He's working for the EU."

"OK. I'm going to take a day or two to see what I can get on Ms Shah and Mr Bukani and this Elissa Global set up, then I might be off to Brussels. Let's keep Jake at bay for a few more days. When we've done what we can we can talk her though it. Are you OK with that?"

"I guess. What do you want me to do?"

"Crunch your way through all the data you have, get everything you can on the four numbers we know about, as far back as you can. See if you can get the current temporary numbers and see what they're up to, especially where they are and who they're speaking to. Voice would be helpful."

"All this without an active operation or an investigation team? If this goes wrong I'll be needing another job. If I'm not in jail!"

"I'd visit you."

"No you wouldn't. You're dead and you're wanted."

"Details, details, Mel. Right, I'm off. See you later?"

"Call first. By the way, who are you? I mean officially?"

"Didn't I say? I am currently Senhor Paulo Silva, originally from Oporto. One of the many Anglo-Portuguese from those parts. I have a passport to prove it. So call me Paulo."

Mel looked at him and shook her head wearily.

"You're one of the most devious people I've ever met, Ferdinand. I don't know what I see in you."

"Bye," he said.

Chapter 16

Julia Kelso took a call from the Senior Investigating Officer handling the Murston case.

"Good news and bad, boss," he said, "we've located Thomas Donohue. That's the good news. The bad news is he's dead. The UN mission in Liberia found body parts on the beach near Monrovia a couple of weeks ago. It's a common occurrence apparently. They've recovered some DNA. It's not on any database they can find, but it is a match for samples recovered from the Murston Roller, the one that Donohue had been driving."

"So the DNA fits, but how do they know it's Donohue's body they've found?" Julia asked.

"Well, two things. First there's the physical description. It's only an arm but it's a white arm from a male around the same age and build as Donohue. But mostly it's because they got information from one of the less nasty rebel units that a white man called Donohue was in the area touting weapons in exchange for diamonds. The rebels took exception and topped him, chopped him up and dumped him in the sea. I've been on to the Foreign Office and the High Commission in Accra - that's the nearest operating mission in the region - looked into it and confirmed it. They're sending a report through in a few days, but for now I'm satisfied that Donohue is dead, so we can move on. I can't wait to tell Murston."

Julia thanked him and hung up. She sent a quick text message to Hugh Cavendish which just said 'thanks. Jx'. She used her personal phone to call Alf's number in Portugal but it went unanswered.

Her next call was to Kim Morris.

"Kim, it's Julia Kelso. Do you have anything on the people who held Flora, this Ilir and his brother Pali?"

"Not much, Julia. Word is they're twins, identical twins, and their family name might be Krasniqi. They're around 30, maybe a bit younger. A casual informant told me they're Albanian and vicious, also not very bright. They aren't the brains behind whatever it is they're doing. I can't find them on any system or with immigration, so I guess they're illegals or on fake papers. No addresses, vehicles or anything, but I do know a couple of brothels they're associated with."

"Any pictures or phone numbers?"

"I've a couple of bad snapshots, but no phones. To be honest I don't have any time or money to do much about them. They're just two of many, and too resource-intensive for me. I've got my hands full with the easy ones and with trying to save as many of the girls as I can."

"Thanks Kim. Let me have the pictures and whatever you have on these two. The identical twins bit makes it tricky if we get DNA from anyone they've abused. I'll see if I can get some effort put in to finding the Krasniqis. How's Flora?"

"She was very quiet after you left. In a way I think she needed to tell the story - she hadn't even told me the half of it before. But it's taken it out of her. I'm thinking of going away at half term with her and the kids, to the seaside or something. Try to be a bit normal for her."

"Good idea, Kim. Get that stuff to me and I'll see what I can do. Bye." Julia hung up.

The next call was to Mel Dunn.

"It's Jake. How are you feeling?" Julia knew Mel had gone sick and wasn't feeling too good.

"I'm OK. It's just one of those passing things. I hope I haven't given it to you."

"You seemed pretty asymptomatic last night. I think you're just overtired. You need a few early nights with hot milky drinks."

"Yuck! What do you want?"

"I want to know if NCIS has come across a couple of twin brothers, Albanians called Ilir and Pali Krasniqi, about 30 years old. They're the charmers who trafficked Flora and probably lots of others. There's another brother too, Luan, I think he's younger but brighter. He's in the Balkans or Bulgaria."

"Krasniqi's a very common Albanian name," Mel said, "can this wait until I'm back in the office? I can make a few calls if it's urgent, but I'll get more by doing the searches myself."

"Up to you, Mel. I want to see if we, the Met, can move against these bastards. We know almost nothing about them, and I promised Flora she wouldn't need to give evidence. Her situation's a bit delicate."

"I'll have a good dig around on Monday. I should be back in work by then. For now I'll put in a call to our liaison office in Rome, they cover Albania from there, and see if they or the Italians can tell us anything. I'll also call the UN intelligence unit in Pristina, NCIS has a small team attached to it. Most Kosovan records were destroyed in the fighting and they're having to rebuild all the criminal and civil records and intelligence files. The majority population in Kosovo is ethnic Albanian. Could be that your pair are Kosovan."

"Thanks Mel. Take it easy. I'm assuming you're not up for a workout this weekend?"

"I'll give it a miss, if it's all the same. I'll take your advice and rest up."

"One last thing before you go. Have you heard anything from Alf?"

"No, why?"

"I tried to call him and he didn't answer. He hasn't called me back yet, which isn't like him. I wanted to let him know that Thomas Donohue is now considered by the Murston investigation team to be dead. He'll be pleased."

"So weird. If I hear from him I'll tell him and get him to give you a call."

"Are you OK, Mel. You sounded a bit distracted then."

"Just felt a bit of a sicky wave. I'm fine now. Must go." Mel ended the call.

"You heard all that, Alf?" she asked. The phone had been on speaker.

"Yes, thanks. So I'm dead again. That's good. I must ask Jake how she fixed it this time."

"Her mates at SIS had something to do with it, that's all I know. If you try to call her from your Portuguese phone or if she tries to call you she'll know you're in the UK. It'll sound different. Just send her a text or something, then turn your Portuguese phone off. I've a feeling she might want you to come over to help out with her Albanians. Now, let's get back to work on this lot." Mel was looking at the various piles of printouts on the table, and she was busy loading data into an analytical programme on her laptop.

******

By mid-afternoon Alf was feeling a bit redundant. Mel was concentrating and he couldn't help much, so he went back to his hotel to think. He needed to be doing something so he took a bus to Wimbledon station and from there he took the Underground to Farringdon. He wandered through the maze of small streets of Clerkenwell, an area fast becoming trendy with lots of loft apartments and office conversions in the old Georgian and Victorian buildings. He eventually found the address of Elissa Global. It was near a small park and he took a seat on a bench to watch and wait, to get the 'feel' he wanted. He knew that Elissa Global was just one of a handful of small companies based in the building, and there was a lot of coming and going. Most people using the building were in their 20s or 30s, in casual clothes and mostly carrying cardboard cups of coffee. Alf gave up and went in search of a camera shop.

He found one near the end of Fleet Street and he bought himself a compact digital SLR camera. Returning to his park bench he sat and experimented with his new toy, taking pictures of buildings and people. No one took any notice of him. It was the sort of area where people get left alone to do their own thing.

By the time the light faded he had pictures of a dozen or so people entering and leaving the building that housed Elissa Global. Maybe one of them would be of interest.

He made his way back to the tube and returned to Wimbledon. The trains were packed and stuffy, and he was glad when the crowds thinned out at Victoria and again at Earls Court. By the time he got to Wimbledon he was ready for some fresh air and a cold beer. After a couple of pints of Guinness he walked along the featureless road between Wimbledon and Raynes Park. He called Mel along the way. She said it was OK for him to come by.

The flat was a tip. Mel looked exhausted. She plugged his new camera into her computer and downloaded the pictures of the people coming and going from the Elissa Global building.

"This one looks a bit familiar," she said, indicating a slim attractive woman in her thirties with jet black hair, strikingly red lips and a very chic designer jacket over her expensive jeans. "I'm not sure, but I think I've seen her somewhere before. Maybe it was in a magazine or the papers or something." Mel moved on, looking at all the pictures and saving them on her machine.

As she closed the laptop down her mobile rang.

"It's Jake," she told Alf. "Hi Jake. What's up?"

"I've a strange question for you. Do you know much about pornography?"

"Apart from the fact that I never use the stuff, not much. Why?"

"You never use it? Not with Sven and Cadi and the others?"

"No, it's one of our unwritten rules. We can't be doing with exploitation. Plus we really don't need to,

I'm sure I don't need to explain. Why are you asking?"

"The team looking into the death of that wee girl in Archway think the flat she was being held in had been used as a set for a movie. I think she was forced to be in really nasty porn. I was wondering if we might be able to find her in other films or images and maybe get to see the people who did this to her, or even identify her. The Met has it's own people who look at and classify porn eight hours a day, but they're swamped and it'll be weeks before they get round to my request. Not that I'm expecting them to be able to identify my poor girl."

"NCIS is pretty much in the same boat. All efforts go on paedophile stuff, not adult, however ghastly it is. Can you send me some pictures of your girl? I'll talk to some of the porn people on Monday. They're trying out some new recognition software and I'll see if I can get them to try it out on her."

The pictures arrived on Mel's email a few minutes later. They were the post-mortem images and Mel paled.

"There's something to look forward to," she said, "this is getting a bit depressing. I'm going to have a long hot bath, a bottle of wine and a good sleep. So I'm kicking you out, Alf. Have you pinged Jake yet?"

"No, not yet. I'll do it later. Don't go looking for the girl tonight, Mel. I've seen some of those porn sites in past cases. They can be really horrible. Leave it to the people who've been trained for it and get the proper support."

She nodded.

97

Alf put his coat on and went on his way. She did what she said she would, but later in bed she couldn't sleep. She lay awake most of the night, replaying the story Jake had told her about Flora and seeing the image of the dead girl from Archway every time she closed her eyes. By 6am she gave up and got out of bed. She put her running gear on and went out. She ran hard for two hours and felt briefly better for it. It was going to be a long weekend.

Chapter 17

Mel was glad when Monday morning came around and she could go back to work. She hadn't seen or spoken to Jake or Alf all weekend, and eventually she had been able to get some rest and a proper sleep.

The first person she sought out was Jerry Keynes. He looked worse than he had the previous Monday, if that was possible. His black eye was now a nauseous yellow, but he had somehow added a cut lip and a bruised cheek. He stank of stale booze and cigarettes.

"What have you been up to, Jerry?" she asked him. "More heated debates?"

"Something like that. How are you getting on?"

"Slowly. I just wanted to run some names past you. Ilir and Pali Krasniqi and their brother Luan. Do they mean anything to you?"

"Not immediately, but Krasniqi's a common name. Why are you interested?"

"I think they might be involved in trafficking sex workers from the Balkans."

Jerry didn't look particularly interested.

"Anything on the corruption angle?"

"It's early days, Jerry. I've still got lots to go through."

In truth Mel had decided that Jerry Keynes was the last person she was going to share anything sensitive with. He seemed to be on a self-destruction mission.

"Oh, well," he said, "I'll go and have a rummage and see if I've come across these Krasniqis. I'll call you later."

She was pleased to get away from Jerry Keynes, who was starting to give her the shivers. She called someone she knew in the paedophile and pornography unit, a neatly dressed middle-aged woman called Barbara who wouldn't look out of place teaching in a primary school in Surrey. Mel had never asked her how or why she had come to be one of the UK's leading experts on extreme pornography.

"Barbara, it's Mel Dunn. How's that new recognition software coming on? Does it work?"

"Good morning, Mel. It's a bit early to tell, it's certainly nowhere close to evidential standard yet, but possibly of some intelligence use. Why do you ask?"

"I've had a request from the Met to see if we can help identify the body of a girl who may have been coerced into making porn films."

"They approached you directly? That's quite irregular Mel."

"I know, it's someone I know who's clutching at straws. It'll go official if it looks like we can help. Can you run some pictures through the software as a favour? I'd like to see how it works anyway. Please?"

Barbara agreed. She wasn't obstructive, just a stickler for rules and the need to segregate people and cases from each other to avoid cross contamination, mental and physical. Mel took copies of the photographs to Barbara's 'lab', which was in different building. Barbara looked at the images dispassionately before scanning them into a computer.

"You can watch it do the processing part, but I'll need to know the classification of any matches or possible matches to see whether I can show them to

100

you, if there are any. The procedure is very strictly adhered to; some of the material we have here cannot legally be shown to any unauthorised person, you included I'm afraid Mel."

"I understand, Barbara. Believe me I'm not keen to see that sort of thing anyway."

"The software scans the image to measure specific body parts and facial characteristics. It produces a numeric classification for the body parts most often seen in pornographic images in the first instance, followed by a second classification for facial characteristics, adjusted for a range of different expressions and activities. It then compares the classification with samples it's already identified from our video and still libraries and rank them in order of likely matches. It only takes a few minutes. The evidential problem is it identifies far too many possible matches - a defence lawyer's perfect get-out. Between you and me Mel, I think this software has immense intelligence value but until it gets somewhere near DNA or even fingerprint probability it won't be going anywhere near a courtroom."

The computer screen flickered and a list of results appeared. Barbara turned the screen away from Mel as she scrolled through the list. After a few minutes she turned the screen back so Mel could see it.

"I'd say it's reasonably likely your girl had a screen name of Venus. She appears in quite a few sado-masochistic videos, poor quality low budget ones. Nasty ones too, not the worst we've seen by any means, but very nasty nonetheless and arguably the wrong side of legal. They're all fairly recent and released on the internet as clips to advertise the full-length films."

"Any idea who's making them?" Mel asked.

"I'd be able to hazard a guess, looking at the camera work, lighting and the storylines, as well as the other 'actors', although I hate calling them that. These look like the handiwork of a freelance director who's been around for quite a while. His stuff is getting more extreme and he'll shortly get promoted to the first division, by which I mean making the sort of pornography that crosses the line between barely legal and completely illegal. Then we can get someone to go after him."

"I might be able to get someone to go after him without having to wait for him to do this to any more girls, Barbara." Mel said.

"That would be most irregular, Mel. I couldn't possibly sanction it. I'm going to wash my hands, and while I'm out of the room please don't, under any circumstances, look at any of those clips, take any screenshots or make any notes identifying the people listed in the index for each one. The index is over there, but you shouldn't look at that either."

"Of course not, Barbara. I would never do such a thing."

"Good. I'll be ten minutes." Barbara left the room.

Mel scanned through a few of the clips and noted the reported names of the director, the 'star' - Venus - and several of the male participants. Two of these, who appeared in several clips, were Ilir and Pali Krasniqi. Mel did a rapid screenshot showing the faces of each of the Krasniqis and pressed print.

Copies appeared from the printer attached to the computer in a few moments.

"By the time Barbara returned Mel was sitting still and calmly, looking away from the screen.

"Thank you so much, Barbara. That was enlightening," she said.

"Anything to help, Mel," Barbara said. She shook Mel's hand and winked at her. "Good luck."

Mel went back to her office and busied herself on her computer for an hour before going out. Outside the building Mel got her phone out and called Julia Kelso.

"Your girl was known as Venus, and she's been in porn films with the Krasniqis. I've got screen shots. The films were made by a scumbag by the name of Bernard Croxley. Your vice people should know him. He used to sell porn around Soho but since the internet happened he's making movies now. Horrid ones too. Fancy a coffee? I've got some pictures for you."

They met at the café by Lambeth Bridge. Mel told Jake quickly and succinctly what she had learned from Barbara and from her own research. Croxley worked freelance making more and more extreme films. He was very close to committing serious crime. Julia took the view that he might be more useful to the Met as a whistle-blower than as a prisoner. He could shed light on some very seedy goings-on. The Krasniqis, on the other hand, needed to be sorted. Julia paid for the coffees and went on her way to get the ball rolling.

Even with her clout as a Commander Julia was finding it difficult to get the resources she needed to get going on Croxley. She put in a call to Kim Morris and told her what she'd found out about the Krasniqis and she emailed pictures of them to her. She also mentioned Croxley to Kim. Kim had heard of him but he wasn't near the top of any vice lists yet, not for any serious attention.

Her next tack was the investigation team looking into the run-up to 'Venus's' suicide. The Senior Investigating Officer told her, in an embarrassed way, that the team had been redeployed and she might like to speak to Deputy Assistant Commissioner Savernake.

Julia did. DAC Savernake, Colin Savernake, was her direct boss. She called his office and invited herself to have a chat with him.

"Julia, how nice to see you. Glad you popped in, I needed a quick word." Savernake was exceedingly smooth.

"There's a coincidence, Colin. Who goes first, you or me?" Julia asked.

"Age before beauty, eh? I wanted a chat about this suicide in Holloway, the unidentified girl. You set a team on it as a possible homicide and rape. I'm afraid, Julia, that my interpretation is different to yours. I see it as a suicide, plain and simple. The preamble, if indeed there was any, looks more like consensual rough sex. Apparently it's quite common these days. That it was being recorded only adds to that assumption."

"I really can't agree, Colin. That girl was chased to her death by someone who had raped her repeatedly, over a prolonged period. The post-mortem clearly shows sequential serious assaults resulting in injuries, the nature of which goes far beyond consent. She may have jumped, but she was murdered just as much as if she'd been stabbed or shot."

"I can see you're agitated over this, Julia. But look, the Met is being beaten up in the media every single day about clear-up and detection rates. The Mayor is on at the Commissioner about it every time they talk. My orders are to improve those rates, and that does not include launching major investigations that are unlikely to bring about a successful prosecution. I'm sorry, but that's how it is."

"So a young defenceless girl gets killed by rapists who probably kidnapped her and smuggled her to London to be forced into prostitution or pornography and we do nothing because the Mayor's office is complaining about clear-up rates? Have I got that right, Colin? Shall I make a notebook entry to that effect?"

"Don't be rash, Julia. This is *realpolitik,* as well you know. It's about making Londoners feel we're here for them, first and foremost."

"And Londoners can't be foreign, is that what you're saying?"

"You're trying my patience, Julia. Don't try to be clever and oversimplify this! You're not doing yourself any favours. I've made my decision and that's an end to it. The girl jumped off the bridge and killed herself. A human tragedy, of course, and we will try to identify her and let her next of kin know, but we won't be deploying scarce and valuable resources on a homicide investigation. Do I make myself clear, Julia."

105

"Oh yes, Colin, very clear. She was known as 'Venus' by the way, the young girl, in the violent porn films she was forced to make. I can get some to show you if you like, and when you've watched one or two we can discuss the legal definition of rape."

"Good day, Julia. Excuse me, I have another meeting." Savernake stood and opened his office door. Julia was seething.

******

Later at home Julia reflected on her meeting with Savernake. She wasn't inclined to admit defeat, but she knew better than to take on Savernake, and probably the Assistant Commissioner above him, head on prematurely. She had seen too many good and keen senior officers talk their way into obscure and meaningless career moves by doing just that. She would get justice for Venus, and for Flora and all the other trafficked girls, her own way and in her own time.

Julia sighed to herself. She had been trying to avoid it, but she knew that for Flora's sake as well as that of the dead 'Venus' she would be needing some of the unorthodox help that Alf provided so well. She composed a text using clouded language but which meant 'I need you here now'. She pressed send.

A few miles away in his hotel room in Wimbledon Alf turned his Portuguese phone on to check for messages. He saw Kelso's message.

"See you tomorrow" he sent back.

"Go to M's" Julia responded.

Chapter 18

Alf sent Mel a text. He would see her at hers as soon as she was home. By 6 he was in his seat at the pub and he saw her walk past around 6.30. He drained his beer and went to her.

"Jake's sent for me. She implied it was urgent. Have you spoken to her lately?"

"No," Mel said, "not about you anyway. I gave her some background on the dead girl and the Albanians who probably smuggled her into the country and forced her to make porn films. I gave her the name of the director of the films she's been identified in. She went off all fired up to get the Met's finest on the case. That was lunchtime, though."

As she was speaking Mel's phone rang. It was Jake, She needed to speak to Mel urgently and was just around the corner. For a second Mel thought about trying to stall her, but it was too late. The entry buzzer went.

"Best duck into the bedroom and play it by ear. She'll blow her top if she sees you here, but she'll blow it twice if she finds you hiding in my bedroom."

Mel went to the door as Alf ducked into the bedroom and closed the door behind him. Julia was steaming down the corridor.

"Jesus, Jake, what's up?" Mel asked. "You look like you could bite the head off a live rat."

Jake entered the flat, casting aside her coat and jacket and kicking off her shoes in her usual fashion.

"I had a run-in with my boss about Venus. He downgraded the investigation without telling me first. I made an idiot of myself with the SIO, who'd already been pulled off the case and redeployed. Venus is just an unidentified body, a probable suicide, and there's to be no investigation apart from a few miserable steps to try to identify her. It's obvious that I'm not going to get any backing to go after the Krasniqis either. West End vice don't have any resources and that arse Savernake's sure to torpedo anything I try to get going myself. So I've asked Alf to come over. I need his help."

"He's already here, Jake. I needed his help as well," Mel said.

Alf opened the bedroom door and stood there, silently.

Jake's eyes flitted from his face to Mel's. She was getting very angry.

"Sit down Jake. I'll get us a drink and then we can talk it through. Just take a deep breath and count to ten while I'm in the kitchen." Mel disappeared.

"Hello, Jake," Alf said, "sounds like you've had a rough day."

"What's going on, Alf?"

"Wait till Mel's back. It's nothing to worry about, we just had to straighten something out before talking to you."

"Straighten what out?" Jake was tight-lipped. "You sleeping with her without telling me? Or are you keeping me in the dark again about something else?"

"It's nothing to do with sleeping with Mel."

"So you *are* keeping me in the dark, then?" Jake was about to blow. She stood up.

Mel came back in with a tray of drinks, just in time.

"I was worried, Jake. Sit back down and drink this." Mel passed her a large gin and tonic. "I took all the stuff I got from Jerry Keynes and started playing with it. I came up with some distinct networks, I'm assuming trafficker gangs, through communications data. No names attached yet, but I'm fairly sure one of them will be the Krasniqis. Anyway, the important thing is there is another network, one that's in contact with all the probable traffickers I've propped up. This one isn't behaving like your usual criminal group. They change the phones they use as regular as clockwork, in fact every month. Nothing too strange about that. But, I've managed to locate other phones which seem to be their permanent ones. These are regular, registered contract mobile phones. I've found four of them so far, but there could be more."

"Where's this going, Mel?" Jake asked.

"We've been able to put names to three of the phones, and we have a pretty good idea who the other one belongs to."

"And?"

"You've been in exactly the same place as two of the phones on several occasions. That's where this is going, Jake. You may, probably do, know at least two people who are members of a covert network which interacts with human traffickers on a regular basis."

"Could these 'interactions' be legitimate, Mel?" Jake asked.

"I can't say for certain they're not. But it doesn't look likely. Given Jerry Keynes thoughts on some kind of corrupt facilitation enabling people trafficking I think these phones could be connected to people in a position to do that corrupt facilitation."

Jake was stony faced.

"Can you see why we didn't want to raise this with you yet, Jake?" Alf asked.

"No I can't! You're telling me you thought, you think, I might be involved?"

"No, Jake," said Mel, "after your reaction to Flora's story I was, am, absolutely sure you're not involved. But I think you do know people who are."

"Who are these people?" Jake asked.

"Andrew Strathdon, for one." Mel said.

"Drew? Drew Strathdon? You're kidding me!"

"Is he your ex, Jake?" Mel asked.

"Yes. What's the link to me you've found?"

"His phone and yours were in the same place at the same time on three occasions in the last month. Twice in Edinburgh and once in London."

"I saw him once in Edinburgh, at that party. I told you about it. Only once."

"The second time was also in Edinburgh, in the Grassmarket area on 3rd January."

"The Grassmarket? I met someone for lunch, but I don't remember seeing Drew. And I would remember, I assure you. You said there was another time in London?"

"Yes. On 7th January. At Dolphin Square."

"I didn't see Drew at Dolphin Square. I didn't tell him I lived there. I haven't seen him in London at all. The fucker must have been following me!"

"Wouldn't you have noticed?" Alf asked.

"What are you suggesting, Alf? That I'm lying to you?"

"No. I'm just trying to figure out why your ex-fiancé suddenly turns up in close proximity to your phone on three different occasions over a 10-day period."

"Mel has been chatty, hasn't she?"

"Don't take it out in her, Jake. Tell me about Strathdon."

"He's a smarmy smart-arse lawyer. He had me suckered for a while and he nearly got me to marry him. Then he asked me to go easy on one of his buddies and I saw through him. End of story."

"What's he doing now?"

"At the party he said he's working for the European Union in Brussels. He said it was legal stuff but he didn't elaborate. I wasn't keen to have a long chat with him."

"Did he ask what you're doing?"

"I just said I was at Scotland Yard. Nothing else. But it wouldn't take much for him or anyone else to find out what I do there, what with all this freedom of information stuff and the bloody internet."

"Have you got any pictures of him, Jake?" Mel asked.

"No I bloody haven't!"

"OK. Let's move on," Alf suggested.

"The second phone I've located near yours belongs to a Jasmira Shah who works at the Foreign Office."

"Jas?" said Jake.

"You know her, then?" Mel asked.

"Yes. She was at Oxford while I was there. We weren't close friends, but I knew her slightly. We haven't kept in touch but I saw her at a drinks do before Christmas. I went with Justin Evans. He'd just been seconded to the Foreign Office from the Army and she's something to do with FCO personnel at the moment. He introduced us and I remembered her. She remembered me too. I met her for a coffee when I got back to London after the holidays. That's all."

"The first time Shah's phone was close to yours was early in December, in Westminster. Does that ring any bells?"

"What date?"

"6th December. It was a Friday," Mel said.

Jake pulled out her diary and looked up the date.

"I was at an awards do. Something about women in public office. I didn't win anything or speak, I was just a guest. She might have been there too, but I don't remember seeing her."

"OK. The third phone we have hasn't been near you as far as we know. It belongs to someone called Bijan Bukani. He's a foreign exchange manager for one of the major banks."

Jake shook her head.

"Phone number four is registered to a company called Elissa Global, based in Clerkenwell. It does something to do with information."

"Never heard of it," said Jake.

"Alf took some pictures of people coming and going from the building where it's based."

"How bloody long's he been here?"

"Just a couple of days. Can you take a look at the pictures?"

Mel opened the file with the pictures on her laptop and scrolled through them while Jake studied them.

"I've a feeling I know that one," Mel said, " the snappy dresser."

"Oh, I know her," said Jake, "she's Dido Sykes! She was at Oxford as well, but not in my circle. She

112

knew Drew and his friends. She's a strange one, very mysterious. I can't remember what college she was at or what she studied, but she hung around with some of the star students, Drew included. I haven't seen Dido for ages."

"The name doesn't ring a bell with me, but it explains Elissa Global." Mel said.

"How so?"

"Dido was the founder and first queen of Carthage. It's tragic really, she killed herself over a bloke called Aeneas. In Greek mythology she's also known as Elissa. I'll have to look up the story again, it's been a while." Mel said.

"Was Bijan Bukani at Oxford as well, Jake?" Alf asked.

"Not that I know of, but it's a big place."

"I'll check it out on Monday." Mel said. "So what we've got is a possible Oxford connection between three of the four phones. Jake's put up sensible reasons why her phone was in the same location as Strathdon's on one occasion only, and twice for Jasmira Shah. There's a possible explanation of the third Shah connection with Jake. We have a picture of someone called Dido Sykes, also an Oxford connection who could be, in fact probably is, linked to the Elissa Global phone. That leaves Bijan Bukani."

"All well and good," said Jake, "but as of now I'm looking for a way to take out these bloody Krasniqis and what's his name Croxley, the porn man."

"What do you know about them, Jake?" Alf asked.

"Not a whole lot. We've got pictures and I can probably get the locations of a couple of places they operate out of. From what Mel told me I'm pretty

113

certain they raped and killed Venus, as well as kidnapping and raping Flora."

"Who's Flora?" he asked.

"She was trafficked by the Krasniqis. She's from Serbia but they snared her in Bulgaria. Once they enticed her to London they sold her off to be raped by the highest bidder, then they used her as a prostitute. She's been rescued and is somewhere safe, at least for now, but her position is precarious to say the least. I want the Krasniqis found and neutralised before I can get Flora sorted out with the immigration people."

"I've had some dealings with Albanian gangs before," said Alf, "and they aren't funny. Anyone going up against them unprepared is going to come unstuck. Let me have a think about it. Right now I need another drink."

The tension in the room started to ease, but Alf saw he had some serious peace-making to do with Jake. It had gone 8 and they still hadn't eaten. Jake said she wasn't hungry but wanted more gin.

"I've a room at the Cannizaro Hotel on the Common. Shall we go there, Jake?" Alf asked.

"Don't you dare," Mel interrupted, "you two can stay here and amuse yourselves. I've always wanted to stay at the Cannizaro. Give me your key and I'll go and give your room service a battering. My bed's trashed already so feel free to trash it some more."

Mel packed an overnight bag in seconds and pulled a coat on.

"Sleep tight," she called over her shoulder as she left.

"Well that's us told." Alf said. "I'm sorry, Jake. I didn't want to upset you but we had to be more sure of the facts before we hit you with those links. I think we've another can of worms on our hands."

Jake snuggled next to him on the sofa.

"Let's think about it tomorrow." She stood and pulled him up by his arms. "Mel told me what you did with her in Portugal."

"And you're OK with that?"

"I can't not be, can I? Not really, given what she and I get up to every now and then. Just as long as you never have to make a choice, or me for that matter. Mel's happy dipping in and out of us, and it kind of makes me happy too. I might be more like her than I thought. But tonight it's you I want, and it's just us. OK?"

Alf led her to the bedroom.

"Let's have another drink first, though," she said.

Chapter 19

Over the weekend the three of them talked at length and Alf started to get an idea of what he needed to do. Jake's first priority was to take the Krasniqis out of the picture and get Flora safely sorted. She was coming round to the idea that human trafficking to feed the sex trade might be getting a helping hand from well-placed people, one of whom could be her ex-fiancé Andrew Strathdon. It was a big leap, and one that needed a whole lot of work before anything official could be done about it. For their part, Mel and Alf accepted that Jake's priorities needed to be addressed before they could get going on the corruption angle, which was what had gripped them in the first place.

Alf set about making some general preparations. On Saturday morning he read the small ads in the local paper and by lunchtime he'd bought himself a panel van with an enclosed cargo area. The seller was a builder who was retiring, and Alf was able to talk him into throwing in a bag of old tools including a lump hammer, several crowbars and some stone-chisels. He told the seller he was setting up a business doing small-scale demolition and he had some work already lined up.

On Saturday afternoon he visited a builder's merchant and acquired steel-capped boots, a hard hat and safety goggles, as well as reinforced gloves and some bolt cutters. He had no idea what he might need all these things for but it was good to have a makeshift armoury and some protective gear if things got rough.

Alf planned to find some accommodation on Monday, or maybe he'd just stay on in the Cannizaro. He bid farewell to Mel and Jake, who was now calm and relaxed, and headed for the hotel. He parked a few streets away and went for a walk on the Common to clear his head. As always the combination of Jake Kelso and Mel Dunn in close proximity was a bit overwhelming. He knew he loved them both, albeit in different ways, but he tried not to think about it any further than that.

It was a cool but clear and sunny Sunday. The Windmill café was packed inside and out. The people outside were wrapped up against a chill that wasn't there, and at first he didn't recognise Elsie. Elsie, Louise Collins, had been the surveillance team leader at his old unit on the National Crime Squad when he was still DCI Alan Ferdinand. She kept faith in him when he was up against some very serious accusations, and she had helped him resolve matters. Elsie sat at a table with her long-term partner Marsha, who people called Matt. They were sitting close together chatting happily over mugs of tea.

He knew it was a major risk, but he wanted to see her, them. To talk to them like everything was normal. He walked up to their table.

"Is this one taken?" he asked.

Elsie looked up. She froze, then slowly lowered her mug, throwing glances at Matt.

"Alf? It can't be."

"Hiya Elsie, Matt," he said.

"Fuck me," said Matt, "you're dead!"

"Not entirely. It's quite a long story. How're you doing?"

The women stared at him. He noticed then that Matt had a bump; she was pregnant. He also noticed that Elsie was neatly dressed and looking tidier than he had ever seen her.

"As you see I'm not dead. Also I'm no longer Alan Ferdinand. I was just passing and I happened to see you both and wanted to say hello."

Elsie was regaining her composure.

"Quite an entrance, Alf. You left a real shitstorm in your wake, you know that? When you disappeared off Beachy Head I had a feeling there was a bit of theatre going on there. What are you up to?"

"Just lending a helping hand to a friend. I'm not normally in the UK, for obvious reasons. Are congratulations in order, Matt?"

"You could say that. We decided to start a family. Elsie's quit the job. She's training to be a teacher, of all things. I always thought she couldn't stand kids."

"And Matt's passed her inspector's. She's with Surrey now, a regular job, not the craziness of serious and organised crime. After your business I lost faith in it all and decided to change direction. I always thought I couldn't stand kids either, but they're quite interesting really. And they're all about looking forward, being hopeful and stuff."

"What brings you to Wimbledon? Do you live round here?"

"No. We're out Guildford way now. Matt's gran's in a home not far from here and we were visiting today. Just fancied a cuppa. And now you turn up. What are you doing with yourself, Alf? Do I still call you Alf?"

"Call me what you want, but Alf will do. Are you still Elsie, or is it Miss Collins now you're a school teacher?"

"I'm not qualified until the end of the summer term, so for now Elsie will do. After that I'll need some proper respect. What are you up to, Alf?"

"Like I said, helping out a friend with a bit of an issue going on."

"Would that be Mel Dunn? She lives round here as I recall. From our chats outside that café in Vauxhall taking pictures for you."

"She's one of them, yes."

"You've got more than one friend? You surprise me, Alf! You're more popular dead than alive."

"No one else needs to know. About Mel being a friend, I mean. Look, I need to go, I shouldn't have bothered you. Good luck with the baby Matt, and with being a teacher Els. I'm sure you'll be great at it." Alf stood to leave.

"You can call me, if you want. I've still got the same personal number," Elsie said. "Have you still got it?"

"I do. Thanks. You take care, both of you."

With that he stood and quickly walked away, not sure why he'd broken cover as he had. Maybe just for a moment of normality, a blast from the past. But what was done was done, and at least Elsie had been quite pleased to see him. Matt was clearly less pleased, but at least she hadn't started shouting at him.

Chapter 20

That Monday evening Kim Morris broke her own cardinal rule. She went out looking for the Krasniqis, but she went alone.

Julia Kelso was awoken at 2 in the morning. She was at home in Dolphin Square, alone and enjoying a good dream-free sleep. The phone ringing on the bedside table dragged her awake.

"Kelso" she said, groggily.

"Yulia? It's Flora. Kim said to call you if something was wrong."

Julia was alert in a moment.

"What's wrong, Flora? What's happened?"

"Kim has gone to work. She is not home and she hasn't called. She always calls. Once when she gets to work, once after four hours, and again when she is leaving to come home. She said that if ever she doesn't call it means she is in trouble."

"OK, Flora, what time did she go to work?"

"She left here about 2pm. She called from work after 3. She said she had some paperwork then she was going out from 5. She should have called by 7. I thought she might be busy. Then I went to sleep and she is not home. She didn't call at 11 when she should have been leaving work. I am scared, Yulia."

"I'm sure it's all fine, Flora. Let me make some calls and I'll phone you back on the number you're using." Julia ended the call and immediately called the front desk at West End Central.

She identified herself to the call operator and asked to be put through to the duty Inspector.

"Commander Kelso, Inspector. It's a long story, but I'm concerned about one of your officers. Kim Morris, a sergeant on vice. Is she on duty?"

"Yes, ma'am, she's booked on. She took a service vehicle out on her own around 5. I thought she'd come back and booked off. It's been a busy evening and we've had a lot going on here. Why?"

"She should have made contact with someone earlier - I can't say more - and she hasn't. She also hasn't gone home. Is the service vehicle still booked out?"

"Give me a second……yes. I'll put out a call to it and see if she answers. I'll call you back."

"I'd rather hang on. Could you see if it has a tracker on it?"

After a few minutes the Inspector came back.

"No answer. The tracker's been deactivated. It was turned off around 7. Last location was Bethnal Green."

"OK," said Julia, "Kim was working on some very serious people. I don't know what's happened to her or why she was alone, but we need to find her. Do an ANPR search for her vehicle. I'll call Information Room to get a street search initiated. They'll need the car details and anything you find on the vehicle's movements."

Julia ended the call and immediately called the Information Room, the 24/7 command centre of the Metropolitan Police. Although London is a huge and complicated city it is also a collection of villages. As such there are police officers who know their villages intimately and plans are always at the ready to conduct very extensive searches, especially for motor vehicles, very quickly.

Thirty minutes after she spoke to Information Room they called her back saying Kim's service vehicle had been found on an estate in Harlesden. Kim was in the boot, beaten and unconscious. The cavalry had arrived just in time as some of the locals had worked out that the boring looking Ford was in fact a police car and they were just about to set fire to it. Kim was on her way to hospital, and it didn't look good.

"Were any of her personal items recovered, a handbag or wallet, her personal phone, anything like that?" Julia asked.

"Let me see.....no. The report says specifically that no personal items were recovered. Sergeant Morris had been stripped to her underwear, not even her clothing's been found."

"OK. Get an officer to stand guard at the hospital and call me the minute I can speak to her. I'm going to make sure her kids are OK then I'm going to the hospital. I take it you'll let West End Central know? Good."

Julia ended the call and pulled on a pair of jeans and a sweater. She grabbed her car keys and handbag and flew down the stairs to the car park. As she was pulling out she called Alf's mobile.

He answered, clearly woken from a deep sleep.

"Alf! Get to Kim Morris's house immediately. I'll see you there." Julia gave him the address. "Kim's been attacked. All her personal stuff is missing. I've a feeling she went out after the Krasniqis and if it was them who took her out they've probably got her home address. They may have worked out her link to Flora and they'll be after her. I'll see you there."

Julia didn't wait for an answer. Her BMW was fitted with concealed flashing blue lights and sirens and she made from Pimlico to Sutton in less than 20 minutes. Her brakes were smoking as she screeched to a halt. She ran to Kim's door, which was mercifully closed. She called Flora.

"Flora, it's me, Julia. I'm outside, let me in please."

The door opened. Flora was tear stained and tense.

"There was banging on the door. Ten minutes ago. I had turned out the lights and I kept the twins quiet. I think whoever it was will come back. I think they are bad people. Where is Kim?"

"Kim's been hurt, but she's safe. And so are you now. A friend of mine will be here in a minute and he'll keep you safe while I sort this out."

With that Julia's phone rang.

"Jake, Alf. I'm outside but we've got company. It's one of the Krasniqis in the pictures. Just one guy in a car up the road, and he's interested in the house. He must have seen you arriving. Looks like he's waiting for back up. Give me a minute to sort him out then I'll be with you. We'll need to get Flora and whoever else is in there away. Get Flora to shove a few things in a bag for her and the kids, and Kim too. Any passports or other travel documents and some clothes for a few days. If I know Albanians they'll be back mob-handed and soon. Get everyone ready to run."

Outside Alf disappeared into an alley. A few seconds later a man who seemed much the worse for wear and booze staggered slowly from another alleyway. He leant on a low wall every few moments and looked like he was about to vomit. Pali Krasniqi watched him with disgust as the drunk made his way towards the Mercedes he was sitting in. The driver's window was open and Pali was smoking a cheroot. The drunk staggered past the car and seemed to bend almost double by the rear passenger door. Pali muttered a foul curse in Albanian, and then the side of his face caved in as a seven-pound lump hammer smashed into his cheek.

The 'drunk' stood upright and ran towards Kim's house.

"Let's go, Jake. Quickly now!"

Alf jogged towards his newly acquired van and opened the rear doors. Jake followed with two terrified children and a tearful young woman who was barely more than a child herself. Each of them was clutching a small backpack. Alf bundled them into the van as gently as he could.

"OK, Jake. I'll find somewhere safe for them. Now you'd better get gone. This place will be crawling with Albanian gangsters or policemen very soon. You'll have some explaining to do."

Julia returned to her car and was leaving the street just as a large dark coloured van turned into it. Under a streetlight she saw that the driver was the other Krasniqi twin. There were two other men in the front alongside him. She didn't hang around to see what happened or what they did when they found the other Krasniqi, who was still slumped in his car and at best very seriously injured. Julia drove calmly but purposefully away from the area. She radioed into Information Room to say she had Kim Morris's children safely housed with their child minder and she was on her way to the hospital.

******

With the immediate danger over Alf was racking his brain about what to do with the children and Flora. He didn't want to take them to Mel's flat, although he was sure she'd take them in temporarily. It was just that she was too close to him and Kelso. There was no way of knowing what Kim Morris had disclosed to the Albanians.

He made a call from his mobile, half expecting it to go unanswered.

"What d'you want?" Elsie grumbled.

"It's Alf. I'm in a jam."

"Fuck me, Alf. Until Sunday morning I was blissfully aware that you were feeding the fishes, then you're suddenly alive and taking a stroll on the common, now you're phoning me at 3 in the sodding morning saying you're in trouble again!"

Alf heard a voice in the background. Matt, and not happy.

"I won't go into the details, Elsie, but I've got three vulnerable and very frightened people in the back of my van and I need somewhere safe for them for a day or two, just until I get something more long-term sorted out. Can you help?"

"Matt's going to kill me, but yes. Bring them round." Elsie gave him her address. It was about half an hour away.

"Flora, can you hear me?" he called over his shoulder. There was no answer. He pulled over and opened the rear door slowly. Flora was poised, crowbar in hand, ready to defend the twins and herself.

"I'm Julia's friend," he said to her, "I'm going to take you somewhere safe while we take care of Kim. You're safe with me for now. I'm not going to hurt you, no one's going to hurt you anymore. Do you understand, Flora?"

Flora's eyes were wide and wildly moving from side to side. She was terrified and in shock. There was nothing he could do for now, so he closed the doors gently and resumed the drive to Guildford.

Alf found Elsie and Matt's neat semi-detached house on a tidy development on the outskirts of the town. A light was on downstairs. He pulled up, went to the door and tapped quietly. Elsie opened the door.

"They're terrified, Elsie, and they don't know me. Can you give me a hand?"

Elsie nodded. She had dressed and she followed Alf to the van. He gently opened the doors. In the back the children had fallen asleep. Flora had her protective arms around them both.

"Flora, this is Louise. She's a friend too. She's going to take care of you for a few days, just until Julia and I can make some arrangements. Do you understand?"

Flora nodded.

"Come along, Flora, let's get you inside with a nice warm drink. What are the children's names?"

"Ben and Sarah. They are twins." Flora whispered.

It seemed she had reverted to her captive state and would comply with anything she was told to do. Elsie helped her and the twins out of the van and shepherded them swiftly into the house.

"Thanks Elsie. I owe you, again. I'll call you as soon as I can."

"Who's Julia?" Elsie asked.

"A special friend, Els. I'll tell you all about it one day."

"I'm not sure I want to know."

She closed the door.

Chapter 21

It was almost 4am by the time Julia arrived at the Central Middlesex Hospital in Acton, where Kim Morris had been taken by ambulance. She found Kim under police guard, still in the recovery room of the emergency department. She was intubated and plugged into a monitor. The two officers watching Kim stood aside for Julia. Kim was going in and out of consciousness. Julia held her hand and waited. After a while Kim's eyes fluttered open.

"It's Julia, Kim. Don't worry everything's fine. I've been to your house and everyone's safe and sound and being taken care of."

Kim squeezed Julia's hand.

"Thanks," she croaked, "is Fl…"

"Everyone's fine, Kim. Everyone."

"Thank you."

"Can you tell me what happened? You don't have to, but it might help."

"I was stupid, went out on my own. Trying to get a handle on the Krasniqis," Kim paused to cough. Blood stained her lips. "They clocked me. One of them drew my attention while the other snuck up. I felt a massive thump and when I woke up I was in the boot of my car. They went to work on me, but only fists and boots. Luckily no knives. They took my bag, my phone, my clothes. They know where I live. They know about my kids. They know about…"

Julia squeezed Kim's hand.

"Ssh now, that's enough. Just rest. I'm going to take care of things. Try to forget all about what happened, think about that holiday you're planning with the kids." Julia held Kim's hand until she fell asleep again.

"How is she, doctor?" Julia asked a harassed-looking young man.

"It's early stages. She was very unstable when she arrived, but she's strong. We need to get a view on her injuries. She'll be going to imaging in a few minutes. Once we know what the damage is we'll work out a treatment plan." He paused.

"What is it, doctor?" Julia asked.

"Her initial bloods weren't too good. We've redone them. Apart from her injuries from the attack it seems that Kim could have some other serious health issues. We won't know until much later, and she'll probably want to discuss it with you."

"I see, thank you doctor. Does her family know?"

"She told us you're her next of kin. I assumed you knew that."

Julia shook her head, momentarily stunned. Her shoulders suddenly felt a huge responsibility resting on them.

She had a brief conversation with the officers looking out for Kim. She advised them that Kim had probably been attacked by organised crime figures involved in the sex trade. They were dangerous, and they should assume they were armed. No fewer than two officers with Kim at any time, and always in contact with back-up. They understood and were armed themselves. Julia thanked them and asked that she be kept informed. She would be back later in the day.

Julia left the hospital and joined the slow-flowing river of tradesmen and early-riser commuters making their way into the capital. She wondered how it must feel to know on a Tuesday morning how your life was going to be the following Friday evening, and the Friday after that. Not to be buffeted by the cruelty and violence of greedy corrupt people, not to be touched by the pain they cause.

She went home to have coffee and get changed. She sent a text to Alf. 'All OK?' it said.

'All fine. Speak later' he responded instantly.

******

In her office Julia logged into the information system and checked for reports in the vicinity of Kim's house. There was no mention of any attack on a car driver, but there was a lengthy account of a suspicious house fire. They had torched Kim's house. It was too early for Savernake, but Julia sent a message to his assistant saying she needed to see him urgently. The she sent for Kim's personal file.

Kim's file was ready for collection by the time Julia's long-suffering assistant Raj got to the office. She asked him to fetch it. It was a slim folder. Clearly Kim was not a high-flier. She had taken a long time to get to sergeant and that seemed to be far enough for her. She had collected a couple of commendations as a constable, one for arresting a violent armed criminal, the other for a well-planned intelligence operation targeting underage sex workers in Soho. She had been on the vice unit for more than six years. No wonder she was tired.

To Julia's surprise Kim was quite a lot younger than she looked, only just turned 40. The file told little about her private life, but Julia noted there was no mention of any family members. There was an old brief report in which Kim had been asking for flexible working arrangements due to a recent relationship break up which left her struggling with child care for her then four year old twins. There was no mention of the children's father. It was a depressing but familiar story.

DAC Savernake's office called her. He was free for a few minutes now. She went to his office.

"If you haven't heard yet, Colin, an officer was kidnapped and severely assaulted last night. Fortunately, she was found before the car she was locked in the boot of was set on fire, otherwise she would be dead. And it would definitely be a murder. As it is she's in a serious condition in the Central Middlesex Hospital. The people who attacked her then went to her home, they got the address out of her - it's a female officer - probably to do harm to her family. They had been moved to a safe place, but the officer's home was subjected to an arson attack and seems to be a total loss. She and her family will need to be compensated and rehoused.

"I'm certain that the people who did this to one of our own were the Krasniqi brothers, the ones you wouldn't let me go after because it would mess with the statistics. So now the statistics will show a kidnap of a police officer, attempted murder of the same police officer, a definite GBH, possibly also with intent, and an arson with intent to endanger life. Now can I get on with my job and sort these bastards out?" Julia hadn't bothered to say good morning to her boss.

Savernake stared at her.

"You are impertinent, Commander Kelso. May I remind you that I am your superior officer!"

"Senior maybe, I wouldn't say superior. Can I have the resources I need? Or do you want something *really* serious to go wrong first?"

"Very well. Now get out. You will regret this, Commander Kelso."

Julia turned on her heel and left Savernake's office. She knew she had gone too far, but she cared more about doing right by Kim Morris than upsetting DAC Colin Savernake.

In her own office Julia rapidly convened an operational team to target the Krasniqi gang. One of them was sent to liaise with the team investigating Kim's kidnap and assault, others to the National Criminal Intelligence Service to enlist the mysterious Barbara's aid and harness her knowledge.

It was swift. By that Tuesday evening one of the Krasniqi twins was in custody along with two henchmen. The other twin was nowhere to be found, but a heavily bloodstained Mercedes saloon with skin and bone fragments had been recovered from a lock-up used by the Krasniqis. Two properties had been identified as Krasniqi brothels. Both had been raided and ten girls had been rescued from them. Late on Tuesday night a body was found on the Lee Valley marshes in East London. Its hands and head had been removed, but investigators quickly linked it to the bloodstained Mercedes and the Krasniqi clan. It was the missing twin, as shown by DNA matches with the surviving one. The investigators found out the following day that the body had still been alive when the hands were removed, and possibly when someone started to saw the head off. So much for fraternal bonds, Julia thought.

The following day the investigation team got the surviving Krasniqi, it was Ilir, remanded in police custody for further enquiries, and he would eventually be charged with a range of crimes including the murder of his brother, rape, unlawful imprisonment, living off immoral earnings and a whole load of other things.

Julia kept Kim updated, but she didn't mention the fact that her house had been burned down. She was still very unwell and lapsing in and out of lucidity.

The frenetic burst of investigative activity had gone a long way towards calming Julia's ire. Now she was able to reflect on the matter of Kim's children, Flora, and the issue of possible complicity in trafficking by at least three people she had a loose association with.

First of all, Julia thought, I need to run and sweat and think. She packed up her things and headed to Dolphin Square with its gym and swimming pool.

Chapter 22

Julia convened a meeting at Mel's flat later that evening – Wednesday. She told Mel and Alf what she had been doing and then looked at them expectantly.

"Kim's kids and Flora are tucked up with an old friend of mine," Alf started. "They won't be able to stay there long because my friend's partner is a serving officer and she's really sticking her neck out. Now that Kim's house is a goner and Kim is still out of action we need to get Flora and the kids somewhere safe where they can stay for a while. Maybe somewhere that Kim can join them as and when she can. Any ideas?"

"My folks have a guest cottage, up in Scotland." Julia suggested.

Alf shook his head.

"If there's a corrupt circle over and above the Krasniqis and it's the people we think it is three of them know you, Jake. Anything to do with you would be too close. Mel?"

"I can't think of anywhere. My lot don't run to a guest cottage, just a shed on the allotment. A hotel, maybe?"

"If I can get them to Ireland I can get them a safe place where they'd have some protection if any hostiles turn up. It'll take a few days to fix, though."

"Do it, Alf," Jake said. "By the way, what's your name at the moment?"

"He's Paulo Silva, at least in England," Mel said.

"OK," Jake said.

"I'll head to Dublin tomorrow and get back as soon as I can."

"Well, while you've been rattling cages, Jake, I've been looking at data. The 'temporary' phones I've linked to our gang of four are busy. They're talking to each other a lot, enough for me to guess a hierarchy. Your mate Dido is top dog, I'd say. The others call her most of the time, not the other way round, like getting her approval to do things or to get instructions. She seems closest to Drew Strathdon judging by the phone contacts. There's also another number that crops up fairly often. Nothing on it yet, but it's also calling Dido. It was hellish busy yesterday and today. Possibly something to do with your well-timed hissy-fit, Jake. It doesn't looks like another temporary phone. It's only activated occasionally but it's been around for quite a while.

"Meanwhile, I took the names we have and images of Dido Sykes, Jasmira Shah, Andrew Strathdon and Bijan Bukani to the encyclopaedic Barbara. I eventually found images of Bukani and Strathdon on the internet, Jasmira's from the FCO yearbook, and Dido's from the snaps Alf took. Guess what? OK, I'll tell you anyway. Barbara didn't recognise the names or images, except one. Your Dido Sykes rang a bell. Only Barbara knows her as something else. She says Dido Sykes used to be a Deborah, Debbi without an e, Saint. She was in some of the 'more assertive' porn movies a few years ago, quite a few years ago, and Barbara said she graduated to high-end escort work. Barbara says she dropped off the scene ages ago, but she's certain it's her.

It got me thinking about where I'd seen her before. It was up on Humberside, East Yorkshire where I'm from. I reckon 'Debbi' was a year or so ahead of me at high school in Hull, only she wasn't a Sykes or a Saint then, or a Deborah or Dido. She looked a bit different too, of course, but I'm pretty certain it's her. She was plain old Carol Jones who lived in a terrace down near the docks with her mum. My dad knows an old retired copper who worked Hull docks back in ancient times. I'm sure he'll remember a thing or two about Carol Jones and her mum, who was a Caroline I think."

"Do some more digging, Mel," Jake said, "we need some substance around the relationship between the four of them. We need to know more about Bukani. Most of all we need to know how they're interacting with traffickers, and which ones they're interacting with. In short, what the fuck are they up to."

"Succinctly put, Commander," Mel said. "Gin?"

******

Paulo Silva was on the early flight from Gatwick to Dublin on Thursday morning. He called a Dublin number from a payphone in the arrivals hall and thirty minutes later the taxi dropped him in Donnybrook. He walked a few streets before arriving at Eugene Flynn's gate. He pressed a buzzer and the gate swung open.

Eugene Flynn and Alan Ferdinand, using the name Thomas Donohue, had become friends years before after Donohue intervened to stop an attack on Flynn and undoubtedly saved the man's life. Eugene was a well-known figure in Republican circles and he wasn't popular with the refuseniks who rejected the peace process in Northern Ireland. In the intervening years

Donohue and Flynn grew to like and trust each other, and other than Jake Kelso and Mel Dunn, Flynn was the only person who knew of Donohue's multiple identities, his past, and his current activities. Eugene's faithful housekeeper Maeve let him in and greeted him with a hug.

"Thomas you're looking grand as ever. Will you be staying this time?" Maeve and her husband Kevin knew Alf as Thomas, and both he and Eugene Flynn thought it best it remained that way.

"Just a flying visit, Maeve. How's your hip these days? Have they fixed it up for you yet?"

"It's just a twinge, Thomas. I'll get round to getting it mended one of these days."

She showed him into Eugene's study and went to fetch coffee. It arrived strong, aromatic and hot, along with a bottle of whiskey 'to give the day a kick start'. Once Maeve departed Alf / Thomas / Paulo spoke at length with Eugene. Eugene called for sandwiches and the two of them continued into the afternoon. Arrangements were agreed, and in the early evening Kevin drove 'Thomas' to Wynn's hotel, his preferred lodging in Dublin, in Eugene's magnificent dark blue 1960s Bentley. 'Thomas', slightly woozy from the whiskey, ordered a hire car for the next morning and had an early night. He had a lot to do and not much time.

After a light breakfast early on Friday morning he set off on the drive south. The long-awaited motorway network guaranteed as a benefit of EU membership was still a distant promise and the drive down to Cork would take a long time. He didn't stop and he made the outskirts of the city shortly after noon. Eugene's niece was waiting in a car in a lay-by as planned. She greeted him with a cool handshake and indicated that he should follow her. She drove swiftly north from the city limits into the rolling countryside. Eventually she turned off the main road on to a narrow lane, and from that on to a long, gated driveway leading to a substantial Victorian-period manor house. The niece, whose name was Roisin, showed 'Thomas' to a sizeable cottage to the rear of the main house. It was warm and dry, and comfortably furnished.

"I live in the main house with my husband and our lot, we've three kids. He travels a lot for work so we're here on our own mostly, with a few staff, of course. They're all Eugene's old pals, or sons of his old pals, and they love the old goat to bits. They'll not let anything happen to your friends. They're welcome to come and stay. Eugene has said so, and so it is. We don't need to know any more than they want to tell us. But it's two children and a sort of nanny is it?"

"Yes, eleven or twelve year-old twins, Ben and Sarah. The sort of nanny is Flora. She's had a rough time but she's a good girl, not much more than a child herself."

"Don't take this the wrong way, but how long will they be staying? That doesn't mean they're not welcome to stay as long as they want, it's just if I need to fix things with the school and all that."

"I can't say, Roisin, the mother's not so well and it all rather depends on how she's doing. I'll let you know as soon as I can. For now, can I get them to you next week? It may be a bit sooner but realistically it'll be Tuesday. I'd like to get them here in daylight."

"That's fine Thomas. Can you find your way back to Cork?"

He could and did, and he returned his hire car to Cork airport. He got the last flight of the day back to London and got a taxi to the hotel. After a quick text message to Jake he collapsed exhausted into bed and slept.

In the early 2000's youthful, and sometimes not so youthful, global travellers still gathered on weekend mornings on the south bank in London to trade equipment, stories and vehicles with each other. Alf was there bright and early as the clapped-out VW campers and other converted vans and buses started to assemble. He was looking for something serviceable and not overly conspicuous. He found a blue VW combi van which was being sold off by a sober-looking Kiwi couple in their late 30s. Keen to talk, they told him they'd taken a delayed gap-year from their jobs as teachers and had driven the van through Europe. It had served them well and was in good order. Now they were selling up and going home.

Alf examined the vehicle, looking for certain features he would need. Satisfied, he haggled for a while and handed over an agreed wad of cash to the New Zealanders. He said he'd sort out the paperwork so they didn't need to hang around. The VW camper joined the battered builder's van in a side road off Wimbledon Common.

That evening he explained the arrangements he had made to Jake and Mel. They approved. As the evening wore on Jake was looking tired and distracted. Shortly after 9 she said she needed to go home, but she gestured to Alf that he should stay. She was fine on her own, for tonight. Mel said nothing.

The next day Mel woke early. Alf was still in a deep sleep but her busy fingers went to work. When he was hard enough she mounted him. He was still half asleep and was dreaming of being deep inside one of the two incredible women in his life. He kept his eyes shut so he couldn't see which it was. At first he thought the gentleness meant he was making love to Jake, and then he felt the unmistakeable ripple of Mel's muscles. He opened his eyes and looked up at her gorgeous face with its brown eyes and slightly crooked smile.

"About time too, Senhor Silva. I've broken at least two of my rules so far, but now you've surfaced we can get going."

After forty minutes of stunning activity she let them both come together, it was a Sunday morning after all. He lay back with his eyes closed while Mel showered. She brought him coffee and sat next to him on the edge of the bed, her bathrobe undone and hanging open.

"That was something to take your mind off why it's called being *in loco parentis* while you're being driven nuts by a couple of bored children stuck in a rattling old VW camper van for two days. I have nieces and nephews. I know these things. Seriously though take care, of yourself and them - Flora and the children. The Albanians are nasty and angry. Jake would be devastated if anything happened to you. I would be too."

With that she stood up, dropping her bathrobe to the floor. Alf watched her as she moved about the bedroom getting dressed, awestruck by her perfect honey-gold body.

"It's just not right, Miss Dunn, that someone should look so sexy just putting on socks."

"Shut up, Ferdinand. Get up and get going. See you in a few days." Mel left the flat.

By 10 Alf was outside Elsie's house in Guildford. He'd called her earlier and his passengers were ready to go when he arrived. Elsie was full of warmth and kindness, while Matt was cordial at best. He could see that Elsie was quite relieved her guests were leaving.

The VW van trundled off. After a while Alf pulled over. The twins were in the back sitting quietly. Flora was in the front. He explained to her what was going to happen. They would drive a long way to a boat, cross to Northern Ireland, which was part of Britain, and then go to a safe place he had found for them in Ireland. The long drive was the way to avoid passport checks and busy international ports. Sometimes Flora would have to be hidden. Beneath the bench that the twins were sitting on was a space for blankets and luggage. Flora would need to go in there when he told her to, and all the time when they were on the boat. It was only two hours and it would be OK.

Flora simply nodded. As the journey rolled on Flora seemed to relax and started entertaining the children with songs and games. They had to stop every couple of hours, and by the time they were in the north of England Alf decided they would need to stop for the night. An anonymous motel did the job. He booked a family room for all of them, and he slept on the couch in a sleeping bag so Flora and the children could have the beds. After breakfast they continued and reached Stranraer by midday. Before arriving at the port Alf stopped and tucked Flora into her hiding place. He told the children to pretend to be asleep. He waved his Declan Walsh passport at the control officer, who wasn't the least bit interested, and a little over two hours later he was on the road south from Larne towards Belfast and on towards the Irish Republic. Monday night was spent in another motel, this time just south of Dublin, and early on Tuesday afternoon the VW clattered up the driveway to where the smiling Roisin was waiting. The journey had been long and, happily, entirely uneventful. Alf was hugely relieved.

Chapter 23

While Ferdinand was piloting the camper van through the Scottish lowlands towards Stranraer Julia Kelso was making coffee for Tim Edwards, the Special Branch Commander who was another old family friend.

"I would have come up to you, Tim," she said, "no need for you to flog down here all the time."

Edwards had a spacious corner office on the eighteenth floor of the tall tower block at Scotland Yard. It had great views.

"More than happy to descend, Jake." Edwards said amiably. "First of all, you've the best coffee in the building, and secondly you have no idea how nosy Special Branch people are. If they saw a strange Commander - no offence - wandering the corridors of power half of them would start a rumour that you've come to shut us down while the other half would be all over you like a rash. Now, how can I help?"

"Can I borrow Niall Morton and Errol Spelman again?" she asked. Morton and Spelman were two detective sergeants who ran one of the operations teams in the Branch.

"You can't have Niall. He's been posted as CHELO to Budapest."

"Cello?"

"With a CH. It means Counter Hostile Extremism Liaison Officer. What used to be a Counter Terrorism Liaison Officer until the politically correct brigade got involved. Hungary is up for EU membership next year and Brussels decided to persuade Budapest to have one of the new CHELO posts as part of the pre-accession process. Niall got the job. He'll be good. Errol's still around and you're welcome to him if you like."

"Thanks Tim, that would be good."

"What do you want him for, Jake? Another one of your 'off the books' numbers?"

"Afraid so, Tim. I think we've come across corrupt facilitation of people-trafficking. I need some good investigators to do some quiet digging so I'm sure of my facts before I light another fuse."

"OK, Jake, but please try not to get anyone shot this time. The paperwork is crippling." Edwards gave her a wan smile.

Half an hour after Tim Edwards departed Julia's assistant Raj knocked on her door.

"Another one of those SB blokes to see you, boss. It's not in the diary."

"Yes, sorry about that, Raj. Last minute thing. Could you show him in."

Errol Spelman was tall and athletically built, and dressed in an elaborately casual manner.

"Errol, good to see you again." Julia stood and extended her hand.

Spelman took it. His hand felt warm and dry in hers.

"Good to see you too, Julia." Spelman had a Jamaican lilt to his accent, despite the fact he was born and bred in London.

Jake looked at him, and she felt momentarily weak at the knees as she looked into his dark eyes. In her mind she had a fleeting and highly inappropriate image of her very white skin next to his rich velvety black one. She had no idea where the thought came

144

from and she busied herself with coffee while she calmed down. She passed Spelman a mug of hot black coffee and they sat at her conference table.

"So, Niall's been sent to Budapest I hear," Julia started.

"Yes. He's got one of the new CHELO posts. I think he'll be good at it."

"Does he speak Hungarian?"

"He's been there nearly two weeks, so by now he's probably fluent. He has an ear. One of his other languages is Russian and almost everyone in that part of the world speaks it too. Hungary doesn't have a specific problem with extremism, at least not yet, but it's the crossroads between Europe and the Balkans. The Hungarians take a close interest in what's going on in their neighbourhood."

"Errol, forgive me for asking but why is it you have a Jamaican accent? I thought you were a Londoner."

He smiled at her and held her gaze. She felt the stirring again.

"I'm London through and through, but the powers that be saw fit to send me to Jamaica for a few years on an extended undercover gig. The accent I adopted then sort of stuck. It feels right."

"I didn't mean to pry. Just curious," Julia said.

"How can I help you, Julia?" Spelman asked.

"I've come across a group of people who are, I think, corruptly involved in human trafficking. Mostly young girls for the sex industry. I need some quick and very quiet background work done on them, the sort of thing you and Niall have done for me before. I've written down everything that I know about them." Julia passed him a slim folder.

"I take it this is urgent?" he asked.

"As ever, Errol, and very sensitive. I should tell you that three of the people on the list are known to me personally, everyone except Bijan Bukani. For openness I was once engaged to Andrew Strathdon. I knew the other two while I was at Oxford, but not that well, just acquaintances. I think you need to know, but please keep it to yourself if you can."

Errol smiled at her. That pang again.

"I'll be the soul of discretion, Julia," he said.

"Thanks. You still have my number? If you need to speak to me that is."

"Of course." He stood.

Julia extended her hand again. He took it. Did she imagine it or did he hold on to it for just a moment too long?

When Spelman had gone Julia sat back in her chair. She was astonished at herself, at her response to the stunningly handsome black man who had looked into her eyes and held her hand. He was around her age, she guessed, but several ranks junior to her, as well as probably married and anyway completely off-limits. The buttons Mel Dunn had pushed in her when they first had sex together a few months earlier had certainly let loose a part of Julia Kelso that she had been keeping locked in for a very long time. It had also whetted appetites she hadn't known she had. While she found her new-found sexual curiosity exhilarating, Julia felt rattled by whatever it was that enabled her to go to bed with Mel Dunn, to have casual sex with Justin Evans, or to fancy the pants off

Errol Spelman. And all that while she had very deep and warm feelings for the late DCI Alan Ferdinand, with whom she slept as often as she could. She needed to get back in control.

Chapter 24

By Wednesday Alf was back in London. While he'd been taking Flora and the children to safety Julia had been visiting Kim, who had been admitted to the critical care unit while the medics worked out how to put her back together again. She had suffered a severe beating and her internal organs hadn't been spared. They weren't telling her, but her survival was by no means a sure thing.

Julia sat with her. She was still groggy and sedated, but she was with-it enough to ask about her children.

"The Krasniqis found your house, Kim. The children and Flora are fine, they're in a safe place with a friend of mine, safely away from gangsters and Flora's safely away from immigration Your house didn't do so well, though."

"I never liked it anyway. I was only there because I could afford it, and the only things of sentimental value in it are the people. I'm glad the kids and Flora are OK. Will they come to see me?"

"Not for a while, Kim. But as soon as you're well enough I'll get you to them. There's plenty of room for you to relax and get better where they are. Is their dad about?"

Kim gave a weak laugh.

"If only! I don't know you that well, Julia, but sadly for you you're all I've got. My mum's dead, I've no idea if my dad's alive or dead and I'm not interested either way. I'm on my own, just me and my kids. When I joined the cops I was 19 years old. I've no idea how I got in, they must have been desperate or something. But suddenly I was a free spirit loose in London with a bit of money and an interesting job. After probation I shared a police flat with two other girls for a few years. It was party central. You wouldn't think it to look at me now but I was a looker, a real good-time girl and I had no shortage of blokes. What I'm getting to, Julia, is that I don't know who the dad is. I can sort of narrow it down to one or two weekends, but not one or two blokes. It could have been any one of five or six, maybe more. Long and short is I was up the duff with the twins so I settled down. Took some time off to have the kids and knuckled down to looking after them on my own and holding down my job."

"You've never tried to find him?"

"No. It was my fault, my life. Like I said, the flat was party central and I was having as much fun as anyone else. Only I got a bit more than I bargained for. You've got to laugh. I do love the kids, though. They've been the making of me."

Julia gave Kim's hand a squeeze and changed the subject. She told her about her whirlwind campaign against the Krasniqis. The gang was effectively out of it now. One Krasniqi was dead, the other was looking at a long stretch and deportation. Other gang members were in the same boat.

"Do you know where I might find a Bernard Croxley, Kim? He's the guy who makes the porn movies for the Krasniqis and probably others too. He's the only one linked with the Krasniqis who I haven't laid hands on yet. I'd like to get the full set."

"Bernie Croxley? He used to have a dirty mag and picture shop in an alley round the back of Wardour

149

Street. I haven't seen him for ages, not that I've been looking for him. He's a bit third-rate, Julia. Why's he interesting?" Kim stopped talking while she coughed up some blood.

"Just for completeness. Don't worry about it, he'll keep. Now, are they looking after you well?"

"Dunno. Every time I start to grumble about something they give me an injection and I wake up the next day. I suppose it's doing me good, to be off the cigs and booze for a bit. I don't know what they're filling me up with but it sure takes the edge off." Kim coughed again.

A nurse approached. It was time Kim had a rest and could Julia come back later? Julia said of course she could. As she left the ward a doctor came up to her, the same one she had seen the night Kim had been brought in.

"Can I have a word, Miss Kelso? About Kim."

"How's she doing?" Julia asked.

"She's making progress with her injuries, but she's not out of trouble yet. There's been some serious bleeding and some of the tissue is badly damaged. We can't sew it all back together for a while, not until the tissue is stronger, that's why we're keeping her sedated. If she fell or moved awkwardly it could be fatal. But I have longer-term concerns too."

"You mentioned some blood tests that you weren't happy with."

"Yes," the doctor continued, "there are some abnormalities. Do you know much about Kim's lifestyle?"

"Not really. We're colleagues, I don't really know her that well. I had no idea she'd put me down as next of kin, not that I mind it."

"Well, her bloods tell me she's been living dangerously for quite some time. We did a full CT scan, and her liver isn't in good shape. It's possible it might still recover some of its function if she never drinks again. If she's lucky, and she sticks to a no alcohol regime, she might get well enough to go on the transplant list, but I'd say it's quite a long shot. On top of that her blood sugar levels gave us cause for concern. Unfortunately, it's justified. Endocrinology need to have a good look at her, but it looks like Kim has untreated and uncontrolled Type 2 diabetes which may have already caused serious organ damage. I'm sorry, Miss Kelso, but even if Kim makes a full recovery from her injuries she still has a mountain to climb, two mountains in fact, and a lot of changes to make."

Julia was stunned and helpless. In her time as a police officer she had seen many tragedies and horrors; mostly they were matters of urgency and suddenness. Now she was looking at a duty to take care of someone who's tragedy would unfold over time, someone she barely knew but felt responsible for. She suddenly felt she would like to have someone she could really lean on, so she wouldn't feel so alone.

******

Mel, meanwhile, hadn't been idle. She had been working up a good picture of the communications of the 'gang of four' as she called them. Her theory about

151

the hierarchy of the group seemed to be borne out. Dido's temporary number was the central pivot, with numerous calls from the other three. The fifth phone Mel had recognised hadn't yet been linked to any permanent number, maybe because the owner of it was more tech, or technique, savvy than the others. She hadn't yet built up a picture of its movements between locations, so she assumed that when it wasn't in use the battery was taken out of it.

Of the remaining three temporary phones those of Bijan Bukani and Jasmira Shah were in most frequent contact with numbers outside the UK. Bukani was speaking to Bulgaria and to Hungary and the Balkan states, as well as to Romania. Shah was also talking to Bulgaria, Hungary and Romania, and also to Italy and Greece and a whole load of other south- and central-European countries. It was clear to Mel that Andrew Strathdon's phone, although a UK pay-as-you-go was based in Belgium but travelling frequently between there, the UK, Holland and France. Classic EU staffer movements. The calls it made were mostly to those countries and Mel was trying to run a tracking exercise to locate Strathdon's contacts. If they were concerned in human trafficking it seemed likely that Bukani was the link with the gangs on the ground who snared victims, Shah fixed it with British Embassies and Consulates to get visas. Strathdon could be coordinating movements of victims both within Europe and into Britain, all on behalf of, or because of, Dido Sykes. That was the theory she was working on. She called her best contact at GCHQ in Cheltenham.

******

The three of them met at Mel's flat that evening. Mel outlined her theory and the others agreed it seemed to fit the pattern of communications and, as far as they could make out the areas of expertise or influence of the members of the 'gang of four'. Mel had established through various law-enforcement channels and liaison officers that Bijan Bukani was a UAE citizen of Iranian heritage who had indefinite leave to remain and work in the UK. Routine checks on port movements showed that he travelled frequently to the Middle East and to southern Europe. A contact in the financial crime team found out that Bukani was regarded as a high-flying trader who made a lot of money for his bank but who also scared the pants off his bosses because of his 'independent actions'. He was a maverick.

Jake told them she had set Special Branch on the gang and she planned to let their enquiries run their course before deciding on the next moves. She did suggest that Alf, or Paulo, should try to get close to Bijan Bukani. Mel said she would see what leads she could get to make that happen.

A plan was starting to form. They agreed that Alf, or Paulo, should try to make a connection with Bukani. Mel would keep going with the phones and communications stuff, all alongside her day job and with no supporting paperwork or an identifiable operational team to work with. Jake could see that Mel was worried by this, it was after all a sacking offence, if not a potentially criminal one. Jake said that as soon as they had enough she would make it all official, but for now - assuming they were on the right track with the 'gang of four' any early disclosure of their suspicions would blow them all out of the water. They all agreed on the plan, and also to keep Jerry Keynes at a long arm's length.

Once the business was out of the way they relaxed over drinks and a Chinese takeaway. As she demolished her second large gin and tonic inside half an hour Jake tried not to dwell on the doctor's words about Kim's lifestyle. She told the others that Kim was in a bad way and that it was long-term. She also told them that Kim was all the children had, except Flora. Jake would speak to Kim about making up a story for the local education authority about the children being absent. Could Alf think about making their stay in Ireland a long-term if not permanent thing? He would work on it.

The night outside was dark and damp. Although it was still relatively early they were tired. The flat was warm and cosy. The bedroom door was open. They all looked at each other. There was a long pause.

"Oh, alright then, I'll take the sofa!" Mel said. "It's only my flat after all."

Chapter 25

Errol Spelman had wasted no time. He had basic biographies and character pen-pictures for Julia's four people within two days. He called her mobile and she asked him to come to her office. When he arrived she was surprised at his appearance. Instead of the really cool clothes he usually wore he was in rough workman's gear. He seemed shorter and two of his teeth seemed to have turned to gold. He noticed her looking at him.

"Just come in off the plot, Julia. I haven't had time to change yet."

"What's with the teeth?" she asked.

"Just cosmetic." He fiddled with the gold teeth and removed a coloured plastic sheath. He also adjusted his posture and before her eyes he turned back into the striking man she was more used to seeing. She was finding it difficult to concentrate.

"That's a very good party trick, Errol. Now, what have you got?"

"Let's start with Bijan Bukani. Bijan Amirzadeh Bukani. He's early thirties, born in the UAE as a third-generation immigrant. His grandfather moved the family to Dubai back in the 1950s from Iran – they were Tehran bazaar traders. Grandfather set up a trading company mostly dealing between Dubai and Iran and did quite well. Bijan's father was in the chair when the Islamic revolution happened in 1979, and according to my information he saw an opportunity to profit from the monarchists trying to get their money and property out of Iran. It seems that Bijan's dad was very good at bribery and smuggling. Bijan was sent to university in the US and then to the UK - the LSE. He's smart. I know someone at the bank where he works. He was hired as an economic strategist but he quickly proved himself to be much better at foreign currency trading. The thing is, your Bijan is an inveterate gambler. He does well overall betting on currency movements and his bosses put up with it. He's under very close watch by the bank's compliance and security teams, but so far they haven't found him using any of their money for his personal gambling, which is hardcore. He isn't married or in any sort of relationship. He's got an apartment down in Docklands but isn't there much. He's banned from a few of the mainstream casinos in London and Paris, but he's welcome at others in Monaco, Macau and the Middle East. My contact says he's seen people like Bijan before. They crash and burn quickly, and usually quite loudly. He says Bijan is about one bad trading day away from summary dismissal, but he doesn't seem to have bad trading days. He always brings in a profit. I've got his passport details if you want.

"Moving on to Jasmira Shah. Not a huge amount available and the people we know at the FCO are quite cagey about staff matters. But we have been told she's an 'intermediate flyer', which means not particularly good and not particularly bad. As you know, she went to Oxford but only managed a Desmond, a 2:2, in International Relations. It was enough to get her into the FCO but not on the fast track. She's not going to end up as an ambassador or Permanent Secretary. Jasmira's from a pushy family, her father's big in pharmaceuticals and her mother is from one of the top Islamabad families, the high-ups or VVIPs as they're known. Jasmira is married but not that happily, it seems. The husband refuses to be dragged round after her on overseas postings, at least not until she gets some proper status. The best she's done so far is first secretary, and she's spent most of her time in consular jobs. Her current job is as a senior manager in the HR department. The FCO encourages its mainstream staff to take head office admin jobs from time to time. It seems Jasmira was the only applicant to make it through to a selection board for the job she's in. It was a small step up, grade-wise, but it's a job where you upset at least two thirds of the people you end up sending to posts.

"Andrew Strathdon. You know most of his background so we've just looked at what he's doing now. He's a senior legal officer in the EU's Migration Directorate. Not the top dog, but not far off. The Migration Directorate looks at all aspects of the free movement of people within the EU, one of its four key freedoms. Their aim is to create a level workforce playing field so that all EU member states can trade with each other on the same basis, so with broadly similar pay rates, working conditions, human rights and so on. One aspect of Strathdon's domain is quite interesting. He looks at legal aspects of the Schengen Information System, which holds information on people and is available to law-enforcement and policy makers across the EU - as long as they're also signed up to the Schengen agreement. Which is everyone except the UK and Ireland. I heard from our CHELO in Brussels that Strathdon takes a very special interest in the Schengen Information System, and in the workings of the units in member states who have pretty much free access to information on people, including criminal records and people who are wanted for crimes or are simply reported missing.

"Finally, Dido Sykes. You say you knew her at Oxford. She was never a student at any Oxford college, or at Oxford Brookes or any of the other 'colleges' with Oxford addresses. We can't find any recent records relating to her in that name, or the other names you gave me – Debbi Saint or Carol Jones. She could have an overseas passport, but it would have to be an EU one or she'd be in the Home Office records. We followed her around yesterday and today. My team is still with her. She uses taxis or a car service, seems to use cash only, and she's hardly ever still. The only point of reference we have for her at the moment is the office in Clerkenwell, and even that's on a short-term rental. She's set my alarm ringing, Julia. No normal person goes around without leaving traces. She's either a spook or she's at it. That's my humble opinion."

Julia had been making notes and now she asked Errol for a few clarifications. What he had told her had brought the four people into a more personal focus but hadn't shone a big bright light on what they were up to. That would be too much to ask for. Bijan Bukani and Jasmira Shah both had flaws, that was clear to see. Drew Strathdon seemed to be taking an interest in an area that would be potentially beneficial to people traffickers. And Dido Sykes was just screamingly incongruous.

Errol Spelman handed over his file of typed notes to Julia. He stood towering above her, smiling down.

She had to fight her impulses and so shook his hand briefly and thanked him for his prompt report. She looked forward to hearing anything further. Julia felt her cheeks becoming warm. Errol was clearly used to having this effect on women. He passed her a card.

"My personal number, Julia. Any time."

After he'd left she leant heavily on her office door, partly afraid he would come back and very afraid of what might happen if he did.

She forced herself to focus on his report and read it through twice more. She called Mel.

"Anything on Bijan, Mel?"

"Are you spying on me? I've just had a call. He's booked business class on a British Airways flight to Sofia tomorrow. I've got the details. I was just going to give what's his name a call. He should go along too I think. I'll give him the booking details and Bijan's seat number."

Chapter 26

The following afternoon Paulo Silva lowered himself into seat 2C on the British Airways flight to Sofia, Bulgaria. To his left was a youngish man with an easy-going expression, but talking urgently into a mobile phone. The cabin door closed and the steward addressed a few words to the passenger in 2A asking him to end his call and turn his phone off. He eventually complied. As soon as they were airborne 2A pressed the call button and asked for champagne. While the steward was there Mr Silva asked for a malt whisky with still water. The drinks arrived. 2A unscrewed the top of his tiny bottle of champagne and poured. Mr Silva raised his glass.

"Cheers," he said to 2A, "it always tastes better when the airline gives it to you for nothing."

"Except the crazy cost of the ticket, you mean!" 2A responded.

"There is that," said Mr Silva, "but it's nearly the weekend so let's make a start."

2A raised his glass and drained it. He signalled for another. Mr Silva did the same.

With the third drink Mr Silva introduced himself.

"Paulo Silva. Have you been to Sofia before? This is my first visit - I'm looking at some real estate."

"Bijan, but people call me BB. I've got some business to see to on Monday but a weekend in Sofia is always good. Lots of fun! Where are you staying?"

"My office booked the Radisson. Is it any good?"

"Best in town. I always stay there. It has everything and it's close to everywhere you'd want to go. Are they sending a limo for you?"

"I don't think so. I was going to get a taxi."

"Bulgarian taxi drivers are completely nuts! I'll give you a ride. The casino at the Radisson sends a limo for me. The London Casino, it's called. They like me there - I go for the roulette and blackjack. Where's the real estate you're seeing?"

"On the mountain - Vitosha, is it?"

"Yes. It's a good place to be if you're living in town. The air is fresher. The gangsters all have places up there too so it's safe as well."

"It sounds wonderful." said Senhor Silva.

Silva and BB talked on for the rest of the flight, drinking steadily. On arrival in Sofia BB led his new friend through the VIP passport lane, which a 50 Euro note folded inside his passport gave him access to. Silva did the same. The ride into town in the casino's limo was a white knuckle one, so god only knew what the regular taxis were like.

"Bulgaria will be in the EU within five years. Between now and then so much money will be pouring into this country. There are fortunes to be made. My advice is to buy as much real estate as you can get hold of - just make sure it's not Soviet era junk. Everything else will make money. It's supposed to be illegal for foreigners to own property here, but a few Euros or some USD here and there makes problems disappear. I know people too, so you just give me a call." BB passed a business card to Silva. It was the bank's, but he had written his own mobile number on the back.

The limo pulled up at the Radisson, a glass beacon in the centre of the city right opposite the parliament building. They both got out and went in. At the check-in the receptionist handed a folded note to Silva. He read it and swore in Portuguese.

"The bastard real-estate vendor has pulled out! Says the properties have been sold!"

"That's too bad, Paulo. But on the bright side you've got some time off in a fun city. I'm seeing some people tonight but why don't we meet up in the morning and I'll show you around. Maybe find some better real estate for you to look at."

"Thanks, BB. I'd appreciate that. I'll call you in the morning." Silva went up to his room.

He unpacked his small case and freshened up from the journey. It was early evening and he went down to the lobby bar. On the face of it the Radisson was a perfectly normal international hotel, but it soon became clear that there was an undercurrent. Outside the building there were ranks of parked Mercedes and BMWs, each with its own phalanx of lumpy young men in black leather jackets. Inside the hotel there were also small groups of other slightly smarter but no less lumpy leather-coated young men, all within calling distance of one or other of the sharply tailored older men with very young women on their arms who were ordering magnums of champagne and bottles of cognac. Sofia's glitterati had come out to play.

Silva noticed another small group, a group which didn't seem to be part of the main scene. This group comprised young men with slightly darker skins, but who were well dressed and seemed quietly spoken. They appeared to be waiting for girls. Silva ordered a beer from a waiter and found a seat from which to take in the proceedings. A second beer followed, then a plate of food. The expensive group with their

162

decorative women had melted away into the casino. Silva had seen his new friend BB go that way too. The lobby bar now held more regular hotel guests, foreign tourists and business people, but the small group of quiet young men still lingered. As Silva watched young girls would hover outside the hotel door and one or other of the quiet men would rise and go to meet them. The young man would take the girl off somewhere and was normally back within an hour. Neither the girls nor the boys looked like prostitutes, and Silva didn't see any of the usual transactional signs. The girls were all young, sometimes very young, and they looked lost and adrift, not at all sophisticated or self-confident. They were all pretty, but in an artless way. These were country girls, poor girls from the estates on the edge of town, maybe Serbian girls from across the border. Just like Flora.

As the black leather jackets started to congregate again Silva decided to call it a day. He went to his room, took a long shower and went to bed.

At 10 the next morning he called BB. He answered groggily. Silva could hear a female voice in the background complaining in broken English.

"See you downstairs in an hour, Paulo," BB eventually managed to say.

Paulo sipped a coffee and watched BB walk across the lobby. He looked better than he sounded, but not much. He ordered a coffee with a cognac chaser.

"A long night, Paulo, but good. I came out ahead and found some female company too."

Paulo assumed he meant the bored looking girl who had come down with BB in the lift, the one who almost certainly must have looked much better the evening before and who had walked away from BB and the Radisson hotel without a backward glance.

"I've asked a friend to meet us, Paulo. He's not Bulgarian but he lives here, up on Vitosha as it happens." BB said.

"How do you know him?" Paulo asked.

"We've done some business over the last couple of years. He knows the real estate scene and is happy to take us around for an hour or two. Here he comes now." BB indicated a man in his late twenties, slim and good-looking, neatly dressed. Paulo recognised him as one of the quiet ones from the night before, the ones meeting girls like Flora. BB stood and waved him over.

"Luan, my friend, how are you? This is Paulo, a friend from London. He's looking to buy a load of real estate on Vitosha."

Luan shook Paulo's hand politely.

"I am pleased to meet you, Paulo. We can talk in the car about your requirements."

His English was accented but carefully constructed.

"Likewise, Luan. Pleased to meet you."

"You are English?" Luan asked.

"Yes and no. I'm from Portugal but my family is originally from England. I went to school in Britain but I live in Portugal now."

Luan didn't seem especially interested.

"BB says you're not Bulgarian but you live here now," Paulo said.

"Yes, that is so. I am from Kosovo, my family is Albanian. I came here while the war was going on and I have a business here now."

"What business is that?"

"General trading, travel, foreign exchange, real estate of course. There is great activity now, getting ready to join EU. Shall we go?"

Luan led the way to a large four-wheel drive BMW. The driving seat was already taken. Luan got in alongside the driver, who was wearing a leather jacket of course, while BB and Paulo took the rear seat.

Sofia was quiet at that time. It was a Saturday morning. Luan pointed out occasional landmarks – the football stadium, the art gallery, the various bars and restaurants imitating the music venues of London and New York. The car made its way to the south of the city centre and started to climb the mountain. Vitosha is an impressive peak that seems to rise out of nowhere. Sofians ski there in the winter, just a short ride from town.

Luan stopped the car periodically to show Paulo various villas and apartment blocks, all of which could be bought for the right price. Paulo asked what the price range was and set himself a fictitious budget towards the top end of it. After a couple of hours it was clear that BB wasn't going to last much longer and Paulo suggested they return to the city. On the winding road down the mountain they had to stop so BB could vomit noisily into a drain.

Back at the Radisson Paulo thanked Luan profusely and asked if he could have a number to call him on. He would arrange to come back in a week or two to look at specific villas, which was what he and his associates thought they wanted to buy. Luan produced a business card with a logo and 'Sofia

International Enterprise' printed on the front. On the back he wrote Luan Krasniqi and a Bulgarian mobile phone number.

BB was looking green and he went off to his room. Luan took his leave. Paulo went to the hotel business centre and composed an email for Mel on their covert email account, giving Luan Krasniqi's name, description, business address and email, and his mobile number. 'Flora's Luan, I think' he wrote alongside it.

He could see little point in remaining in Sofia so he called British Airways to secure a seat on the late afternoon flight back to Heathrow. Before leaving the hotel he left a message for BB saying he would call him in London next week. He was back in the quiet casino-less and gangster-free civilisation of the Cannizaro Hotel by 11pm. He slept well.

Chapter 27

"Alf's done well." Mel was on the phone to Julia on Monday morning. "He made contact with Bijan Bukani on the plane. Seems Bukani fancies himself as a playboy but got pissed pretty quickly. He spent Friday evening in the hotel casino and rented a companion for the night. On the Saturday, and this is the best bit, he introduced our man to one Luan Krasniqi with whom he does business. Flora told you about him. I've got Krasniqi's mobile number and email address - Cheltenham are looking out for him but I'm going to need paperwork soon, Jake. Very soon. Alf's going to meet up with Bukani again this week."

"Brilliant, Mel. I'll speak to your DG today. I don't suppose he'll be happy about it but ho-hum. Errol sent me a load of pictures his team took outside Dido Sykes's office. They were there for two days and Errol reckons Dido comes and goes pretty frequently. I'm going to try to bump into her to see how she reacts."

"OK. I've put together a summary of what we have so far. Once you get it all together there's a reasonably strong circumstantial case supporting Jerry Keynes's theory, and pointing at our gang of four. There's some big holes in it though, not least there's not much intelligence pointing towards their direct involvement in criminality."

"I need to see what you've got, Mel. Can you come over here with it? I'm in my office."

Mel arrived an hour later with a briefcase full of charts and papers. She spent another hour talking Julia through a series of connections between gangs strongly suspected of trafficking girls and Bijan Bukani. She also showed Julia the connections between Bukani - on his successive temporary phones - and the other three members of the gang of four. If you accepted that the temporary phones were just that, and that they belonged to the respective members of the gang of four, the case against them started to stack up. Now all they had to do was confirm the linkage between the temporary phones and the four 'suspects', and to work out just exactly what each of them was up to.

Mel drew Julia's attention to the other phone she had mentioned previously, the one that didn't seem to be a temporary one in the same way that the others were. This phone had been in use for quite a long time. It was only ever used to contact members of the gang of four, nearly always Dido Sykes, and in between times it was deactivated, meaning turned off with the battery removed. Mel had done some geolocation on it and it was used primarily in central and north London, and once or twice in rural Hertfordshire.

"I'm not sure if this one belongs to a fifth gang member or not," Mel said, "but the behaviour is definitely dodgy. The most innocent explanation I can come up with it that it might be Dido's bit on the side and he or she doesn't want to be found out. If that's the case, whoever it is knows enough about mobile communications to make the phone completely untraceable between calls. It's a faff to take batteries in and out of phones - the others don't do it. It's a long shot, but I've put in a request to look for other phones that join or leave networks in the same place and at the same time as the fifth phone. It might give us a pointer towards whoever number five is."

"You do have a devious mind, Mel, thank god. I can't get to your DG today but I've a meeting with him at 10 tomorrow at your place. Can you be ready for us?"

"Sure, but I wouldn't be surprised if the DG starts to smell rodents with you and me repeatedly cooking up corruption cases between us. Will you give me a job after he fires me?"

"I suppose I could. Your coffee's much better than Raj's. Can you type slowly and answer the phone in a surly manner?"

"You'd only hire me as your gofer? You are a rude ungrateful Scottish person - after all I've done for you!"

"I'll see you tomorrow." Julia said.

******

Julia had almost forgotten how hard it is to look as if you're doing something while essentially just hanging around. It's the most crucial of surveillance skills, and one that few people have. The advent of mobile phones had helped enormously, as had the explosion of takeaway coffee shops. It was a cool but pleasantly dry afternoon, and Julia found herself a perch on a low wall. She sipped at a coffee while having a pretend conversation with someone on her phone. She was about 50 yards from Dido Sykes's office front door.

Just as she was running out of credible time Julia saw the door open. She recognised Dido instantly.

Her jet-black hair and striking make-up complemented her expensive designer outfit. Julia made her move. She walked towards her, still talking into her phone with a cardboard coffee cup in the other hand.

"I know all that, but I've really got to complete the purchase this week!" Julia had raised her voice. "No! That's your job. Please, just get it done and let me know by the end of the afternoon."

"Bloody lawyers," Julia muttered, as she careered into Dido Sykes and dropped her cardboard coffee cup.

"Oh God! I'm so sorry. Have I splashed coffee on you? Dido? Dido Sykes? It's me, Julia Kelso - from Oxford? Gosh, I haven't seen you in years! I'm so sorry. I was so busy shouting at my solicitor I didn't see you there."

"Julia!" Dido exclaimed. "What a surprise! You're looking great. How are you? Don't worry about the coffee, it's just a tiny drop. You can hardly see it."

The women talked at each other excitedly for a few minutes.

"So, what are you doing round here?" Julia asked.

"I've got an office near here. I run my own media and information company now. What about you?"

"I've been in London for a couple of years now. I moved down from Scotland. To get away from the wind and rain mostly."

"I hear you're a big hitter in the police now. At Scotland Yard, too!" Dido said. She had a slightly affected mid-Atlantic accent.

And who told you that, I wonder? Julia thought to herself.

170

"That's right. I decided on public service after Uni and the police got the short straw. It's interesting though. What did you do after graduation?"

"I went to the States for a while. I did an MBA in Boston and then worked in Europe," Dido said vaguely. "I've only been in London a short while, there's such a vibrant business culture here now. Too good to miss."

"Do you keep in touch with anyone from Uni?"

"No, not really. You?"

"I bumped into Drew over New Year. You know we'd split up?"

"No, I didn't. I always thought you two were so solid. What happened?"

"That's a long story for another time, Dido. Oh, I also saw Jas, Jasmira Shah, remember her?"

Dido shook her head.

"She was at a drinks do I had to go to," Julia continued. "We had a quick chat, but other than that I haven't really seen anyone. Look, why don't we get together for a natter over a coffee or a drink? I'll give you my number."

"Yes. I'd like that," said Dido, digging in her bag for a business card.

"Elissa Global? You must tell me all about it next time. It's so good to see you, Dido. I can't believe I literally just bumped into you like that! I'll call you."

They parted company.

'What's she after?' thought Dido.

'The lying bitch,' thought Julia.

Chapter 28

After the encounter with Dido Sykes Julia returned to her office. She called Mel and passed on the details from Sykes's business card, which included an email address and more phone numbers. As she finished the call Raj popped his head round the door.

"Hello boss," he said, "Mr Savernake says can he have a quick word in his office?"

Julia went to Savernake's office on the 8th floor wondering what she had done now.

"Julia!" Colin Savernake beamed at her. "I just wanted to say good work on rounding up those Albanian thugs. How is Sergeant Morgan doing?"

"It's Morris, Colin, Sergeant Kim Morris. She's still in hospital. They're hopeful she'll recover from her injuries, but she's not at all well. I think it'll be a while before she's back at work, if ever. I've had a word with the CPS and they're going to up the charge from GBH to attempted murder, for what it's worth."

"I see. Look, Julia, we got off on the wrong foot over this business. I wouldn't want you to think that I'm soft on crime or want you to go easy on criminals. Far from it. When we spoke I had a lot on my mind, pressure from above and all that over the figures. I'd like us to kiss and make up, figuratively speaking of course. How about a drink after work this evening at my club? Then we can get to know each other a bit better, to help us with our working relationship."

Kelso was watching Savernake carefully. He was clearly uncomfortable, and his words did not have any ring of truth about them. She was curious.

"Yes, why not? Shall we say 6.30?"

"Splendid. I'll meet you downstairs and my driver will take us. My club is in St James's, the Carlton."

"I'll need a breath of air after my late meeting. I'd like to walk across the park and meet you there if that's OK."

"Of course. I'll see you there." He was put out and barely concealed it.

Back in her office Julia called Mel again.

"You just can't leave me alone, can you?" Mel said.

"I've just had a weird experience. My boss just tried to apologise to me and he's asked me for a drink. He's a rubbish actor and he's obviously hating being nice to me. Something's prompted it, and I have no idea what but it's since I spoke to Dido Sykes. Can you have a snoop about at whatever's coming in on your side?"

"I'll have a look, but what I can get my hands on isn't that quick. You only saw Sykes and hour or so ago."

"Thanks Mel. I'll call you later if I can and see you around 10 tomorrow." She hung up.

At 6.30 Julia was in the lobby of the Carlton Club. As a female she wasn't allowed past the porter's desk until her host arrived. She waited as patiently as she could. Colin Savernake arrived ten minutes later, full of blustering apology and rude words about the rush-hour traffic. He showed her to the lounge where female guests were permitted. He had changed out of his uniform and was wearing a slightly stale grey pinstripe suit. There was dandruff on the shoulders. He was a thin, tall man with greying hair, neatly cut. He still wore old police-issue spectacles, and while his suit was Savile Row it was a ready-to-wear and didn't quite fit properly.

"Interesting club, Colin. Have you been a member long?" she asked.

"I was put up when I became a Commander, so five or six years ago. It's a convenient watering hole, discreet and no damn journalists."

"Except the ones who are members?" Julia asked.

"There are a few, but they wouldn't snitch on fellow members. The food isn't too bad. Now what can I get you?"

"I'll have a gin and tonic, Colin. Ice and lime, not lemon."

He ordered. Julia noticed that he only ordered singles - he was having a very mediocre blended Scotch.

"Didn't Margaret Thatcher make a big fuss about joining this club when she became Prime Minister?" Julia asked.

"She did, the Blessed Margaret. It's always been a Tory club, not that I'm in the party or anything, and the leader has always been invited to join. But it's a men only club, so even when she became party leader she wasn't invited in. When she became Prime Minister she did what all Conservative Prime Ministers do and had her first Cabinet dinner here. Of course, the club couldn't refuse and they offered her immediate honorary membership. She didn't like it, of course, but it was a compromise. I suppose the club will go the same way as most of the others and allow women to join sooner or later. The last to fall will be White's. They don't even allow ladies through the door, even as guests."

"Very forward looking of them. What do men see in clubs like that? I mean, what are they afraid of?"

"So you're a bit of a feminist, are you Julia?"

"Not as such. I just don't see the sense in locking out interesting people. I wouldn't join a women only club, and I don't see the appeal of a men only one. Let's change the subject. Where's home for you, Colin?"

"We're out in Hertfordshire, near Broxbourne. Do you know it?"

Julia shook her head.

"It's pleasant enough, we're in a village but still close enough to London. I'm glad to have a driver, though. The commute on the train used to be tiresome. Of course my wife doesn't need to work anymore. She looks after the homestead, and the kids have flown the coop. We have two. One's on a gap year working in Australia, and the other's finished university, she wanted to be an engineer of all things. She's gone off to Canada to work in the oil industry. If I'm working late or have a function to go to I stay here at the club, but I'm thinking of getting a bolt-hole in town, just for convenience. What about you?"

"Home is in the Highlands, north west of Perth. My folks still live in the family place and I use a flat in London which dad's had for years. He was with the Foreign Office. We lived abroad while I was young, but they have a policy to send diplomats' children to boarding school in the UK once they hit secondary age. But I'm Scottish through and through. I came here to London for the experience and a change of perspective, and I'll go back when the time's right."

"Are you ambitious, Julia?"

"Am I ambitious? I'm 38 next birthday, Colin, I've got a first class degree from Oxford and I'm a Commander in the Metropolitan Police. One of the youngest you've ever had, or so I'm told. What do *you* think?"

"Fair point, Julia. Look, don't take this the wrong way, but it's a good idea to try to make friends while you're here. Sure, you're capable and bright, but often that's not enough. Sometimes you need a sponsor, someone to speak for you, to put your case and maybe smooth the feathers that you seem to ruffle." Savernake leant forwards towards Julia. She smelt his stale breath.

"I could help you, Julia. I could be your sponsor, be on your side."

"Why would you do that, Colin? What would you want in return? I'm not wet behind the ears and I do understand that almost everything in life is a transaction."

"I don't want anything from you, Julia, at least nothing that you wouldn't want to give willingly. I would need to know what you want, what you're doing and thinking, what your plans and ambitions are. I'm just offering some friendly support, support from a superior officer."

Julia smiled at him.

"Senior, Colin, senior. I'm not unappreciative, and I'll think about what you've said. I've never felt the need for sponsorship before; I believe in merit. But I do see that above a certain level the police is as political as anything else and sometimes you need to play a different sort of game. Thanks for the drink." Julia stood up.

"I'll see you in the office, Colin. Goodnight."

Savernake stood as well and moved to try to kiss Julia on the cheek. She was too quick for him and had already turned away from him and was half-way out of the door.

She hailed a cab in the street and fifteen minutes later she was behind her own front door. She kicked off her shoes and made a proper drink, then she reflected on the rather strange conversation with her boss.

She reached for her private mobile phone, then hesitated. She changed her mind and used her official one. She called Errol Spelman. He answered after two rings.

"It's Errol," he said.

"Hi. Julia Kelso."

"Good to hear from you, Julia. I was half expecting a call."

She ignored the insinuation.

"It's been a long day, Errol. Could you add another name to the list I gave you? It's Savernake, Colin Savernake."

"You mean DAC Savernake? The Bubble?"

"The Bubble?"

"Sorry, it's his nickname. He got it because he kind of rose to the top without any effort and without leaving a trace."

"I get your point. Can you do it?"

"Yes, I can do it, Julia, but I'll have to do it myself. I can't ask my team to go after a Deputy Assistant Commissioner off the books. It's career ending stuff."

"But you're willing to do it?"

"Yes. I've got some insurance in the bank, and I trust you. If you say it needs doing, it needs doing."

"Thanks Errol. I owe you."

"We can discuss that. Later." He chuckled softly. His deeply silky lilting voice was playing havoc with Julia's insides. She ended the call.

Julia finished her drink and took a bath. In bed she tried to read a book but was too distracted. Errol Spelman's voice was replaying in her head, and all she could see through her closed eyes was his sculpted body, but inexplicably shirtless. She gave in and reached into her bedside drawer for one of the toys Mel had recommended during one of their late night conversations. Mel had said this one was great 'in an emergency'. Twenty minutes later Jake Kelso was asleep.

Chapter 29

In Sofia things weren't going well for Bijan Bukani. Luan Krasniqi was blanking him. Krasniqi had pushed Bijan about what was going on in London. They had lost two girls, expensive girls. One dead, one a runaway. One of his brothers, Pali, was also dead, the other one - Ilir - was in a British jail. Two of his houses had been lost and all the girls in them taken away. He hoped he could get at least some of them back. The deal had been, Luan Krasniqi had said angrily, that Bijan and his friends would make sure things like this didn't happen and in return they got a big slice of the profits from the girls. A very big slice. The Krasniqis met the not insignificant cost of getting the girls to London, or Paris or Rome or wherever, a cost charged by Bijan's friends. A load of girls gone, expensive and high-value assets written off, would have a big impact on the profits for all of them.

Bijan protested, quite truthfully, that he knew nothing at all about losing girls or Luan's brother getting killed. His job was to make and maintain contact with people like Luan Krasniqi, pimps and gangsters, in the bars, clubs and casinos of Sofia and Skopje and Ljubljana and Bucharest and Budapest, and just about anywhere else. His message to them was that if they found a young girl and they wanted to put her to work in London he could fix everything. For a fee and a cut of the earnings. Most gangsters weren't interested, but those who knew the commercial advantage of young, pretty, unwilling and ideally virginal girls could see the value in what Bijan was offering. Business was brisk. What the gangsters didn't know was that all Bijan did was get a full description of each girl and send it with a quick snapshot to Dido Sykes, not that he knew her name. She took care of everything else, as far as he knew.

Luan Krasniqi didn't believe that Bijan knew nothing about what had happened in London. Bijan wasn't used to this turn of events. He dealt with winning and losing on the roll of a dice or the spin of a wheel or the movement of a currency price. The consequences lasted only as long as it took to play again. Only losers got angry. Luan Krasniqi was not a large man, but he was a scary one and he had large scary people around him. Cousins, he called them. Was there anyone in Albania who wasn't related to everyone else? Luan Krasniqi had let two of his apes loose on Bijan for ten minutes, just to make sure that the message that he was extremely displeased was getting through. Bijan had been hurt and humiliated. He was very frightened. He'd missed his flight and failed to make the business meeting he had ostensibly come to Sofia for. His boss at the bank would be furious. He needed some help. He made a phone call to her.

In his frazzled state Bijan wasn't thinking properly and he used the wrong phone. He called her temporary phone from his own permanent phone, from Sofia.

"Hello, it's BB. I have a problem with Krasniqi. He's really pissed off about losing two girls or something. He's talking about pulling the deal with the four who are already in the system."

As soon as he started speaking she realised what he had done and was furious.

"Shut the fuck up, you moron! You're through!"
She disconnected.

Twenty minutes later Bijan was back in the Radisson, distraught and getting drunker. An hour or so later a pageboy walked through the lobby bar with a sign with his name on it.

"Telephone for you, sir. On the house phone in the lobby."

Bijan Bukani made his unsteady way towards the bank of phones near the hotel entrance. As he picked up a phone and spoke his name a man in a black leather jacket shot him in the back of the head with a silenced pistol. The killer walked calmly out of the hotel and was driven away. Bijan Bukani remained mostly vertical, slumped against the side of the phone booth. It was quite a while before anyone checked to see if he was OK. He wasn't, he was dead.

******

"It came through early this morning," Mel said to Jake, "Bijan was shot dead in his hotel last night. It happened shortly after he'd made a call from his own phone to the temporary one being used by your mate Dido Sykes. Cheltenham got it. It's short - he says he's having trouble with Krasniqi who is pissed off about two girls and is talking about pulling the deal on the four already in the system. She calls him a fucking moron and hangs up. Ninety minutes later Bijan gets shot in the head. Just after Bijan's call to Sykes the boffins see another call from an unknown UK mobile to a Bulgarian one. They don't get the whole thing, just one side, but the call contains Bijan's name and the name of his hotel, the Radisson. One and one makes six, but it could be that the second call was an instruction to take out Bijan. If we can tie it to Dido Sykes…well, there we are."

"Indeed. Now we know there are probably another four girls being trafficked to London right now. And that the people we're after are in on it. How can we find out who and where they are?"

"As my old grandma used to say I'm buggered if I know," said Mel. "We can talk about it after you've seen the DG. I think he's quite cross with me. I'll wait for the summons."

Julia went up to the fourth floor of the DG's building. He was waiting for her, his usual charming self.

"Julia! How nice. We still haven't got round to that lunch, have we? Now, what pile of poo are you going to dump on my desk this lovely grey damp winter morning?"

"Do I hear a hint of cynicism, Richard? Someone must have put salt in your coffee again."

"I wish they would! It could only improve it. Now, what have you got?"

Julia told him the story.

"So it looks like yet another case where malign influences are at work, Richard," she concluded. "In this case it's further complicated by my personal connection with at least three of the people involved. The fourth, Bijan Bukani, was murdered last night in Sofia. It's going to be a tricky one. I think there are another four girls being shipped to the UK right now, all destined for the sex trade. What I'd like from NCIS is as much intelligence as possible to help me identify and intercept these girls, and to nail the bastards responsible - including those facilitating the trafficking."

"Has Mel Dunn been helping you already? I had a call this morning from a colleague in Cheltenham about the murder of your man Bukani. It seems he made a call to the UK from a number that Cheltenham got to know of only yesterday, from Miss Dunn. I put my neck out and said it was all in order, just that the admin hadn't quite caught up yet. My colleague was concerned about the legal aspects, and rightly so. I'll send for Miss Dunn while you're here, but between you and I Julia take this as a yellow card. Get the paperwork sorted before you ask your friend to start bending the rules. For all our sakes."

Julia hesitated for a second.

"I'm sorry, Richard. I take full responsibility and I take your point. It won't happen again."

"Thank you, Julia. There's an end to it. Let's get Mel in and start the ball rolling. Good luck."

******

After their meeting with the Director General Julia and Mel went for a coffee.

"I'm sorry I dropped you in it with Richard, Mel," Julia started. "He gave me the most polite bollocking I've ever had and he says that's the end of the matter. I hope he's right."

"I was expecting it. He called me before you arrived and said I'd been rumbled. He said he knew you were behind it and said I should be careful. He said he doesn't want to lose me, which I suppose counts as a verbal warning that I'll be fired if I do it again, getting intelligence out of Cheltenham without the right paperwork. Fair enough, I suppose." Mel sipped her coffee. "What do we do now?"

"There are too many loose ends. Let me have a think and we can all meet up this evening. Can we use your flat again?"

"Yes, but I need my sleep, in my own bed. You're both going home afterwards."

"Snippy!"

Chapter 30

They met that evening. Alf / Paulo listened as Mel and Julia filled him in on what had been happening.

"So with Bijan gone and both Krasniqi brothers in London either dead or out of circulation it's likely that Luan Krasniqi might be feeling a bit desperate about the London operation. How about I go and have another chat with him, see if I can give him a hand?"

"I think that would be good," said Julia, "we need to try to get an inside view on how the whole thing works, and what the gang of four, or should that be three now, have to do with it. Until Bijan's call to Dido I was starting to think we might have got it wrong. That said, I do know Dido was lying. There's no way she could have known what I was doing if she hadn't spoken to either Drew or Jasmira Shah, and she said she hadn't seen or spoken to either of them."

"What was she like at Oxford? If she wasn't at the University what was she doing there?" Mel asked.

"She was always just around. We did socialise with the same people sometimes, Drew was the link mostly - he'd bring her along or get her invited. He always told me they were friends, nothing more, and that she was interesting. She drifted in and out of different circles; I don't know where she lived or who with. She was quiet but could throw some very astute questions into conversations. Although she was and is very attractive she could sit in the corner of a room and no one would notice her unless she wanted them to. I'm pretty sure I saw her at a few lectures and talks, which seemed quite normal at the time. It's not

186

so normal now I know she wasn't a student." Jake paused. "You said you knew her in Hull, Mel?"

"Yes. She was pretty much the same there too. Quiet and a bit in the background, but always about. Almost like she was watching people. She seemed to try to hide her looks, like you say she's an attractive girl. But she could turn it on if she wanted anything. I got my dad to ask his old police mate. Her mother, she was a Caroline, worked the streets near the docks. She was on the game and made no secret of it. Carol, aka Dido, was her only daughter and there was no sign of a dad. It can't have been easy for her trying to do homework while her mum was upstairs being banged by strangers. Dad's pal thinks Caroline came to a sticky end. He didn't think Carol followed her mum into the trade, but if what Barbara said was right she did, only down here in London. Are you going to follow up on your chance meeting with her, Jake?"

"I think I'll leave it a bit. Now I've squared the admin with your DG it would be good to go all out on Dido's communications, and on anything coming from Luan Krasniqi. Alf, you go and see if you can push him into trying to rebuild his London operation. I'm going to talk to Jasmira Shah about a career change."

******

Paulo Silva called Luan Krasniqi using his Portuguese mobile while sitting in the lobby of the Radisson Hotel in Sofia. He had arrived in Sofia the day before and had made his preparations.

"Luan? It's Paulo Silva. We met last week when I was here. I've been trying to get hold of BB. We were going to meet up in London but he doesn't answer his phone."

"You didn't hear? BB had an accident. He was killed outside the hotel - a hit and run. Are you here now, in Sofia?" Luan was lying.

"Yes. I got in late last night. I'm shocked, about BB I mean. I was hoping to do some good business with him. Can we meet up? I've still got that real estate project on the go, and after we spoke last time it seems there are other opportunities here."

Luan readily agreed and twenty minutes later he walked into the Radisson. Paulo noticed the two minders discreetly shadowing him.

"They with you, Luan?" he asked.

"Just staff," Luan replied, shaking Paulo's hand. "Did you come in from London?"

"Yes, last night. I had a few things to do in the UK. Do you have business there?"

"Some family business."

"What sort of thing."

"Just family. Nothing special. Now, what about real estate here?"

"Well, Luan, as you know when Bulgaria joins the EU people from all over will be interested in buying property here. It has a good climate for year-round holidays. Warm and sunny in the summer with nice beaches, and in the winter there's snow for skiing. Perfect. North Europeans, especially the Dutch, Germans and the British have a passion for buying real estate. I'm thinking holiday homes, resorts, that sort of thing. I want to buy a lot, cheap and run-down, fix them up quickly and sell or rent them as vacation properties. I think now is the time to buy. What do you think?"

"So you aren't interested in Vitosha?"

"I was last week. I've been doing more research and I think there's more to be made down by the Black Sea and in the mountains. Vitosha real estate is good but the market is local. Dutch people want smaller easy to run places, flat enough for a swimming pool or close to a ski lift."

"That makes sense," said Luan, "I know people down near Varna, but you need to know there are already some foreign business people doing the same sort of thing. Russians."

"That doesn't surprise me. No matter, there's enough for everyone."

Luan let out a laugh.

"You don't know these Russians, or their Bulgarian partners."

"You saying they're gangsters, Luan? Russian mafia and all that?"

"You make your own mind up. All I know is I keep my business away from them and they leave me alone."

"You said you're Albanian, am I right? I've heard about Albanian mafia too. Is that your business, Luan?"

"You are asking questions that you shouldn't, Paulo."

Paulo grinned at the handsome Albanian.

"I'll take that as a yes, then, shall I?" he laughed, " shall we get some lunch? I'm buying."

"OK. But not here. We can go to a place I know, just outside the city."

He didn't let it show but Paulo wasn't comfortable being taken to a strange place in a strange town by a gangster he hardly knew. He was unarmed and he didn't know the territory, but he didn't have much of a choice, not if he was going to get under Luan Krasniqi's skin.

"Great," he said, "let's go."

They drove in Luan's big BMW. Paulo sat in the back beside Luan, who was talking into a phone in a language Paulo didn't recognise, although he did hear his own name mentioned. The two 'staff' were in the front, one driving, the other on lookout, both wearing the familiar lumpy black leather jackets. Paulo glanced at his watch and made a mental note of the time. He gazed out of the car window, his eyes scanning for landmarks and clues as to where he was being taken. After twenty minutes the car pulled off the highway on to a small road into a forest. To Paulo's relief the BMW stopped in a car park by a rustic restaurant. The place was quite busy, which was a good sign. As Luan descended from the BMW a small man, apparently the restaurant owner, scuttled forward to greet him. He spoke in heavily accented English.

"*Zotëri* Luan, welcome! I have your table ready. Come inside." The little man was effusive.

"Thank you, Boris. This is my friend Senhor Paulo. He is new to Bulgaria. We want your finest traditional cooking today." Luan smiled.

Boris showed them to a corner table with a view out on to a pretty courtyard. It was pleasantly cool in the restaurant, a nice change from Sofia's ubiquitous and ferocious central heating, which was compulsory until the beginning of May regardless of the weather.

No menus were offered or consulted. After a few moments Boris ushered a waitress to their table. She carried a tray with plates of colourful salad of tomato, cucumber, peppers and finely grated white cheese. She placed one in front of each of them. Alongside the plates were shot glasses into which Boris poured ice-cold raki.

"Shopska salata!" Boris announced proudly.

"In Bulgaria every meal starts with a plate of salad and a glass of raki. I think it gets the healthy vegetables out of the way early. *T'bäft mir.* This is *bon appetit* in Albanian." Luan raised his glass.

"Cheers, Luan," said Paulo.

The salad was fresh and crisp, the raki cold and potent. The salad plates were replaced by bowls of fiery-looking deep red soup. Its accompaniment was a large glass of cold beer and chunks of dark bread.

"This is *shkembe chorba*," Luan explained, "it is very good if you have had too much to drink the night before. Boris makes it good and spicy. Bulgarians put even more spices into it, but that is because they are crazy."

Paulo spooned some of the red soup into his mouth and felt his eyes begin to water. He reached for the beer.

"Jesus, Luan, what's it made of?"

"You probably don't want to know. It is made with the stomach of a cow, tomatoes, a lot of chilli pepper, garlic and onions. It is strangely addictive."

Paulo had some more. It was no less fiery but Luan was right, he did keep going back for more, followed by a mouthful of cold beer, of course. The main course was a more or less familiar version of moussaka, but made with a layers of meat and potato instead of the usual aubergine and pasta. It was served with plain yoghurt and a bottle of rich red Plovdiv wine. When it was over they ate some fruit and sat back. Luan's phone beeped and he glanced at the screen. By now the restaurant had emptied and they were alone apart from the staff.

"So, Paulo. Are you going to tell me why you are really here? I have friends in London. They have been doing some research while we have been eating. They can't find anyone who has ever heard of you."

"Why would they? London's a big city and I'm not from there. I told you, I live in Portugal."

"They can't find anyone in Portugal who's heard of you either."

"I don't know who your friends are, Luan, or how well connected they are, but I can't imagine anyone being able to look all over London and all over Portugal for someone who knows me, all in the time it takes to eat lunch. I could start to get offended. I thought we were just here to talk about real estate and have a friendly bite to eat."

Krasniqi was watching him closely.

"My staff will take you outside and search you. After that we may talk some more." Luan nodded at his two goons, who had been seated at a table near the door. One of them came over. Luan spoke to him tersely in the same language he had used on the phone.

"Vrite ate!" Luan said sharply.

The goon nodded grimly.

"As you wish, Luan," Paulo said, rising slowly to his feet. He hadn't understood the words Luan had used, but there was no mistaking their meaning.

He followed the man out of the door on to an elevated veranda. The second one followed behind Paulo. They were moving towards the large BMW, more or less in a row. As he turned at the bottom of the short steps Paulo saw that the one behind him had his hand inside his leather jacket, moving towards his lumpy armpit. 'Here we go,' he thought.

The first goon was several feet away now, close to the big BMW. Paulo chose his moment. The secret of winning at fighting is to start and finish it as quickly and violently as possible. Maximum force and maximum surprise. Paulo spun round and drove the heel of his clenched fist upwards and hard into the face of the goon behind him. Paulo aimed his blow not at the man's nose but at a place two feet above and behind it. The nose exploded, but not before its cartilage and the shards of bone attached to it had been forced deep into the main's brain. He had been killed in an instant by a single massive blow. The first goon hadn't seen or heard a thing. Paulo reached inside the fallen thug's jacket and withdrew the gun. As he expected is was a Makarov, and fitted with a silencer. Paulo was familiar with this type of weapon and he slipped off the safety catch. The first goon had been busying himself at the rear of the BMW but now he came to see what was delaying his partner.

He gasped and started to say something as he saw his fallen comrade. As the man reached for his weapon Paulo fired. The weapon in his hand spat twice with barely a sound. Two small red spots appeared on the remaining gangster's forehead and he toppled forward. Paulo turned, removed the magazine and threw the pistol as far into the forest as he could manage before taking the other thug's gun and pocketing it.

Luan looked startled as Paulo walked back into the restaurant alone.

"You'll be needing much better staff if we're going to work together, Luan," Paulo said.

Paulo placed the gun on the table between the two of them, keeping his hand on it.

"Now, shall we stop fucking about or do you want to go the same way as your apes?" Paulo's expression was icy.

Luan paled.

"What do you want?" Luan was struggling with rising panic.

"I want your London operation. All of it. Now that one of your brothers is dead and the other is locked up forever, and two of your 'houses' are closed down, your business isn't going to last long. The vultures will be circling. I'll take it from you, or someone else will. With me you'll get something from it, with the others you won't. That's what I want, Luan. Your London operation, and your supply chain. The only reason I'm interested in you is you've a very profitable range of merchandise, not your run of the mill girls. Yours are special. Young, fresh. There's a good market for that. By the way, if you're thinking of doing something silly, like having me over, you need to know it's not just me. I've a group of associates, we go way back to a different time and we've eaten people like you for breakfast. Your people didn't find me because I don't want to be found. Are you getting my drift, Luan?"

"You think you can just take over our operation? Just like that?"

"That's right, Luan. Just like that. How do you think it fell apart so suddenly? By accident? No, Luan. We wanted to send you a message. This is the second part of the message. You're working with us, or you're not working at all. Not just in London, but anywhere. You're with us, or you're a dead man."

Paulo reached for his wallet. He withdrew a thick wad of Lev notes and laid them on the table.

"I did say lunch was on me. Now let's go. You're driving."

Chapter 31

Paulo searched Luan by the car, he wasn't armed. He made him drag the bodies of the fallen goons into the back of the BMW. Then he told Luan to drive back towards Sofia, keeping the silenced Makarov pointing at him all the time.

"Where are we going?" Luan asked, trying to stay calm.

"I'll show you when we get close. I've found somewhere private where we can work out our business arrangement."

Just the day before Paulo had hired a short-term serviced office in an anonymous block just north of the airport, paying over the odds in cash. It had a secure underground car park. Paulo directed Luan to the place and told him where to park. He walked behind Luan keeping at arms length, not that he sensed any fight in the Albanian gangster. Paulo used a key card to activate the elevator to the second floor, where his temporary office was located. They didn't see anyone else in the building, and Paulo was quietly pleased to note that while the mounts and cables were in place the CCTV cameras hadn't yet been installed.

He unlocked the office, two rooms. The outer one had a desk and chair, with a small sofa for guests. The inner room had a large desk, several leather swivel chairs and a massive TV. In a small fridge there were bottles of cool water. He passed one to Luan. They sat on opposite sides of the desk, quite a normal sight apart from the Makarov which lay beside Paulo's right hand.

"So, Luan, who else is on your team?"

Luan shook his head.

"For London it is only me, Ilir and Pali, and a few hired hands. We have a large family in Albania and Kosovo, but they aren't interested in the girls - they don't even know about them. They have other things to keep them busy. I do other things for them here in Bulgaria, but the girls are my operation."

"How does it work, Luan? Where do you get them from?"

"They are all around. You see them everywhere. After the war in Serbia and Kosovo, and with everything changing in Bulgaria and Romania girls are looking for opportunities."

"But not your girls, Luan. Yours aren't the usual 'opportunity' types."

"No. I just know one when I see one. The best ones are the ones who think I'm going to marry them and they love me because I won't touch them before then. The virgins. I take some others too, not virgins but still very young and pretty, innocent looking. I don't want whores who look like whores."

"So you find a girl, you get to know her, get her to trust you. What happens then?"

Luan hesitated. Paulo moved the gun slightly, just a reminder.

"Before I used to call BB. He let me have a new number for him every month. I would just ask him for the best exchange rate on a currency conversion, the currency for wherever the girl came from. He would say a number - any number. Then an email would arrive with a form to fill in. The form was for a description of the girl, very detailed. I would complete it and send it back with a picture of the girl.

197

If she already had a passport I would get that too and tell BB. If he wanted to use it he would tell me where to send it."

"Who was the email sent to?"

"Always a different name. Made up. Always a different address. Then I would wait. I would keep the girl, sometimes more than one, in my apartment. They didn't go out. I spent time with them, always being very nice to them, saying how good it was going to be when I came to meet them in London and we could get married." Luan was actually smiling.

"After a while, usually about ten days, I would get a call from BB telling me where I could collect a package. The package would have in it a passport, always a European one or the girl's own one which would have a tourist visa or work permit for the UK stamped in it, and travel tickets. By boat and train, not so much by plane, destination London. But going through France or Germany or somewhere else."

"Are the passports from BB fakes?"

"No, always genuine ones. The name was not the girl's name, but the face was always similar, and the description. If the passport was from France, for example, the travel would always be through Germany and Holland; if it was German travel would be through Italy and France. That way the girl didn't have to speak a language. They all speak a little English."

"OK," said Paulo, "then what?"

"Once I saw the tickets I could get Ilir and Pali to meet the girl when she arrived in London or Dover or wherever. I sent them her picture. I tell the girl that my cousin would meet her and look after her. They would pick the girl up and take her somewhere, then they send the passport back to me by DHL. When I get the passport back I call BB and he tells me what to do with it. Normally pack it up and leave it for him at a hotel somewhere in town.

"I don't see the girl again, or the passport. Ilir and Pali keep her and run the sales end."

"What was in it for BB?"

"He took thirty percent of all earnings, before costs. I pay a fee for the passport and travel, 5,000 Euro per girl. I pay for the houses, the food, security, everything out of my seventy percent."

"That's hefty. How much does a girl make for you?"

"For a pretty young virgin some people will pay a lot, especially if they want to do it rough. Sometimes we have an auction. We once got 50,000 for a Serbian girl, very sweet looking, very innocent, for front and back by the same guy the same night. That's pounds, not Euro. After the first time we don't get so much, but a girl will still make eight or ten thousand a week. Pounds. If the first time isn't too rough we can make the girl a virgin again and do it all over, but no more than twice. If the first time is very rough and there is a lot of damage you can't fix it, so we ask a lot more for the rough ones."

Luan was getting into his stride, talking about his business.

"How long do the girls work for?"

"They bring in good money for four years, sometimes five. Then some of them stay with us and help with the operation, the ones who are really compliant. Others do work that isn't so well paid. We

199

can rent a few girls out to clubs in the north of England for weeks at a time. Sometimes we say the clubs can have them, if they're troublesome or get sick or ugly. Other ones we dispose of or sell on when they are no longer useful for us. We have to keep standards up to keep the prices high. We are like the premier league. Like Manchester United." Luan grinned.

Paulo suppressed the desire to shoot him on the spot.

"OK. With BB out of the way what happens now?"

"BB said once there was someone else. I don't know who. I have an email address to send a message to. Someone will contact me."

"What email address, what message?"

"I am not so stupid as you think, Paulo."

"I'm glad about that. So the deal is this: you keep paying the thirty percent to whoever arranges the passports and travel. You and I split everything else after costs 50/50."

"That doesn't sound like a good deal."

"It's the only deal. Fifty percent or nothing. Fifty percent or all the other houses you have in London go the same way as the first two. For the fifty percent I get paid you get something too. You get protection, not like the protection you thought you had which didn't work, proper protection. By my people. It's the deal of your life, son. Unless you'd like to join the goons in the back of your car."

"You threaten me?"

"You'd better believe it. And if you think getting rid of me gets you another chance you can forget that straight away. There's plenty more where I come from, but they're not so reasonable. Now you go home and send your email. You call me in exactly 24 hours on this number," Paulo passed a slip of paper across the desk, "and I'll tell you what happens next. If you don't call me you'll be dead by the end of the week, and you'll be wishing it had happened sooner. Like I said, I'm the reasonable one in my outfit. Do I make myself absolutely clear? Say 'yes, Paulo'."

"Yes Paulo."

Paulo stood. He motioned Luan to do the same and stepped towards him, smiling. Luan was uneasy with this strange foreigner. He tentatively extended a hand towards him. Paulo maintained his smile as he drove his knee hard into the Albanian's balls. Luan fell forward, retching. Paulo aimed a kick at his head, connecting with a satisfying crack. Luan fell to the floor, unconscious.

"Just in case you had any ideas, sonny Jim. Also, that's from Flora, just for starters."

Paulo caught a bus to the airport and sat quietly in the business class lounge with a malt whisky trying to get the foul taste of the tripe soup out of his mouth. He was back in London by the evening.

Chapter 32

While Paulo / Alf had been in Sofia Julia Kelso had been meeting with her old University acquaintance Jasmira Shah. They met over a light lunch at the Royal Horseguards hotel, not far from the Foreign Office. The women chatted while lunch was served. Neither was drinking alcohol so they sipped their sparkling water. When the food arrived Julia started.

"Tell me about the FCO, Jas. Has it been good to you?"

"It's civil service, Julia, only they make you work in places with no running water or mains electricity. No, I'm being unfair. It's great to live and work in other places, as long as your expectations are reasonable. I've mostly been in Europe, which has been marvellous, especially Vienna which was my last post before the one I'm in now."

"Vienna? I've always liked the city but never got on with the language," Julia said.

"Me neither. I'm no linguist, which is just as well. I've mostly worked on consular matters, dead Brits abroad, lost passports, visas and that sort of thing. In Vienna I had a policy role but with the UN agencies based there, and they work in English. Some FCO types who have to deal with host governments need to be fluent before they arrive in post. It makes somewhere like Budapest a nightmare to staff. Hungarian is only useful in Hungary so no one is keen to spend a couple of years learning it unless they want to live on goulash for ever."

"I know someone who's been posted to the embassy in Budapest, Niall Morton, do you know him?"

"The new CHELO? Yes, I was on his interview panel. Don't tell him, but he wasn't everyone's first choice. His language skills swung it, but he didn't come across as a loyal team player." Jasmira was sneering.

"I'm sure he'll exceed expectations; he's a very capable man. You don't sound like a big fan of the new CHELO posts."

"Between us, I'm not. I believe that government to government liaison should be left to trained diplomats. Having policemen involved can foul up all manner of things, no offence."

"So policemen can't be diplomatic?"

"That's not what I meant, Julia. Diplomacy involves considering all manner of complex threads and facets; getting the best of all possible results rather than scoring a single goal. It's hard enough to get politicians to understand that, let alone CHELOs and all the other 'specialist liaison officers' who are multiplying like rabbits."

"Let's talk about something else. What are you doing now?"

"My current post is in the human resources department. The Office likes to have serving diplomats in the HR team so we can decide who is the best fit for a post. People can bid for posts, but if you're respected you get sought out and invited to put your name forward. If you get invited you inevitably get the job. That's working level, of course, anything below head of mission. Once you get to

203

those dizzy heights it can get very political - just look at Washington and Paris! How's the salmon?"

"Very nice. And your risotto?"

"Acceptable. I'm heading up a project now to get more diversity into the consular teams abroad. It was my idea. I've filled about half the vacancies in Europe and the EU accession states with under-represented minorities, Asians, blacks, that sort of thing. The next step is to increase the lifestyle-diverse numbers, but sexuality is still contentious in a lot of places."

"What about females?"

"They're already pretty well represented in consular roles. Chancery is a different matter, but progress is being made. Why are you interested in all this?"

"Oh, I'm just weighing up career options. My move down to London from Scotland isn't panning out quite as I'd have liked. Being young, female and Scottish doesn't go down so well with senior colleagues who are none of those things. I'm not one to give up easily, but there are times when you've just got to put yourself first."

"You are so right, Julia. Being young, female and Asian isn't so easy in the Foreign Office either. I know exactly what you mean. One benefit of being in HR is that people need to start respecting you and being nice, otherwise one quick slip of the pen and they're in Ulan Bator or Brazzaville for the next three years. A lot of people owe me now, people in jobs they wanted. It is very satisfying!" Jasmira laughed loudly. "Seriously, though, if you really are interested in a change of career and are thinking about the FCO it could be possible. I could certainly put in a good word for you and steer you through any selection process."

"Thanks Jas. I'll think about it. By the way, I bumped into Dido Sykes the other day, quite literally. Do you remember her?"

Jasmira tried to cover her shock, not very successfully.

"Dido Sykes? Yes, I remember her vaguely, Wasn't she part of Drew's circle? I haven't seen her in years. Where was this?"

"Here in London. She told me she has her own company now, over in Clerkenwell. Doing media and information stuff, whatever that means. Maybe we should all get together, the three of us, and have a girls' night out? I didn't even ask her if she's married or anything. Are you?"

"Yes. My husband has his own career so he doesn't tend to come abroad with me, except to visit. You never married Drew then? Everyone thought you would."

"I did too for a while, but it didn't work out. Shall I see if Dido fancies a night out?"

"I'm not sure, Julia. I didn't really know her that well. I think I'd rather not, if you don't mind."

"Not at all, that's fine. Just a thought. Look, I have to dash. It's been lovely seeing you and having this chat. Thanks for the tips; I'll think about the FCO. Let's catch up again soon." Julia left a folded banknote on the table. "My share. See you, Jas."

She could hardly get away fast enough.

Chapter 33

The three of them regrouped that evening in Raynes Park. Alf was last to arrive having been stuck in the evening traffic from the airport. Mel went to kiss him but recoiled in horror.

"Jesus, what the hell have you been eating? It smells truly disgusting!"

"Spicy tripe soup with extra chilli and garlic. Believe me it tastes worse than it smells, especially now." Alf said.

"Well you're definitely not staying over," Mel said. "How did you get on?"

"It was an eventful trip. Luan Krasniqi tried to have me done away with but it didn't go his way, obviously. I've found out more or less how Bijan fitted into the trafficking, and I think I know why. Now that he's dead and Luan's operation here in London's been deprived of the Krasniqi brothers he's a bit stymied. Essentially the operation was just the three brothers and a few local hires. The Krasniqis got seventy percent of the revenues but paid all of the costs, but they still made good money. Luan told me that the girls he uses bring in eight to ten grand a week each for between four and five years. Jake's onslaught took out two brothels, each with four to six girls working them. I reckon he's got at least the same again, if not more, still operating. He's very keen to get his show back on the road, and he's got a new business partner."

"Who's that, then?" Jake asked.

"Paulo Silva."

"I should have guessed," she said.

"According to Krasniqi, he identifies and recruits the girls from all over the Balkans. When he's got a good one groomed and trapped he contacts Bijan and supplies a description and a photo, and the girl's own passport if she has one. In a week or two he gets a genuine passport that allows travel to the UK or the girl's own one with whatever visas and permits are required. He also gets travel tickets for a route determined by whoever's in Bijan's food chain. Once the girl gets to the UK Krasniqi's brothers pick her up at a port or train station and send the travel documents back to Luan. He returns them to Bijan. Bijan's lot get a fee of 5,000 Euro per girl, plus thirty percent of her earning before costs."

"Why would he pay that? Surely he could get the girls to the UK himself more economically." Mel was curious.

"Good question," Alf said, "I reckon it's because Bijan's lot, let's assume it's the gang of four, provide a reliable and ris-free documentation and transport service, and then claim to have protection for the operation in London. Luan bragged about having the most valuable girls, young, attractive and innocent, and therefore they command a premium. He was particularly proud of his record of making money selling virginities, sometimes more than once.

"My guess is that one member of the gang of four can get hold of genuine passports and 'borrow' them. Using them makes it safer than using forged or altered passports. He or she must have access to lots of them because they seem to be able to provide genuine documents with descriptions and photographs that are close enough to the actual girls

207

being unwittingly trafficked. Another member of the gang must be able to get visas and work-permit stamps which are either genuine as well or good enough to withstand scrutiny."

"How many trafficking networks do you think there are, Mel?" Jake asked.

"I've firmly identified five, including the Krasniqis, with another two or three possible. All in touch with the gang of four. With a guestimate of forty girls each and assuming a similar arrangement to the Krasniqi one the gang of four are pulling in almost £500,000 a week, every week. No wonder Dido Sykes wears posh frocks. Even with costs and overheads that's an awful lot of money."

"So, Alf, why did Luan Krasniqi invite you to be his business partner?" Jake asked.

"I kind of invited myself. I had to scare him into it, of course. I expect he'll have woken up now but he won't be feeling much like partying tonight. Let's not dwell on it. He's going to call me tomorrow afternoon. He thinks he'll be killed if he doesn't. He's a bit short of bodyguards at the minute so I'm pretty sure he'll call. I want to get to the gang of four through him, and I think I can do it quickly. Luan Krasniqi won't be trafficking any more girls though, that's for certain."

"I'm not even going to ask what went on in Sofia, so please don't tell me," Jake said plaintively.

"How did you get on with Jasmira, Jake?" Mel asked.

"She's an ego in high heels, that one. We chatted over a lunch that was a lot less stinky than Alf's. I came away with the impression that Jasmira feels slighted and undervalued. She's bitter and she thinks she's amazingly capable."

"I take it she's not," Mel said.

"I'd say she's middle of the road capable. Never going to set the world on fire, and I think the Foreign Office has the measure of her. She likes to win petty victories. She's been consigned to consular jobs, and while they're necessary they're not the glamourous or headline-making ones. Our Jas sees herself negotiating treaties and solving global crises. The FCO sees her as a visa clerk. If you're right, Alf, Jas will be behind the visa and work-permit part. She's in HR and she told me she's been filling posts in Europe and pre-accession states with her own selected candidates. It means she'll be able to put people in key consular posts who are personally indebted or beholden to her. I'm not saying for a moment that she isn't appointing competent and capable people too, she wouldn't last long if she didn't, but she certainly has the opportunity to place her own people too."

"So," said Mel, "Looking at the personalities of Bijan and Jasmira what have we got?"

"Bijan was a hyper-active playboy," Alf said. "He was a drunk and also a gambler, and I think for him that was both a strength and a weakness, the gambling I mean. He made good money gambling for the bank, but he lost an awful lot gambling for himself. I think he was Dido's foot soldier, and probably the most dispensable and exposed of the gang. I'd bet that Dido had him killed. She'll have a replacement lined up already."

"And Jasmira is vain and opinionated. I think she could be easily flattered into doing almost anything." Jake said.

"What about Strathdon, Jake?" Mel asked.

"If only I knew. I thought I was close to him for years but I don't think he ever really let me near him. He's partial to the finer things in life, so his motivation could simply be money, but there's got to be more to it than that. I've been thinking back to Oxford and his relationship with Dido Sykes. I can't put my finger on anything, not yet anyway, but it'll come."

"And what about Dido? Carol Jones, Debbi Saint?" Mel asked.

"What indeed. A dock-side prostitute's daughter turned kinky porn-star turned escort turned criminal entrepreneurial people-trafficker specialising in young unwilling sex workers. A psychologist's dream project. I've no doubt she's behind this, but we don't have any evidence and very little intelligence."

"We've got a bit more intelligence now, though," said Mel. "I've been looking at her email. Her email address was on the card that she gave you, Jake. Of course that gave us absolutely nothing, as you'd expect. But while there are no two email addresses the same, it doesn't mean than one email address can't be lots of others. The email address she gave Jake is hosted on what seems to be her own server. I'm saying this because the server hasn't got millions of other email accounts on it, so it's not a commercial email provider. The server does have a few hundred email addresses associated with it, but only about half a dozen actual email accounts."

"You're losing me, Mel."

"Keep up, Jake. Alf said that Krasniqi and Bijan communicated for the most part by email using a lot of different email addresses, each usually used only once. That's what's on Dido's server - she has email accounts for each network she services, and for each account she creates endless email addresses, they're known as aliases. To an outsider all the emails are going to different addresses but in fact they're only going to one for each network. Now I've worked that out we have a decent chance of intercepting most of her email traffic."

"Why only most?" Jake asked.

"Because I don't think the server is in the UK. If it was you could just get a warrant and grab it. It's hidden among a load of others which on the face of it seem to be in Russia but could in fact be anywhere at all. All I can be sure of is that her server has a specific Internet Protocol address that shows an email where to go. How it gets there is a whole different problem, so the boffins need to be quite lucky. That's why we only have a *decent* chance of getting *most* of her email. Which is better than having no chance of getting any at all. They're working on it. Now, I'm going to kick you out. Not because I don't like you both very much, I do, it's just that Alf is getting smellier by the minute and I'm not sure I can take much more."

"I second the motion," said Jake, "he's getting unbearable. When will it wear off, Alf?"

"I wish I knew."

Chapter 34

The following Monday evening, across town, Colin Savernake was lying face down. His hands were strapped above his head, which was encased in a tight black leather hood. Otherwise he was completely naked. He was exhausted and his chest was heaving. Dido Sykes pulled the hood roughly off his head and unfastened his hands.

"That's enough for now. You don't deserve any more. Did you do what I told you, Colin? Have you reined in that bitch Kelso?"

"I have spoken to her, yes."

"Mistress!" Sykes hissed.

"I'm sorry. I have spoken to her, mistress." Savernake corrected himself.

"She's cost me a lot of money and caused a great deal of upset. I won't tolerate it, Colin! If you won't keep her under control I will! And if I have to do it myself you will be sorry. Do I make myself clear?"

Dido Sykes punctuated her speech with a slash at Savernake's exposed genitals with the whip in her hand. He flinched.

"Now get dressed and get out of my sight!"

"Yes, mistress."

******

An hour later Dido Sykes was sipping champagne in the bar of one of London's numerous casinos. A young man was sitting beside her. She had already forgotten his name and was renting him by the hour. She had already told him she had no intention of

212

letting him touch her, he was just for decoration and to deter others from trying it on with her. She was watching another young man closely. He had been drinking steadily for over an hour while playing blackjack. The house had let him win a few hands but was now taking him to the cleaners. Dido thought he must be at least fifteen thousand down. She had done her research and was satisfied that this young man would be a suitable replacement for the redundant, and deceased, Bijan, who she'd also found in this casino. His name was James, Jamie, Linmouth and he was about to be fired from his job as a trader at one of the larger brokerages in the City. Dido had made sure of that. Jamie would be stony broke and homeless by Friday if he was foolish enough to turn her down.

Dido watched as the dealer stood stony faced. Jamie was asking for more short-term credit, which was not going to be forthcoming. She rose and walked over to him.

"That's enough. Come with me now," she was looking right into his eyes.

He hesitated, then despite himself he stood up and left the table. Dido took a large wad of banknotes from her handbag and left them in front of his empty seat. The dealer nodded. Dido walked towards the door. Jamie Linmouth followed her. Dido's escort looked forlorn as he watched his 'date' leave with another man.

A large BMW saloon was waiting for Dido by the curb. She told Jamie to get in and slid in beside him. She pressed a button and a screen rose between them and the driver.

"You are James Linmouth?"

He nodded.

"I will call you Jamie, like everyone else does. If you haven't realised it by now you are barred from this casino, and very soon from almost every other one in town. Tomorrow morning when you get to your office you are going to be dismissed without notice because you have been making unauthorised trades using your employer's money but for your own benefit."

"I haven't..." Jamie started to protest. She silenced him with a glare.

"Your employer is certain that you've been doing it and they have all the proof they need to get you arrested and prosecuted if they choose to. Your current account at HSBC is twelve thousand pounds overdrawn. The bank will cancel your overdraft agreement on Thursday morning and they will want all of their money back immediately. Both of your credit cards are on their maximum limit and they too will be revoked on Friday. So you will need to find forty two thousand pounds by the weekend or you will become bankrupt. You are three months behind on your car lease payments and your Porsche was repossessed one hour ago. The leasing company wants nine thousand pounds from you."

"Repossessed?" Jamie asked.

"Yes," she continued, "your rent is also due, and you're two months in arears already. Unless you pay three months rent on Friday your landlord will evict you, as he has already informed you. That's another nine thousand pounds. So, on Friday evening you are going to be penniless and sleeping in the street."

Jamie stared at her. His alcohol-clouded brain was struggling to comprehend what this strange and beautiful woman was telling him.

"What do you want?" he eventually asked her.

"To throw you a lifebelt. You will work for me. I will pay your debts but you will owe me instead. I will pay you for the work you do for me."

"What work is that?"

"It is illegal and dangerous work. You don't need to know any more. This isn't a negotiation."

"If I say no?"

"Even if you say yes everything I said is going to happen will happen. If you say no you will feel the full consequences. Now get out. A car will be waiting for you outside your place of work at 9.30 tomorrow morning. You will have been fired by then."

Dido reached across him and opened his door. He slid out. The car drove her away and left him speechless.

Jamie made his way home. He was puzzled and confused, and not at all sure that what had happened was real. His apartment was on the riverbank on the south side of Tower Bridge. He went to the basement garage and saw the empty space where his Porsche had been parked when he left home that morning. He lay awake all night, unable to sleep. Everything the woman had said about his finances was true. Was she right about him losing his job too? If she was then it was all over. He would lose everything.

He showered and dressed. After a coffee he walked across the bridge and made his way through the backstreets of the City to his place of work. He swiped in and took his seat in front of his three computer screens. He tried to log on but he password was rejected three times. The screens went dark. A secretary walked up to him.

"Mr Challoner wants to see you in his office immediately," she said.

She hadn't used his name, even though she usually called him Jamie and they had been out for a drink once or twice.

The interview with Mr Challoner was brief.

"It has come to my attention, Linmouth, that you have been conducting unauthorised trades using the firm's money. This in contrary to your employment contract on two counts and is punishable by instant dismissal without notice or compensation. The details are in this letter. You are hereby dismissed from the firm and will be escorted from the building by the security guards who are waiting outside my office. The firm will commence legal proceeding against you to recover any losses you have incurred once we have audited your trading activity. That is all."

Jamie hadn't been invited to sit down. The office door opened and two uniformed security staff were waiting. The few personal items he had in his desk were in a plastic carrier bag which one of them handed to him. The other removed Jamie's office pass from round his neck and held out his hand for Jamie's company mobile phone. They walked him down the stairs, not even letting him use the lift one last time. He was escorted across the lobby, the humiliation burning his cheeks. The security officers stopped outside the main door and stood still. Jamie kept going. A grey people carrier was waiting at the curb. The driver held a sign up with the name J Linmouth written on it. It was 9.30 precisely. The woman had been right. Jamie Linmouth nodded at the car driver and got in the back.

The car took Jamie to the Waldorf Hotel at the Aldwych. Dido Sykes was waiting for him, sipping a green tea. She nodded at him to sit down.

"Sixty thousand pounds has been deposited in your bank account this morning. Use it to settle your debts. If you don't you'll be sorry and I will make sure you return it to me. I don't use the courts. You now owe *me* the money. You will use the rest of the day to get yourself a new passport from the passport office in Victoria. Here is an envelope with the completed application form in it complete with photographs and witness signatures. All you have to do it sign it and queue up. Tomorrow morning you will meet me here at 9am and I will tell you exactly what you will be doing."

She pushed the envelope across the table and stood up. She left Jamie sitting there.

Dido Sykes was driven away from the hotel and over Waterloo Bridge. She was meeting Drew, who was on the 11am train from Brussels. She shivered with anticipation.

Chapter 35

Luan Krasniqi called Paulo Silva at the appointed time. He sounded angry and surly. Paulo didn't apologise for kneeing him in the balls or kicking him in the head.

"Send the email at exactly 17.00 Sofia time. Exactly 17.00. When you've done it call me and tell me where you were when you sent it and what email account you used. When you hear back from BB's boss call me too. Now, you've four girls already in the system. Where are they now?"

"Two are in my apartment. The others are somewhere else in Sofia. They are all safe and well."

"Good. That's all for now. Call me after you've sent the email at 17.00." Paulo cut the connection.

He called Mel's mobile and told her to alert Cheltenham to look out for the email communication. Then he went for a run on Wimbledon Common to help him think.

******

At that moment Dido Sykes was in bed with Andrew Strathdon in the Chelsea Harbour apartment she rented, high above the Thames. She let him use her as he wished - he was the only man who had ever been allowed to do that. Everyone else had always been under her complete control. He was the only man she respected. She didn't really know why, but since she had first met him at the Oxford Union all those years ago she had wanted to please him. Even when he'd said he was going to marry that bitch

Kelso she had let him continue to use her for his pleasure. She let him do things to her that Kelso would never allow, and she did things to and for him that she knew Kelso would never ever do. Drew had spoken to her as an equal back then, and he spoke to her as an equal now. Despite his privileges with Dido's body he was never arrogant or superior with her.

Dido got up to fetch him a glass of champagne. He watched her exquisitely sculpted body as she moved across the bedroom. She was stunning and sensuous. She stood in front of him as she passed him the champagne flute, which she sipped from first.

"I've replaced Bijan," she said as she slipped back into bed. "Jamie Linmouth, another gambler and weak, but he'll do as he's told as long as we want him to. Shah is getting annoying and pushy. You might need to have a word with her. Your ex made a clumsy attempt to pump her the other day."

"Julia?"

"Yes. She had lunch with Jasmira and gave her some bull about a possible career move to the FCO. I'm worried, Drew. Does she know what we're doing?"

"I don't think so. If she thought she had anything we'd have seen clear evidence of it by now. And that other asset you've got would have told you. I think it's coincidence. I saw her at a friend's party in Edinburgh over New Year. She mentioned that she'd seen Jasmira in London before Christmas. I kept an eye on her in Edinburgh and here in London from a distance, just to see if she was on to something. I didn't see any sign of it. Now, what's the issue with the Albanians all about?"

"That could have been avoided. One of the Krasniqis tried to kill someone in the uniform vice squad, a female police officer who'd been about for years. We could have neutralised her easily, but the Albanians decided on their own that she had to go. It went wrong and the police went after them. Ilir Krasniqi did the right thing and got rid of his stupid brother, but then the police grabbed him and closed down two of his houses. He'll be locked up for a long time. There are still three of his houses working, but they'll need to get someone else in to run them. I've got hired help on it for now but we need to keep our distance. I've yet to get a message from Luan. The last I heard from Bijan was that he's got four more on the way. He was panicking after what happened in London. I'm going to send Jamie out to Sofia to calm him down."

"So soon? Is Jamie whatsisname up to it?"

"If he isn't he won't be coming back, Luan will see to that. Luan needs us a lot more than we need him, so we'll see what happens. How are things in Brussels?"

"Tedious and bureaucratic, but useful. The project I set up to facilitate rescuing trafficked girls is working well. Details of all missing girls who might have been trafficked are collected on my central database, and all their passports or identity cards are sent to my office too. There are an awful lot of missing girls across Europe. The explanation is that if one of the missing girls is located anywhere in the EU we can get her legitimate travel documents to her quickly so she can be rescued, wherever she happens to be found. So I've got access to hundreds of travel documents for girls in the right age range. I just borrow one or two of them now and then. I've got the ones we need for now. Two each for Budapest and Bucharest, and one for Ljubljana. When I get the information from Sofia I'll get another four."

"Don't border people check the names against missing girls listed on police and immigration systems?"

"Yes, but all that's centralised now. When I borrow a passport I temporarily remove the owner from the database and put her on it again when I've got the passport back."

"I'll get the passports to Shah tomorrow. You are so clever to have thought of using genuine documents, Drew."

"And you're clever too, to do all the planning and coordination and communications you're so good at." He kissed her lips.

Dido kissed him too and turned her back to him.

"You can do it again if you want, Drew. As hard as you like."

******

In her office Julia Kelso was on the phone to the hospital. Sergeant Kim Morris was making steady progress, and while she was a long way from being fit for duty the hospital thought she could be discharged in a week or so. Julia said she would visit over the weekend and arrange somewhere for Kim to go when she left hospital.

Raj knocked on her door.

"DAC wants to see you again, boss."

"Well why didn't he call me himself. Don't answer, Raj, it's a rhetorical question. I suppose he said now, please?"

"He did."

Julia sighed. She decided to change into her uniform and when she was satisfied with her appearance she went up to Savernake's office. He was all smiles.

"I've some exciting news for you Julia. The Commissioner is setting up a new task force to get the service in good order for the next decade. He's expecting major advances in technology which will bring changing social trends. The sixth floor feels that the service needs some fundamental restructuring and reskilling to meet the challenges ahead. He wants a DAC to head it up. I've nominated you, Julia."

"I'm not a DAC, Colin," Julia said.

"But you can be. The Commissioner and I spoke about it. He can't commit to anything in writing, obviously, but he said that if you pass the Intermediate Command Course at Bramshill he will appoint you when you come back, provided you'll take the restructuring job, that is. The next course begins in two weeks, and you have a place reserved on it."

"I see. Can I think about it?"

"Of course, but not for too long. I must say, Julia, I was expecting a little more enthusiasm from you."

"Sorry to disappoint, Colin, it's just that I wasn't born yesterday and I can see when I'm being sidelined. You'll have my answer by the end of the week."

She left Savernake's office, fuming and furious. Surely even Savernake wasn't daft enough to believe she couldn't see through his waffle. Restructuring task force indeed! A sure-fire way to stick her in a dark cupboard where she couldn't be seen or heard, and where she couldn't rock any boats. But why now, she wondered? Back in her office she changed back into her civvies.

Errol Spelman had asked to see her. Not fully trusting herself Julia called Mel and asked if she could come over for the meeting. She was sitting at Julia's conference table when Spelman arrived.

"Errol, this is Mel Dunn, she's a senior analyst from NCIS and she's working with me on this. You can talk freely in front of her."

Mel nodded at the tall Jamaican and tried to be discreet while surreptitiously appraising him.

"Pleased to meet you, Errol. Julia's told me a lot about you."

Kelso blushed slightly and busied herself with coffee.

"I looked into the people you told me about Julia. I'm assuming you know that Bijan Bukani was killed in Sofia last week? The Bulgarians are saying it was a robbery, but my contacts say that's rubbish. It was a professional hit. I can probably put a name to the gunman, but I have no idea who ordered the hit or paid for it.

"Bukani was an inveterate gambler. His finances are, were, precarious to say the least. He was also drinking very heavily. He hasn't got a criminal record, but the financial crime people have come across him a few times in Suspicious Transaction

Reports. They think he was connected with money laundering, but then again so's half the workforce in the City.

"Jasmira Shah isn't well liked. She thinks she's tremendous and could run the whole Foreign Office, but she's just really average. I asked a friend who's on the Foreign Secretary's protection team to have a sniff around. She's currently in the HR department, not that unusual for an officer of her grade. She's had a few postings, nothing particularly major or challenging. She's got a reputation for attention to detail, which helps with her consular work but not with her interpersonal relationships with colleagues. She's a bit brusque and shouty with subordinates. Nothing criminal in her background. She's got a bit more money than she ought to have, but her husband is a businessman and that might explain it. She hasn't got any debts. I can't get any financial information about her house; it seems to be owned by a family trust. I can have another try if you think it's relevant."

"I think we can leave it for now, Errol," Julia said.

"OK. Andrew Strathdon, someone you know well. He's working for the EU in their migration policy team. He's high up in the legal affairs department. It's more important than it sounds as migration and free movement of people is one of the main pillars of the EU, so his is a significant job. My contacts in Brussels say he's good at it, personable too and well liked. They say he's been working on projects to make tracing and recovery of victims of trafficking easier and more efficient. They involve a lot of centralisation of data, which has upset some people, not least the Brits who want to share other people's information but not their own. Strathdon travels between London and Brussels frequently. He has an apartment in Brussels, modest, rented, and a house in Scotland where he hardly ever goes. In London he seems to use hotels or sometimes stays with friends.

"He's very comfortably off, financially. He has a healthy bank balance and no debts that I can find. He doesn't seem to misbehave with drink, drugs or sex. The only reddish flag I've found is a name similar to his linked to a dodgy offshore account in the Cayman Islands. It was in one of those exposé pieces, leaked inside information. The spelling isn't quite the same and there isn't enough information to properly identify him as the subject.

"Dido Sykes. Well, as you rightly suggested that's not her real name. As you know originally she's Carol Jones from Hull. You say she was in the sex industry as Debbi Saint, and if so I can't find any record of that. She may have used other names I suppose. In fact I'm pretty sure she must have other names because I can't find any financials in any of the three names you gave me, and these days everyone has to have a financial profile, even if they haven't got any money. Her company address in Clerkenwell is rented on a rolling one-month lease. It's a serviced office. I had a quick look around it over the weekend on the quiet. There isn't anything to speak of in the office, although it's well furnished. There are two ordinary looking desktop computers and a couple of phones, and one locked security cabinet that I couldn't get into. Nothing unusual in power usage, so I don't think she's got any serious computers in there.

"Other office users say there's a lot of coming and going with couriers and temporary staff. Sykes herself isn't there every day but isn't absent for too long either. I can't do much more on her without a full team. I did get a few pictures. She's certainly a striking woman, and I'd bet the clothes shops love her.

"Last, but not least, Colin Savernake. Well actually he is pretty much the least. Nothing at all unusual about his lifestyle or finances, except for one thing I'll come to in a moment. He's mister dull, lives at home with the wife, mortgage paid off a couple of years ago. His kids have flown a long way away, one to Australia the other to Canada. He doesn't seem to have many local friends and doesn't belong to local clubs or societies. He plays a bit of golf. Word is his wife is a bit of a secret drinker, sherry and wine.

"You know him as well as anyone at work. He's reached the dizzy heights of Deputy Assistant Commissioner by not doing anything wrong, or maybe by just not doing anything much at all.

"The one interesting thing about him goes back a long while. When he was a junior officer he was swept up in a raid on a sadomasochist party place somewhere out near Watford. He claimed he had never been there before and was simply investigating a complaint from a member of the public, even though he was off-duty, a long way from home and in another force area. Nothing was done about it by Hertfordshire Police and he was let off with an informal warning, but I've been told, off the record, that he was actually a regular punter at the place. A submissive, into being dominated. He may have grown out of it, but you never know."

Julia and Mel asked Spelman a few clarifying questions than Julia thanked him profusely. Errol left a folder with his notes in it on her desk. As he and Julia shook hands Mel noticed the lingering contact, but couldn't tell who was doing the lingering. When Julia sat down again after Errol had gone she looked a little pink.

"What do you make of all that, Mel?" she asked.

"I can see you've gone all gooey-eyed, not that I blame you for a moment."

"I meant, what do you make of what he said? Are you getting any insights?" Julia ignored Mel's earlier comment.

"I'd say we're looking at a fairly clear hierarchy, with Strathdon and Sykes more or less at the top. Maybe Strathdon has the edge, I don't know. Shah is definitely lower down, as was poor old Bijan. I think he was the expendable one at the bottom. As for your boss, I'm not sure he's in the hierarchy at all, but if he's still into S and M there could be a link between him and Dido. That's what Barbara in the NCIS porn unit says she was famous for, back in the day.

"I think we should have a close look at what Strathdon's up to in Brussels. It sounds very laudable, but it could be giving him access to all sorts of information to help with trafficking. Shah too could be actively facilitating through influence over consular activities and staff in EU and accession states, like Bulgaria, Romania and Hungary – even tiny Slovenia."

"I agree. Have you got anyone in Brussels?"

"Of course. We've a liaison office there, and also at Europol in the Hague. I'll give them a go first rather than the Brussels office, which is always busy just trying to figure out how the Belgian police system works. I'll call someone when I'm back at the office. Look, Jake, are you OK with all this? I mean, you were very close to Strathdon. If he *is* behind this trafficking operation how will you feel about it?"

"I don't know. I'm hoping I'll be so furious that I'll be laughing when he's sent down. And if he is behind it I *will* get him sent down. Just don't let Alf kill him first."

Chapter 36

Drew had finished and he lay back with his eyes closed. Dido got up and put on a robe. She went to the room she used as her office. The passports were where Drew said they were, and she put them neatly in a padded envelope. She wrote an address and called down to the hall porter, and a few moments later her doorbell chimed. She handed the envelope to him, together with a twenty-pound note. She asked him to call a courier to deliver the package and charge it to her service account. The address was that of a 24-hour convenience store in Kennington that did a neat side- line in taking delivery of packages for customers who didn't want them sent to their homes. No questions asked. Shah would collect it on her way to work the next morning. Shah had access to the stamps and labels needed for permits and visas that had to be issued in London. If only locally issued stamps were needed her minions in consular sections of Embassies would attend to it. The passports would be in the Diplomatic Bag to Budapest, Bucharest and Ljubljana by the next afternoon.

Dido went back to the bedroom and sat in a chair watching Drew sleep. She poured herself another glass of champagne and listened to his steady breathing. He was sated and relaxed. She was happy. She neither enjoyed nor disliked having sex with Drew. The act in itself meant nothing to her, but she liked the way it made him behave towards her. She reflected on the time she had spent with him in Oxford. He knew very soon after meeting her that she wasn't a member of the university but it didn't seem

229

to matter to him. When she fled Hull and after her brief but fairly lucrative career as a porn actress, which she had found ridiculous, she wanted to go to one of the famous university towns. She wanted to see if she could learn proper things through osmosis, through geographical proximity with people who studied there. She tried Cambridge first but found it bleak and too self-absorbed. She preferred Oxford with its industrial heritage, its factories and its sizeable working-class population. She felt more at home.

Drew had still taken her to debates and talks at the Union and had showed her how to gate-crash interesting lectures. He was the male role-model she had never had. He was mature, thoughtful, considerate. He listened to her and spoke to her like she was a real person, not just someone to hire for a while to dump your juices into. He introduced her to his friends with vague explanations that she was 'doing some research'. He'd even introduced her to that bitch Kelso when she turned up at the university the following year. He said she'd been his girlfriend in Scotland, and it soon became apparent that she was still his girlfriend in Oxford. That was when she decided she would let Drew have whatever sex he wanted with her, whatever he wanted that he couldn't get from Kelso, or that he wouldn't even ask her for, and whenever he wanted it.

She still smiled to herself when she remembered the look of astonishment and horror on his face as she wordlessly unzipped his jeans and slipped her hand into his pants that first time in a punt on the Cherwell. Kelso had her back to them and was discussing something political with the other couple who were on the boat, which was moored to a post. Drew's lap was partly concealed by a rug, and Dido's steady hand movements weren't apparent to the others. Every time she felt he was close to coming Dido would stop and throw a question into Julia's conversation to make her turn around and look at her - while her hand was wrapped around Drew's cock beneath the rug. It was early evening and the light was fading. When she thought it was time Dido ducked her head under the rug on Drew's lap. She could barely contain her giggles as the punt rocked from side to side when Drew came in her mouth. By the time Julia turned round to see what was going on Dido was sitting upright and gazing vacantly at the water. Drew was staring in the opposite direction.

"Sorry, bit of cramp in my leg," he said.

"Is there any more of that wine, Julia?" Dido had asked, holding out her plastic glass.

Julia poured her some of the inexpensive South American red. Dido drank.

"Delicious," she said, swallowing. She was looking right at Julia.

The next day Drew sought her out. She was at the Union reading a book.

"That stuff in the punt yesterday," Drew started, "what was that all about?"

"I thought you'd like it. You can have it any time, you know, and lots more besides. Any time at all. Even now if you want, right here."

She took his silence to mean yes. She pulled him down next to her on one of the long wooden benches. There were a few people around, but no one too close.

She bent her head forward into his lap and started. It didn't take long.

"There," she said afterwards as she repaired her lipstick, "doesn't that feel good? It's only right that you should feel good, Drew. You should have everything you want, when and where you want it, and bollocks to all the rules that say you can't or you should have to wait. Life's too short to obey rules, don't you think?"

After that she and Drew had sex frequently and often bizarrely, never discussing themselves or making or expecting any promises. They even continued after he said he was going to marry that bitch Kelso.

Dido Sykes, as she had become by then, supported herself at Oxford with her hastily assembled collection of gags, masks, manacles, whips and latex suits, all tricks of a trade she had seen her mother pursue. Her earliest memories were of her mother spreadeagled on the kitchen table with no knickers on and her skirt pulled up in front of a short queue of Latvian sailors. She learnt that seemingly all men, and some women, will pay for strange sexual things. And that was how her mother kept the squalid roof over their heads and some food on the table, when she wasn't getting fucked on it for money.

Dido left school with nothing but her humiliation. Her mother's reputation had rubbed off on her and she was treated with disdain by both fellow students and most male staff members alike. Some of the women teachers patronised her and offered her pointless advice. She developed a shrewd ability to read people, to determine their weaknesses and where her advantage over them might lie, if she needed one. She knew she was clever. She also knew there was no way she would ever get into a university, but she went anyway. She absorbed knowledge and she understood concepts. By the time she left Oxford for the other Cambridge, just across the Charles River from Boston in America, she had probably learned more than most real Oxford graduates.

Splitting her free time between Harvard and MIT she learned about this new thing called the Internet and quickly saw what it could mean to the world. She grasped how to hack and learned how to code. She also made good money the same way she had done in Oxford. And now here she was. In a plush apartment in London on the river, with everything she wanted, with a thriving if criminal business, just one of several she had, and the only man in the world she had ever wanted to please.

Dido finished her champagne and stood up. She dropped her robe and got back into bed.

Chapter 37

Wednesday morning. Errol and three of his team were covering the Clerkenwell office from various vantage points. Errol had two of the team on motorbikes while he and one other were on foot. Just after 8am a large BMW drew up and Errol watched as Dido Sykes and a tall, well-built suited man got out of the car and went to the office. Pictures were taken. Errol called Julia and described the man. She guessed who it might be and asked to see one of the pictures, so Errol sent one of the bikes back to the Yard with a memory card. Twenty minutes later Julia called back and confirmed that the man was Andrew Strathdon. The team kept watch.

At 8.45 Dido Sykes came out alone. She walked briskly through the streets of Clerkenwell and Holborn and arrived at the Waldorf Hotel just before 9. One of Errol's team had followed her. She had been at the Waldorf for less than five minutes when she emerged with a young worried-looking man in tow. They hailed a taxi and drove off. Errol's man called his boss.

Errol saw the taxi arrive a few minutes later and he took pictures of Dido and the young man as they went to the office.

******

Dido and Drew read the email from Sofia. It was brief.

"I need four urgent conversion to sterling from Lev. Send contact details."

Dido composed and equally brief reply: "Pineapple will call you." She sent it.

******

Jamie Linmouth was rattled. He had done everything the strange woman had told him to. He had his new passport, he had paid his debts. For the first time since he had started life as a trader he was almost completely broke. His bank account now held precisely £134.79. It was all the money he had in the world. Now he sat in an uncomfortable chair opposite the woman and a man he had never seen before. The man was speaking.

"What we do, Jamie, is help people travel. We help them find opportunities. The problem with European governments, and the British one in particular, is that they don't want people to be able to travel to find opportunities and they do their best to stop us helping them. Your job is to be a representative for us. We will send you to places to meet with customers. You will take and collect documents, but not across borders. You will be the point of contact between customers and us. We will give you a new phone every month and you will use it only to contact us. You will obtain other phones to speak with customers, but where possible you will only speak to them face to face. The phone you use for each customer will be one from the country in which the customer resides, if possible. Are you following me?"

"Yes, sir," said Jamie.

"Good. Apart from the phone we give you we will provide an email address each time you visit a

235

customer. You will use that to send certain documents to us. You will only ever use hotel business centres or Internet cafés to send or receive emails from us. We will provide email accounts for you to use. Confidentiality of communications is key to our business. It is up to you to maintain it.

"Now, your first job for us will be tomorrow. In that envelope you will find a booking reference for the afternoon British Airways flight from Heathrow to Sofia. There is also some Bulgarian currency and a hotel reservation. When you land you will buy a local pay-as-you-go mobile phone from the kiosk at the airport, then take a taxi to the hotel and make a local call from a payphone in the area. The number is in the envelope, but you must subtract 1 from the first digit, 2 from the second and so on. So 784 379 would become 661 923. Do you understand?"

"Yes sir."

"Good. When the call is answered you will ask if there are pineapples in the market today. The answer is irrelevant. Say you need 12 to be delivered to the London Casino on Friday. Then hang up. On Friday take a taxi to the Radisson Hotel. Sit in the lobby and a man will come in at exactly 12 noon. Ask him if he has the pineapples. If he understands you, introduce yourself to him as Jamie and say you have taken over from BB. Give him your Bulgarian phone number and the email address that is also in the envelope. Say that arrangements are being made for the four conversions and you will be in touch. He will give you a number on which to contact him. Is all this clear?"

"Yes sir. I am good at detail. It is, or was, my job."

"Good. After you meet the customer in Sofia you return to the airport and get the evening flight back to London. Phone the number entered in the mobile we have given you once you land at Heathrow. Two thousand pounds will be paid into your bank account on Monday if you complete this task satisfactorily. That is all. You may go. And please do not discuss this with anyone at all. You owe us a large amount of money, which will be repayable immediately if you breach our confidentiality or disappoint us in any way. You've already been told that we don't use the courts for debt recovery."

The man stood, the woman remained seated. She hadn't spoken at all.

Outside Errol watched the young man leave. He sent his other foot soldier after him and waited. Within 10 minutes Dido and Strathdon emerged. The BMW appeared from nowhere and they both got in. Errol sent the bikes after the car and made his way back to the Yard.

Ninety minutes later his mobile rang. It was one of the bikers.

"They went to the tall apartment block in Chelsea Harbour. I've got the floor number but can't do any more here without showing out. The bloke stayed about half an hour then left in a taxi. Milly followed him on the other bike and took him to Waterloo International. She spoke to the port control office and they managed to track him to the 12.30 to Brussels. He had an overnight bag but no other luggage."

"Great stuff, Lee. Give me the floor number and call it a day. Let Milly know." Errol was pleased.

After another hour his foot soldier reported in with a home address for the worried-looking young man. Errol stood him down too. By early afternoon he had enough to go to Julia.

"Boss, it's that SB bloke again. Can you get him to make an appointment next time?" Raj was annoyed.

"I'll see what I can do," said Julia, "show him in."

"We've been busy, Julia," Errol started, after another slow handshake. "I know why we can't find anything on Dido Sykes. She's got another name. She's Christine Leclerc on a French passport. She's renting a flashy apartment down at Chelsea Harbour, which is where Andrew Strathdon stays when he's in town. He's gone back to Brussels. They met a guy this morning, we've identified him as a James Linmouth with an address near Tower Bridge. Initial enquiries show he's a trader in the City, but the financial team found out he was unceremoniously fired on Tuesday and he's been blacklisted. They have informal arrangements for that sort of thing in the money world. He won't get a job in the City again, unless it's in a sandwich shop. Passport office says he stood in a queue most of yesterday waiting for an fast-track new passport. I've flagged it with ports and I'll get to know if he travels. I've got someone looking into Christine Leclerc, which is about the most common name in France."

"That is amazing, Errol. I can't thank you enough," Julia said. "I need to get some of this actioned and I'll give you a call later."

******

238

Over at NCIS Mel scanned the reports on her desk, including details of the email from Luan Krasniqi in Sofia. She called Julia.

"Pineapple?" Julia asked.

"Codeword I expect, not a real pineapple. The interesting thing is it's given me a bit of a steer towards the email server. The boffins tracked this email pretty well and it seems to have ended up in the north east of the USA or lower Canada. We're looking to see if we can see it crossing the Atlantic back to the UK, but there's an awful lot of traffic to go through. Cheltenham has asked the US and Canada to help.

"I've analysed previous traffic on similar routes and I've got a handle on the overarching email addresses for each of the networks, and it's pointing towards the alias addresses I was talking about the other day. The boffins are trawling back to see what they can still find. I'm going to pull it all together in a report for you, all official and above-board like."

"Why do I think you're always taking the piss out of me, Dunn? Now, can you meet me for a drink tonight. Errol's done some great work and I thought I'd ask him to meet me after work."

"And I'm your gooseberry?"

"Bodyguard. But I'm not sure if you'll be guarding mine or his. He's come up with another name for Dido. It's Christine Leclerc. She's on a French passport – I'll email the number to you. Drew's been staying at her place in Chelsea Harbour."

"Interesting. I'll see you at 6.30 then." Mel hung up.

******

239

Meanwhile in Sofia Luan Krasniqi was not happy at all. His face still throbbed; he had a cracked cheekbone. He cursed Paulo Silva, a man he had grossly underestimated. At least the hardened criminals of the Balkan region did you the courtesy of looking the part, not like a well-dressed polite middle-aged businessman. Without turning a hair Silva had killed two of his most loyal and, he'd thought, best men, and then stolen most of his business and finished off by mashing his balls and kicking him unconscious. He was going to fix the son-of-a-bitch. He started working his phone, seeking out contacts and potential allies in London. He emailed the address he had used before, asking - trying not to plead - for any information on one Paulo Silva who seemed to be a threat to their business. A suitable contract would be put out when someone found this Silva.

Unbeknown to him Luan's anger was being noted at GCHQ and faithfully reported to Mel Dunn, who was concerned. But the angry Albanian had given her and colleagues a whole load more to focus on, like a lot of UK phone numbers linked to Balkan organised crime and more than a few hit-men. Plus more links into Dido Sykes and her inner circle. Mel would need to discuss all this with Alf and Jake later on.

Chapter 38

As a busy day drew to a close Julia Kelso and Mel Dunn sat in their usual corner of the bar at the St Ermin's Hotel waiting for Errol Spelman.

"I need to talk to you and Alf together, Jake," Mel said, "maybe after this. A few new things have come in today that you both need to know about."

"OK. Let's go back to yours afterwards. Will you tell Alf?"

"Already done, in anticipation. He'll be there at 9."

"Good. At least Errol's safe for one more night."

"Are you being serious, Jake, about Errol? I mean, how well do you know him?"

"Not serious serious. I'm taking a leaf out of your book, Mel. Enjoy what you want if no one gets hurt."

"That's just it, Jake. No one gets hurt. I'm not one to give advice, but you really need to get to know him better, and him you, before you even think about the beast with two backs. And what about Alf?"

"I'm pretty sure Errol's not his type. Here he is now, we'll finish this later."

Jake stood up. She stood and instead of taking his hand she stretched up to kiss his cheek. Errol nodded as if he'd expected this. Then he noticed Mel and he deflated himself just a little.

"Hi Errol, how are you doing?" Mel asked.

"Good Mel. I didn't know you and Julia were social friends too."

Mel just smiled at him.

Julia ordered drinks for them all. Gin and tonic for her and Mel, a dark aromatic rum and still water for Errol.

"Thanks for finding the time, Errol," Julia said, "you've been so helpful I just wanted to say thank you, and give us a bit of time to get to know each other better. I like the way you work."

"A pleasure. Now what's a nice girl like you doing in a place like this?" Errol wasn't paying much attention to Mel. She understood.

"St Ermin's, London or the Metropolitan Police?" Julia smiled.

"Let's take it in reverse order, although St Ermin's is self-evident. It's a nice place."

"I was in the police in Scotland, Strathclyde. I love Scotland but it's a bit like a funnel, and sooner or later you run out of professional room. I needed a deeper pond for a while and the Met foolishly said they'd have me. So here I am. Which explains London too. Now, what about you?"

"My parents weren't much more than kids when they arrived from Jamaica with their respective folks. London was crying out for people to do the rubbish jobs that the war survivors didn't want. Government found an answer by inviting lots of us over from the Caribbean, but they seem to have forgotten to tell the locals we were coming. My folks had a rough time. They struggled to make a living and keep a decent home, but they managed. They're about to retire soon. Dad's worked on the Underground for nearly forty years, Mum did more than twenty in a civil service canteen. He wanted to be an accountant - he's good with figures – and Mum wanted to teach. That wasn't the sort of thing that the government had in mind for them. They had kids, three of us. My big brother died when he was eighteen. Stabbed. My dad talked me

242

out of going after the white kids who'd done it, he said it wouldn't bring him back but would take me away from him and Mum too. So I calmed down, looked after my little sister and went to catering college. I was going to be a chef in a smart restaurant - I had a dream of creating fine dining with a Caribbean twist. Obviously that didn't happen, but that's for another time.

"I decided to take on the system. I joined the cops. My Dad worked it out, but my Mum was horrified. Not because she hated the police, she wasn't too keen on them but certainly didn't hate them, it was just she thought I'd get killed or corrupted. I'd made up my mind to be a cop, and a good one. Special Branch saw something in me and pulled me in. Not so good for promotion but it's a great job. I've done fifteen years and should get another couple of promotions if I stay with them. Maybe more outside. Who knows?"

"What about your family now?" Julia asked.

"Never married, and no plans to as long as I'm in the job. I share a flat with my sister. She's a project manager for one of the big IT companies. She's away a lot, and it's a big flat so we have our own space."

Errol called the waiter and ordered another round. He hadn't asked Julia or Mel if they wanted another.

"And you, Julia?" he asked.

"Like you, never married nor likely to be. It's a personal choice. I've a couple of very good friends down here, Mel included, and they keep me on the straight and narrow."

"I'm sure you don't need that, Julia," he said.

"You'd be surprised!"

The drinks arrived and the interrogations turned to casual chat, which Mel joined in with. After a while she looked at her watch.

"Crumbs, I've got to be somewhere. Are you coming, Jake, or will I see you later?"

"Jake?" asked Errol.

"A kind of nickname," Mel said.

"I'll finish up and come with you, Mel. Give me a minute," Jake said. "Errol, it's been good getting to know you more. When I first borrowed you and Niall from the Branch Tim Edwards told me you were a great cook. Is that so?"

"They say I am. Just a hobby, though."

"Maybe you should cook dinner. Next time."

"On one condition, Julia."

"And what might that be?"

"Bring a proper wine. Every time I ask someone round to eat they think it's funny to get some Thunderbird. I said the next person to do that would get thrown out. And I wouldn't want to do that to you."

They all got up. Julia kissed his cheek again, he shook Mel's hand, but not for long. He left.

"Easy tiger," Mel said, "I can smell you smouldering."

"You can pay for the cab, just for that." Julia said.

******

Alf, or Paulo, they couldn't decide which, was loitering in his usual pub and he appeared at Mel's door before Julia had chance to kick her shoes off. He

244

was startled when she threw her arms around him and kissed him warmly.

"What's got into you, Jake?" he asked.

"Just feeling affectionate."

Mel stifled a laugh. Jake glared at her.

"Drinks first, then business," Jake said.

"Right. Let's sum up," said Mel, "we're getting more to link Dido Sykes, aka Christine Leclerc to mischief in the Balkans. The Krasniqi guy that Alf pissed off has gone on the rampage and is trying to find Paulo Silva by reaching out to everyone he knows in London, including Dido by email. I'm sure she'll be furious. It's enough to keep Jake's team going for a month of Sundays. On a serious note, Krasniqi is talking about taking out a contract on said Paulo Silva."

"Before you start, Alf," said Jake, "I'm thinking if we can get Luan Krasniqi to London I can get him accommodated with his brother for a very long time. I'll be setting up a team to look at all these Albanian gangsters he's pointed a telephonic finger at, but I'm more interested for now in the four girls that Krasniqi has his mitts on, and in disrupting the other four trafficking networks that Mel's identified."

"Four of them?" asked Alf.

"Yes," said Mel, "it looks like Dido's outfit chooses only one per country to deal with. Clearly a commercial strategy to keep their prices up and their cut high. We've got Budapest, Bucharest, Ljubljana, and Skopje. Sofia too, of course. Judging by the communication traffic I'd guess that Sofia, Budapest and Bucharest are the biggest operations, while Ljubljana and Skopje are the second tier. I've unearthed historical communications going back more than two years, and looking at the numbers of girls - they call them 'conversions' in the emails - being brought into the UK each year from these five places is 35 or 36. I'm assuming there's some replenishing going on, but even so that number of girls represents a total income of around 16 million a year. On top of the ones who are already here, so you can multiply that by three, conservatively. The 'fee' for travel and documentation is just window dressing. I'm guessing it might be in place so that the finger can be pointed at someone lower down the chain if it all goes wrong, some clerk in an Embassy or similar who will suddenly find they have a bank account stuffed with tens of thousands of pounds which they've never heard of and can't explain."

"So how do we get hold of the four in the pipeline?" Jake asked.

"I think they're safe until they get to the UK, unless Krasniqi is bounced into doing them harm." Alf said. "So I think we can let plans for their journey proceed, especially now we've a bit of a handle on it. If we lose the intelligence feed I can jump on Krasniqi again and get him to London to meet the girls, then they're safe and he's all Jake's."

"Why not do that anyway?" asked Mel.

"Because of what you said earlier about Krasniqi being a bit pissed off. If I jump in too early there could, more likely will, be a showdown and one or both of us won't come out of it well. I reckon I've got a 50/50 chance of getting Krasniqi here at the right time. Going in too early will reduce that. Apart from the intelligence stream Mel's worked out we've another good lead on BB's replacement, the boy Jamie. He'll be off to Sofia very soon I reckon. I'd like a chat when he gets back if you can tip me the wink, Mel."

"He's right, Mel. Getting Jamie wrong-footed early will be good. I don't know what Dido has on him, and I don't think he's a willing volunteer judging by Errol's description of him, but I'm sure he'll not want to give up the next twenty years because of it. With Errol's handle on the ports and yours on the communications we should get to know what Jamie's up to and give him a fright when we want to."

"OK. Next thing is how is Dido pulling the strings? Or is she pulling the strings?" Mel asked. "Could it all be down to Strathdon?"

"I think it's Dido," said Jake, "she's an ace manipulator. I wouldn't be surprised to find that both Strathdon and Shah think it was all their idea when we get to the bottom of all this. Dido has them eating out of her hand. She's probably massaged Shah's ego and done the 'all girls in this together' thing, 'it's so unfair how you've been treated, you should show them, get your own back'. I think she's been playing Drew as well, since Oxford. I wasn't there for the first year he was, but she was around. When I turned up it all seemed perfectly normal and friendly, but when it became clear that Drew and I were together she changed. She kept trying to score points off me She never tried to take him from me, but there was something going on. Drew would get a bit shifty from time to time, like he'd almost been caught out. Drew's always fancied himself as a high-achiever. I think she persuaded him that there are more ways to be one of those than he'd thought."

"So," said Mel, "we've got Dido or whatever her name is pulling the strings and doing the coordination at the centre. Drew Strathdon and she are more or less on the same level. You mentioned he stays at her place in Chelsea Harbour - do you think that means they're a couple?"

"That probably depends on your definition of a couple. Dido never had a boyfriend or girlfriend at Oxford. If she was doing anything with Drew it must have been for his benefit, not hers. I do know that Drew isn't the type to sleep on the sofa if there's an alternative," Jake said.

"I don't recall her having anyone special, or at all, at high school come to think of it," Mel said. "As I was saying before I interrupted myself, Jasmira Shah is lower down the food chain than the other two, and poor old Jamie is just fish-food. From what Alf learned from Luan, with what we've got from various places, it seems reasonable to think that Drew Strathdon finds and 'borrows' genuine travel documents belonging to missing persons, mostly girls. To get the best ones he gets a detailed description from the trafficker who has groomed the girl which comes via Dido. We think by email mostly, but it could come by another route. Strathdon finds a travel document for someone the right sort of age with similar features and colouring. He purloins it gets it to Dido.

"Dido gets it to Shah. Shah attends to any necessary visas or permits, either in London or at an Embassy somewhere. Whoever Shah's corrupted gofer is in the Embassy delivers the document to

Jamie, or BB as was, who gets it to the trafficker together with any travel tickets.

"Jamie formerly Bijan gets paid the five grand per girl, which presumably goes back to Dido the same way, via Shah's network. Girl travels to London. The trafficker arranges to get her met and that's the end of it for her, or rather the horrible beginning. Trafficker retrieves the travel document which is sent back to the trafficker upstream, in Sofia for example, and it also comes back to London via Shah and then to Strathdon.

"To my mind that confirms that Dido is behind it all. If anything goes wrong the person most exposed is Jasmira Shah. She has her fingerprints, literally, all over the flow of documents one way and money the other. Strathdon is also in play and he's taking a risk. I think he brings documents with him when he comes to London and retrieves them again. Literal fingerprints again. Even if Dido is in the chain I'll bet she never has one of the documents with her. Everything will be remote. So she's running it and taking least risk of getting caught. Cunning cow."

"What about the missing link?" Alf asked, "the other unidentified phone that floats in and out?"

"Thanks for reminding me," Mel said, "it popped up briefly on Monday, just for a minute or so. It was in the Bloomsbury area. I haven't got the latest data for Dido's phones yet. I'll check tomorrow. Do you have an idea who's it is?"

"No," said Alf, "but it's getting to be time to find out."

"I'll do some mapping and maybe Jake can get her new best mate Errol to do some snooping about."

"He's not my new best mate. Good idea, though. I'll need to know who it is before we can start planning Dido's downfall. I've a nasty feeling it could be significant. I think that's it for now, Mel, I'm exhausted. Now let's all have a nightcap and think about how to put a stop to it all in the morning."

They had a last drink, then there was an awkward pause.

"It's OK," said Mel, "I'm on the sofa. Just don't break him, or my bed."

"What do you mean?" asked Alf.

"You'll find out! G'night." Mel went off to the bathroom.

Chapter 39

On Thursday morning Mel and Jake left the apartment before Alf was up. Neither could face the train so they hailed a cab.

"You feeling better now?" Mel asked Jake.

"Yes and no. Your bed's fine but I think I may have over-startled Alf, and myself for that matter."

"But the flame of Errol still burns?"

"Let's talk about something else. You know I said I thought the missing link phone might be significant? You said it popped up on Monday?"

"Yes, in Bloomsbury. Late afternoon, early evening."

"Well on Tuesday morning I got a summons from that arse Savernake. He gave me some old pish about a restructuring job that came with a promotion. Basically, he wants to send me off to Bramshill Police College for six months to do the Intermediate Command Course, and then come back to do a nothing job. He wants to shove me out of the way."

"And?"

"Well, the day after I 'bumped into' Dido Savernake came over all smarmy and took me out for a drink. Shortly after I'd seen Jasmira he's trying to send me to Siberia. I want to know where Dido's phones were on Monday. If one was anywhere near the missing link's one on Monday I'll put money on the missing link being Colin Savernake. God only knows what his connection with Dido is, if there is one. If it is Savernake there's going to be another almighty shitstorm."

"Happy days," Mel sighed, "here we go again. I'll check and let you know as soon as I can."

They both sat in reflective silence for the next ten minutes as the taxi chugged its way through Clapham Junction towards Vauxhall.

"Would you take the job, if it exists, for the promotion?" Mel asked eventually.

"If it exists? You're right though, it could be Savernake trying to sink me. You don't get a second chance at the Intermediate course, and it's not beyond the realms of possibility that he could scupper me, all it takes is a couple of unsupportive appraisals and I'm sure Savernake could manage that. To answer your question, Mel, I don't think I would take it. There's a lot in the Met needs fixing, and I wouldn't mind having a go at it, one day. Just not now. Hugh's been nagging me about joining his lot."

"Hugh Cavendish, from Six?"

"Yes. I'm thinking about it. There's also something coming up at Europol that I've been asked by their DG to have a look at and consider. The Met doesn't know, and they wouldn't like it if they knew I was looking elsewhere."

Mel squeezed Jake's hand.

"I'd miss you, Kelso."

"I'd be taking you with me wherever I go, Dunn, you don't get away from me that easily." Jake smiled for the first time in a while. "Onwards and upwards, as they say."

The cab pulled up on Albert Embankment. Julia paid it off and said goodbye to Mel. Then she walked in the chilly morning mist towards Lambeth Bridge and the distant gloomy tower block that was New Scotland Yard.

Mel wasted no time. She grabbed a coffee and walked briskly to her office. Dumping her coat on a spare chair she got to work on the call records and cell site searches. She almost didn't want to find it, but it was there. The missing link phone and Dido's current temporary one were active in the same cell within an hour of each other. Not at exactly the same time so no clincher, but too close to be a likely coincidence. She looked at past cell site data for the location and found two other occasions when one of Dido's temporary phones was active within an hour of the missing link one. Mel could narrow it down to one of the terraces just east of Woburn Place, the sort of place that although being in the middle of London was unlikely to have too much CCTV coverage. She phoned Jake.

"I think you need to get Errol, Jake. Dido's was in the same place as the missing link on Monday, not at exactly the same time but close enough. I've got them both there at the same sort of time on another two occasions over the past couple of months. Too much of a coincidence in my book. We've got nothing in our records for the street in question. I'd say that there's probably a safe-house or somewhere else for Dido and the missing link to have their little get togethers. No identifiable pattern yet.

"Just a thought, could Errol's team sit on Savernake while you give Dido's cage another quick rattle? It might prompt another meeting or at least some contact."

"Good idea. I'll set it up. Have you heard from Alf?"

"No, why? Do you think you actually killed him? I'll give the flat a call."

******

Alf / Paulo wasn't dead, but he was a bit stunned. Despite it being almost 10 in the morning he was still in Mel's bed. Jake had been astonishing the night before, with few signs of her usual warmth and tenderness towards him, no matter how passionate she was feeling at the time. While he had quite enjoyed her lustful energy he had been unsettled by her need for self-satisfaction, which was so unlike her. Mel Dunn had sort of warned him that she was in a strange mood, and he would try to find out just what was going on when he next saw her.

He heard the phone ring. It stopped after two rings then rang again four times. The third time it rang he picked it up. It was a code they'd worked out if they needed to speak on the landline.

"You survived then?" Mel asked.

"What was she on, Mel? I'll spare you the details but it was scary. Is she OK?"

"Just an emotional thing, no drugs. Between you and me I think she's scared."

"Scared of what?"

"Scared of being in love with you."

"What?"

"It'll keep. She'll be fine again soon. Now, what are you up to?"

"I was just lying here thinking."

"Lying? You're still in bed?"

"Consider it my day off. It was a long night shift. I'm planning on going back to the hotel in a bit, then I'm going to get some exercise, not that I think I need it today. Then I'm going to think about my next moves with Krasniqi and Dido's new boy."

"I just heard that the new boy Linmouth is on his way to Sofia. He's off on his first mission. He's supposed to be back tomorrow night, landing around 9."

"Is he now? Well, I might just introduce myself tomorrow evening."

"By the way, Jake has an idea that the missing link might be her boss Savernake. She's going to get Errol's team to follow him after she's made another contact with Dido. I'm covering the phones so we'll know if there's any contact."

"Savernake? He doesn't strike me as the type, but then Dido's a strange one. If she has something on him or some kind of hold who knows?"

"Where are you going to be tomorrow night, Alf?"

"Depends how I get on with Linmouth. I'll probably go to the hotel. Why?"

"No reason. Just curious. Let's speak later."

Alf got up and made himself some coffee and toast. He tidied up, tried to make Mel's bed but gave it up as a bad job, and then he left. He walked slowly, deep in thought, up hill towards the Common. In his room at the hotel he took a long bath, suddenly aware of the stinging scratches Jake had left on his back. After a while he got out and dressed in fresh clothes. He decided against going for a run and instead he had a leisurely lunch overlooking the hotel gardens and the trees beyond.

He spent the afternoon dozing and thinking in his room. It was dark early and he felt he could just collapse back into bed and sleep, but he needed to get going. Just after 6 he left the hotel wearing casual jeans and a loose jacket. He found the battered builder's van which started on the second attempt. He drove through the sluggish winter-evening traffic into central London and by 8 he was parked up near Jamie Linmouth's apartment block. He spent an hour walking the streets of the neighbourhood and getting the 'feel'. He was able to get into the underground garage under Linmouth's building and he sized up the assortment of flashy motors stored there. This was a place where the young men and women who did 'something in the City' slept and played.

He made careful mental notes and went back to Wimbledon.

******

It was almost 9 on Friday evening and Paulo was back outside Jamie's building. The City types would all be out on the town for a few more hours yet, and it was quiet. He found a local convenience store and bought a small selection of groceries, milk, bread and the like The assistant put them all in a plastic carrier bag. He went back to the van and sat and waited. He had a good view of the entrance to the block. He had seen one of the photographs that Errol's team had taken of Linmouth and he was sure he'd recognise him when he saw him.

Just before 10.30 a taxi pulled up. Alf saw Jamie Linmouth get out and pay off the driver. He waited

256

for a receipt. Linmouth had a shoulder bag but nothing else. He walked wearily into his building. Alf watched as lights were lit in an apartment on the third floor. He went to the door and pressed the buzzer for Jamie's flat.

"What?" a tired and grumpy voice said.

"Cabbie. You left something in the cab," Alf said.

"I'll be down."

Alf was relieved to know that Jamie Linmouth was neither astute nor wary, which was good for Alf but not so good for Jamie if he was going to succeed in his new profession as an international criminal. Alf waited in a shadow with his face turned away from the light, the plastic carrier bag in his hand. Jamie opened the door. Alf stepped forward and put his weight on the door to prevent Jamie closing it.

"You're not the cabbie. What do you want?"

"Just a little chat Jamie, about your new job. Can I come in?"

The way the stranger said it made Jamie think it wasn't a question. Maybe she had sent him? He had done everything he'd been told to do, except he had forgotten to call her when he landed back at Heathrow. Maybe the visit was a good thing? Jamie stood aside and let the man in. They rode up to the third floor in silence. Jamie let them into his apartment. They both stood in the hallway.

"So, what do you want?" Jamie asked again.

"Let's make ourselves comfortable first, shall we?"

The man took off his jacket and sat in one of Jamie's armchairs.

"How was Sofia?" the man asked. "Did you see Luan?"

257

"What do you know about Sofia?" Jamie asked. "Who are you?"

"The name's Paulo. Paulo Silva. I'm Luan's business partner. So I know you've seen him. I know a lot about you, Jamie. I also know you've not done this sort of thing before, and you probably don't know exactly what it is you are doing. Am I right?"

No answer.

"As you wish. Let me tell you something about myself then. I met Luan no more than two weeks ago. Just two days before your predecessor was shot dead in Sofia. Oh? She didn't mention that then, when she recruited you? The vacancy you filled was created when a guy called BB, Bijan, was murdered. I take it you met Luan at the Radisson? Well that was where BB was shot dead. Not so many days ago.

"I went to meet Luan because I wanted to invest in his business. He tried to have me killed but clearly that didn't succeed. In return I decided not to invest in his business, but to take it from him. Which I've done. Are you with me? The difference between Luan and me, though, is that I do know my arse from my elbow. So I've come here tonight to see you so you can take a message to the crazy lady you're now working for. What's she got on you, anyway? I'm assuming it's gambling and money, that's how she got BB."

Jamie nodded. Speechless.

"OK. The message is this. Tell her that she's not to deal with Luan Krasniqi anymore. Just with me. Paulo Silva. You'll remember my name I hope. Tell her we'll be meeting soon, at a time and place of my choosing. You can also tell her not to even think about getting one of Krasniqi's contracts on me carried out because he will be dead long before I am and she will lose not only the four 'conversions' in transit but also the whole of the Sofia operation in London. The last part of the message is the most important. Tell her that Sofia is just for starters. I, or rather we - I'm not alone in this - aren't stopping with the Krasniqis. We're taking everything. Budapest, Bucharest, Ljubljana, and Skopje as well. Be sure to tell her that, just so she knows what I want to talk about when we meet. Have you got all that?"

Jamie nodded.

"Now, before I go, one last thing. Give me your phone. Both your phones."

Jamie started to refuse so Paulo stood up. He didn't touch Jamie, he didn't need to. Jamie was already terrified of this intimidating stranger. He handed over two mobile phones. Paulo held them in his hand.

"Which one did she give you?"

Jamie pointed to the one on the left. Paulo pocketed them both.

"Good lad. You're to give the crazy woman the message, in full, but not until 11am on Monday morning. I'm going to rip out your landline now. If you set foot outside this apartment before 10am on Monday morning you will be killed before you get to Tower Bridge. Do you understand that? You are not to contact or meet with anyone at all before that time. Do you understand?"

Jamie nodded.

"Good. Now here's a few provisions just so you don't starve. I really hope I don't have to see you again, Jamie. If you think I'm scary now just wait until

I get angry. Give my love to Dido. That's what the crazy lady calls herself. At least at the moment. But don't forget, not before 11 on Monday. Go to her office. You know where it is. I won't be far away but you'll not see me."

Paulo stooped and ripped the phone socket off the wall. He put the phone itself in a bin. Then he left.

Jamie Linmouth was left shaken and trembling. There had been no violence, but this Paulo Silva was the most frightening human being he had ever met. He went to the bathroom and vomited. He sat up all night and all the next day before falling into an exhausted sleep late on Saturday night. He didn't open his front door until 10 on Monday, and even then only with extreme trepidation.

Chapter 40

Alf / Paulo made his way back to Wimbledon, stopping on the way to get a bottle of Bushmills. He parked the battered van in a side street and walked back to his hotel. In his room he poured himself a large whiskey and sent a text message to Mel.

"Need to see you both tomorrow."

A reply came in a few minutes.

"We're running at 10. See you at mine 2-ish?"

He said OK and finished his drink. After one more he climbed into bed and slept fitfully, beset by strange dreams.

Unbeknown to either Mel or Alf, Jake Kelso had spent an interesting Friday evening with Errol Spelman. She'd called him on his mobile to say she had a job for him and his team on Sunday morning and could they meet to discuss it. He had suggested immediately that she come round and take him up on the offer of a home-cooked dinner. She accepted eagerly and had butterflies in her stomach for the rest of the afternoon.

She left the office early and went home. She bathed and changed. She slipped a clean pair of pants and a toothbrush into her handbag, just in case, She took a taxi to Errol's place in Streatham via a decent wine shop where she bought a bottle of red and another of white, again just in case. She pulled up outside his apartment block feeling like she was seventeen years old again.

Errol opened the door for her. He had a broad welcoming smile and was wearing a white tee shirt under a chef's apron. He was wearing jeans and was

261

barefoot. He stooped, but she still had to stretch to kiss his cheek. He thanked her for the wine.

"Great timing, Julia. Everything's ready, it just needs last minute stuff when we're ready to eat. Let's have a glass of something."

She opted for a glass of red wine. He had already opened a very decent rioja.

"Let's get business out of the way first. What do you need us to do on Sunday?" he asked.

"It's going to sound nuts, but I've an idea that DAC Savernake is connected to the people-trafficking gang I'm investigating. I think he has an association with Dido Sykes."

"OK," Errol said cautiously, putting down his wine glass.

"So on Sunday I'm going to engineer a contact between myself and Sykes which could, or should, provoke a contact between Sykes and Savernake. I'm expecting a crash meeting between them to be arranged hastily, probably in the Woburn Place area. I need evidence of that meeting."

"Nothing much then," Errol said. "Can I ask why you think there's a connection between the two of them?"

"It's just suspicion based on communications data, coincidences, and interactions between Savernake and me that could be linked to events in the investigation. That's why I need evidence."

"Fair enough. Leave it to me."

They spent the next fifteen minutes going over details of times and places. Errol would have his team covering Savernake's house in Hertfordshire from 10 on Sunday morning. He excused himself to make some calls to warn his team.

In his absence Julia looked around the room. There was no one else in the flat, which was spacious and comfortable. There were pictures - photos and paintings - on the walls. Blues music was playing quietly on a fancy stereo. Still feeling incredibly nervous Julia took the plunge and slipped her shoes off, tucking her legs underneath her on the sofa. Errol came back and saw that she was relaxing. His smile broadened.

"What are you cooking for us, Errol?" she asked.

"I hope you like fish. If not, it's going to be fried chicken from the takeaway. I've done a ceviche, lots of lime but not too much spice or onion. It's a favourite of mine. Then fish, I've used fresh tuna but with a Jamaican style marinade, lightly curried then poached in coconut milk. With saffron rice. I've done a special rum and banana dessert. How does that sound?"

"My mouth's watering already."

Errol stood and walked to the kitchen. He returned with the wine bottle and approached Julia on the sofa. She looked up at him expectantly. He poured the wine and she reached for his hand. They touched.

The front door of the flat flew open and Julia heard voices. One female, the other male.

Julia withdrew her hand and looked at Errol's face. He had a bemused and slightly mischievous smile on his face.

"That'll be Sasha and Steven. Sasha's my sister."

They entered the room. Sasha was tall and graceful, sharing her brother's warm broad smile. Steven was in a paramedic's uniform, slim built with a healthy outdoor complexion and slightly red hair. Steven threw his arms around Errol and kissed him on the mouth. Errol kissed him back.

"Julia, meet Sasha, my baby sister, and Steven, my partner. Sasha, Steven, this is Julia, a friend and colleague."

Julia was stunned but recovered herself in an instant. She started chuckling and rose to shake hands with Sasha and Steven, who disregarded her hand and kissed her on both cheeks. Her chuckling turned to full on laughter which she didn't try to explain.

Steven and Errol were a little taken aback by Julia's laughter, but it was infectious and they soon joined in. They all started chatting over drinks.

"Right!" said Errol, "let's eat."

******

On Saturday morning Mel and Jake were on their regular route through Battersea Park It was a mild grey gloomy London winter morning. They were back at Jake's flat by 11 and took turns in the shower.

"I went to Errol's last night, for dinner." Jake began.

"Oh? And?"

"It was delicious."

"What was?"

"Dinner."

"Did you?"

"Did I what?"

"Do it, with Errol?"

"You are *so* nosy! No I bloody didn't."

"I thought you were gagging."

"I was. Then his sister and his partner came in. We had a great evening. They're super."

"Partner?"

"Are you having trouble with sentences this morning? His partner. Steven. He's lovely."

Mel collapsed in a giggling heap.

"Errol's gay?"

"Completely, and very happily too. Steven's a great guy."

"What did you do when you found out?"

"I laughed my head off." Jake collapsed in giggles too.

When they could speak again Mel got serious for a moment.

"Alf wants to talk to us. I said we'd meet at mine around 2. Are you OK with that?"

"Yes. Any idea what he wants to talk about?"

"He was going to pay a visit to Jamie Linmouth last night. I told you Linmouth went to Sofia. Knowing Alf he'll have dropped a grenade down the toilet and he wants to tell us just before everyone's covered in shit. Can I have some coffee?"

Chapter 41

They met that Saturday afternoon. Jake had driven Mel to Raynes Park and the three of them sat in her living room.

"OK, Alf," Jake started, "what have you done?"

"Such trust!" he said. "I paid young Jamie Linmouth a visit last night, and before you say anything he's fine. Well, he's maybe a little bit terrified, but I didn't touch a hair on him. I gave him a message from Paulo Silva to give to Dido at 11 on Monday morning. I told him to tell her that Paulo Silva has taken over Krasniqi's operation and she's only to deal with him now. Also that the Krasniqi operation is just step one. Paulo Silva and his associates will be taking over the other trafficking operations too, Budapest, Bucharest, Ljubljana and Skopje. Silva will be seeing Dido at a time and place of his choosing."

"I told you so," Mel said to Jake, "he's lobbed a massive bomb in the septic tank."

Jake considered what Alf had told them.

"And the message won't be delivered until Monday morning? You're sure?" she asked him.

"Yes. Linmouth's too scared to open his front door before then, and he's without any means of communication for now."

"Well Dido will be having an interesting couple of days then. I plan to give her cage a rattle tomorrow myself. Not as hard as you're doing, but it could work out well. Mel told you, didn't she? I've got Errol's team out tomorrow morning, on Savernake. I'm going to call Dido at 10 to have a wee chat. I'm expecting her to summon Savernake, if he *is* the missing link, and I want it evidenced."

"Sounds good," Alf said.

"I'll have Errol's guys out again to see what she does after Jamie's delivered your message on Monday."

"I'll be around too, but I'll stay out of their way."

******

Julia left them to it that afternoon and drove out to see Kim in the hospital in Acton. When she found her in a day room Kim was sitting in a chair looking listless. She had turned a pale yellow and had a drip in her arm. She gave Julia a weak smile when she saw her.

"First friendly face in days," Kim said.

"Sorry," said Julia, "work's been a bit manic. How are you doing?"

"The medics told me you know about my 'underlying issues'. The damage done by the Krasniqis is the least of my worries it seems. That's on the mend, by the way. My inner workings are knitting themselves together on their own so no need for any more sewing, which is good. They explained to me exactly what's wrong with my liver. They said it's bolloxed. They actually said that. I'm on a transplant list but I'll have to sign the pledge. I don't mind. I only ever drank to calm my nerves anyway, or to get pissed. It just became a habit and I can live without it. The chances of getting a new liver aren't that good though.

267

"The diabetes is manageable, but I'll need a proper diet. Being a working copper isn't good for one of those. Police canteens even deep-fry salad. Sorry, am I sounding gloomy?"

"You've every right to be gloomy, but no you're not. I can see you've got the measure of this and you'll do fine."

"I won't make old bones, though, Julia. I'm concerned about the kids, and Flora too. I'd like to see them, it's their birthday in two weeks. Can you fix that?"

"If you want to see all of them it can't be here in England, but I'm sure it can be fixed. If you want to see the kids I can get them here, but if officialdom gets to know about it they'll want to put them in care. I've heard they're very happy where they are, and settling down well. It might be easier and better to take you to them. I'll speak to the doctors to see when it's safe for you to leave the hospital. You'll be able to recuperate where they are. There's plenty of room and fresh air."

Kim reached for Julia's hand and held it. She was getting tearful but held it in.

"Why are you doing this for me, Julia?"

"You've no one else. And why wouldn't I?" Julia smiled.

Kim sat back in her chair. Her eyelids flickered.

"Sorry Julia. Sudden nap coming on. It happens all the time - must be the drugs or old age. I don't need to go back to bed. I'll just snooze here for a bit."

With that Kim's eyes closed and her breathing became slow and even. She was fast asleep. Julia found a doctor and discussed Kim's care. Medically speaking she wasn't too far off discharge, another week or so of regular treatment should stabilise her liver and the diabetes, and give the internal injuries a bit more time to heal. After that she would need regular medication and a lot of care, but it could all be done at home. Julia didn't tell the doctor that Kim was effectively homeless. She would speak to the ever-resourceful Alf and get something sorted out. In the meantime she made a mental note to speak to the Met's welfare people so they could visit Kim and get her kitted out with new clothes and essentials for when she was ready to leave hospital.

Julia drove slowly back into London. She thought about going home, but instead diverted south and headed back towards Raynes Park. She called as she pulled up, just in case. There was no need. Mel let her into the flat. Alf was at the dining table poring over Mel's laptop, a half-empty coffee mug beside him. A second mug was on the table opposite him.

"How's Kim doing?" he asked Jake.

"She's a bit low. Physically she's improving, at least from the injuries, but she's starting to feel the pressure of all the other things she's got wrong with her. She's alone and lonely, and she's missing her kids. It's their birthday in two weeks. Do you think we could get her to them by then, Alf?"

"I was going to give Roisin a call anyway to see how things are going. I'll do it now."

Alf went into the bedroom and closed the door. If all was not well he wanted some time to think things through before discussing it with Mel and Jake.

"Roisin, it's Thomas. How are you?"

"I'm grand. I'm enjoying the company too. Flora's teaching me to cook foreign food and in revenge I'm teaching her to drive in that old Volkswagen you dumped here. The kids are doing great. How's the mam?"

"A bit up and down, Roisin. She's getting over the attack on her, but they've found other things wrong. She's going to need a change of lifestyle and a bit of peace and quiet. She's wanting to see her kids too."

"Bring her over. There's bags of room in the cottage. The kids would love to see her too."

"This could be long-term, Roisin. She'll need some care, and the kids will need schooling. And there's the matter of papers for Flora."

"We've a fine doctor and the hospital in Cork is good. I can arrange the school, I'm on the management board of the community school here. I'll leave the documentation to you and Uncle Eugene if you don't mind."

"You're a star, Roisin. They'll have their own money, of course, and you'll let me know what they've cost you so far so we can settle up."

"You'll do no such thing. They're my guests and that's that. Now, when will you bring the mother across?"

"In a week to ten days if all goes well. Don't tell the kids yet. It'll be a nice surprise for them, and they won't be upset if we have to delay things a little."

"OK, Thomas. I'll see you soon." Roisin hung up.

Back in the living room Alf filled the others in on his conversation. Jake was visibly relieved.

"Right, now that's sorted let's work out how to get this thing finished," she said.

They discussed and planned for the next couple of hours. After a while Alf's contributions petered out.

To Jake this could only mean he was planning what he needed to do in his own way, things he didn't want to burden her with. It still made her very nervous, but she was starting to learn to live with it. When she felt it was time Mel went into the kitchen and came back with drinks. Jake and Alf took the hint.

"So what do you have in your list of things to do this year, Mel?" Jake asked.

"On New Year's Day my resolution was not to be involved in anyone getting shot, at least not by one of you two anyway. Alf hasn't said as much but I think that's out of the window already. My second resolution was to get into archaeology again. There are some interesting explorations going on in the Mediterranean, all underwater stuff. So I've booked myself on a scuba diving course, two in fact, in Crete at Easter. Only for the interest mind. I don't plan to do it for a living, not yet, but it would be nice to have something to fall back on when Jake gets me sacked from NCIS."

"So you don't want to replace Raj then?" Jake asked.

"I spoke to him about his job. He says you're a terrible boss. So no, thank you. I'll take my chances in the sea."

"Good choice, Mel." Alf commented.

"Are you two ganging up on me?" Jake asked.

"Someone has to," Mel said.

Much later, after takeaway food had been cleared away and glasses drained they all sat together on the sofa, just being quiet. Jake stood up.

"I want the sofa, please," she said, "you two go in there." She nodded towards Mel's bedroom. Mel understood.

"Do I get a say in this?" Alf asked.

"Are you saying you don't want to?" Jake asked. "Or are you making a choice?"

"No to both questions. It's just a bit strange."

"Strange is what we do," Jake said.

Alf shrugged. Mel stood up and took his hand.

Chapter 42

Sunday morning. Jake's phone beeped. Errol's team were in place. She waited until just after 10 then called the mobile number that Dido had given her. It was picked up on the second ring.

"Dido? Julia Kelso. I hope I didn't wake you or interrupt your Sunday morning."

"Julia? I've been awake for ages. I was just going out. This is a surprise."

"I just wanted a quick chat. I was passing Chelsea Harbour the other day and I thought I saw you. Do you live down there?"

"You must have been mistaken, Julia. I'm sure you didn't call me on a Sunday morning just to say you thought you'd seen me somewhere."

"No, you're right. I just wanted to check what you'd told me. About not seeing Drew Strathdon or Jasmira Shah since Oxford. Are you sure about that?"

"I may have passed them in the street but I really don't recall. What's this about?"

"Just an ongoing case. It's probably nothing. I'll let you get on. Bye, now." Jake disconnected the call.

"That'll do it," Mel said.

******

In rural Hertfordshire Colin Savernake was in his conservatory reading the Sunday papers over his tea and toast. The hall telephone rang twice and stopped. A moment later it rang, two more rings. Silence. It rang for a third time. Just one ring this time.

"Colin? Was that the phone?" a voice floated down the stairs.

"Must be a wrong number, dear," he called back.

He went to his study and opened the security cabinet under his desk. He withdrew a mobile phone and turned it on. He looked up the only number it had ever dialled and pressed call. When she answered she was hissing.

"What the fuck is going on, Colin?" an angry voice said. "I told you to get rid of that bitch."

"I don't know what you mean."

"Mistress!"

"Sorry. Mistress."

"The bitch just called me. I want to see you now! Be at the place in one hour. If you are so much as a minute late I'll come to see you at your house, where you are with your wife and where your neighbours can see you. Do I make myself clear?"

"Yes. Mistress." The phone went dead.

Savernake called up the stairs again. "I have to go into work, dear. It shouldn't take long."

He was shaking and sweating as he pulled on a weekend jacket. He unlocked the garage door and started his pale blue Rover 75. A comfortable and safe car. He manoeuvred gingerly out of the drive and into the lane. He didn't notice a car pulled in to the curb a few doors up, nor did he notice the motorbike that settled in two cars behind him as he joined the A10 and drove towards London.

The two bikes alternated the follow. It was an easy job. Savernake took no interest in anything around him. One of the bikers did a close pass and reported that Savernake was pale and seemed agitated, distracted. His lookout, thought Errol.

Savernake followed the A10 as far as Seven Sisters then took Seven Sisters Road towards Holloway and Islington. Along Euston Road and into Bloomsbury, Savernake made it to 'the place' with a few minutes to spare. The Sunday traffic had been light.

Savernake let himself in. He rented the flat and had the second key. She had the other. She was already there. She was sitting tensely in the armchair, her coat draped across the back. Her eyes blazed, but when she spoke her voice was icy cold.

"You told me you were going to get her out of the way. You haven't done it!" It was a statement.

Savernake began to stammer.

"It's not that easy. There are processes to…."

He was silenced by the crack of a whip. Even from her sitting position she was able to flick her wrist so that the tip of the whip stung him between the legs. He let out a brief yelp.

"I don't give a fuck about processes, Colin," she stood up, "take off your jacket and shirt."

He did so. He stood in front of her, skinny and pale, shaking. She slowly and casually positioned herself, and as she looked him straight in the eye the whip hissed again. A red weal appeared across his chest. A second hiss, it struck the same place. The weal started to ooze blood.

"What is she doing, Colin? Why did she call me?"

"I don't know." He realised his mistake as the whip hissed and cracked twice more. He now had a diagonal red cross on his pale chest.

"You are her boss, you pathetic piece of shit!" Two more hissing cracks. "She is investigating me and she wanted me to know it. I want you to tell me why?"

"I'll find out, mistress." Savernake was trying not to sob. The pain from the razor-like cuts in his chest was exploding as his nerve endings responded to the outrage.

"You have precisely twenty-four hours. If she isn't gone by then I will deal with her myself and then I'll deal with you. Now remove your trousers and pants."

He did as he was told and stood, just in his shoes and socks, in front of her. He would normally shudder in anticipation, but now he was simply terrified. Ten minutes later he lay in the floor. The cross on his chest was replicated on his back. His buttocks were striped. His testes let as if they were alight. She had gone.

As she ascended the steps from the basement flat Errol took a stream of photographs from his vantage point in the back of an observation van. It was enough for Julia. He signalled to the driver to move and he drove off. There's nothing more suspicious to a criminal than an occupied static van, and now he had what Julia wanted there was no point in hanging around. He stood all the team down except one bike, just to see if he could get a snap of Savernake leaving, and called Julia. He told her what he had seen.

"Bingo!" she exclaimed to Alf and Mel in the flat in Raynes Park. "Savernake is definitely the missing link."

Mel had been on the phone too.

"We've got an unidentified mobile calling Savernake's home number, looks like a coded contact, then the missing link mobile calls a number we've seen before. The missing link number is located in the cell that covers Savernake's house. It's him alright," Mel said.

"Right," said Alf, "I've got things to do to be ready for phase 2 tomorrow. I take it you'll be having words with DAC Savernake in the morning, Jake."

"I think I probably will."

"I know I don't need to tell you this but be careful. If Sykes is responsible for what we think she is she's got to be a psycho. We don't know what kind of hold she's got on Savernake, but if it's powerful enough to make him collaborate with her in what she's doing even he could be dangerous."

"You're right, you don't need to tell me. I'll be careful but if it's just me and Savernake in a room it won't be me needing carrying out."

Alf nodded. He was going to kiss them both goodbye, but thought better of it. It wasn't the moment.

******

In Bloomsbury it took Colin Savernake a good hour and a half to staunch the blood, but he couldn't stop the stinging. His torso, buttocks and genitals felt as if they were immersed in boiling acid. The sort of pain his mistress normally inflicted was pleasurable shortly afterwards. She was very skilled. The pain he felt now was most certainly not at all pleasurable. It was excruciating. When he thought of his mistress now he didn't feel excitement, he felt terror. Kelso had not only humiliated him at work with her condescension, she had also robbed him of one of his few remaining pleasures, an hour every now and then with his mistress. It was time she paid for it. He would do what his mistress had demanded, he needed to please her.

As he climbed the stairs slowly and painfully a camera caught it all.

Chapter 43

Monday morning. Julia Kelso was in her office just after 7. Mel was across at NCIS not long after. Alf was having a leisurely shower in his hotel on Wimbledon Common, followed by an even more leisurely breakfast. At 10 his taxi arrived and took him to Waterloo International station. He was wearing a smart business suit with a dark blue raincoat. In his briefcase he had a few random bits of paper, a paperback novel, a clean shirt and underwear and a washbag. In his jacket pocket he had his Portuguese passport in the name of Paulo Silva. He found a coffee shop with a good view over the concourse and he waited. He turned on the phones he had taken from Linmouth. There were missed calls on both, as he had expected. He turned them off again.

At 10.15 a timid Jamie Linmouth opened his apartment door for the first time since Silva's visit on Friday evening. He hadn't been able to eat or drink anything that morning and he was trembling as he walked through the City towards Clerkenwell. As he neared the office Errol's team clocked him. Errol called Julia. Game on.

He arrived at Dido's office at 11 precisely. She was not pleased to see him, and he stood in front of her as she lambasted him for not being in contact. She demanded to know what had happened in Sofia. He told her very briefly and stood silently, composing his words for the next part.

"So everything seemed to go OK in Sofia. I got back and was going to call you as instructed. But then he appeared."

"Who appeared?"

"Paulo Silva."

"Silva? Where did he appear. How do you know it was him?"

"He was outside my apartment, near Tower Bridge. He was waiting for me. He knew I'd been to Sofia. He forced me into my apartment and said he had a message that I was to give to Dido. Is that you?"

Dido said nothing. She was staring at him.

"He said my predecessor was murdered. Shot dead in Sofia."

"He had an accident. Hit and run." Dido said.

"Silva said he had gone to meet Luan Krasniqi to invest in his business. Krasniqi tried to have Silva killed, so Silva decided not to invest but to take Krasniqi's business from him. He says he's done this, and you are not to deal with Krasniqi anymore. Only him, Silva. Then he said Sofia isn't the end of it. I've no idea what this means, but he said he's going to take Budapest, Bucharest, Skopje and Ljubljana as well. He's going to take everything. He said he'll be in contact with you at a time and place of his choosing. Those were his words. I don't know what any of this is about. He told me not to tell you before now. He was adamant. Not before 11 on Monday morning, and to do it here. I don't know why."

"Here. In this office?"

"Yes."

"Why didn't you tell me before?"

"He took my phones. Both of the ones you gave me. I haven't got myself another one yet. Then he ripped my home phone out of the wall. He said if I

280

opened my front door he would know about it and I'd be dead before I got to Tower Bridge."

Dido had gone pale. There was no reason for Linmouth to lie, unless he was a plant, a very clever plant. She had checked him out thoroughly before choosing him as Bijan's replacement. He had been lined up long before Bijan had to go. He couldn't be a plant, it just wasn't possible. But if what he said was true the London operation was compromised. Not by the police, but by other criminals, ones she had never heard of. She had control of the thuggish gangsters who provided the livestock and ran the revenue end, the ones who thought they were partners because she let them have 70 percent after costs, the ones who were too stupid to see that essentially she took the big profits and they took the big risks. She had never heard of Silva, no one had. She couldn't find him on her extensive internet information web. She thought for another moment and made her mind up.

"I want you to stay here, Jamie. I need to go out but I'll be back. Just take any messages if anyone calls. Don't let anyone in. I'm not expecting any visitors. I'll make you a coffee before I go. I'm sorry that you've been caught up in this. It's not what you think, and you've done nothing wrong."

Dido left the office and he saw her busy herself in the small kitchen area next door. She came back with a steaming mug of instant coffee.

"Drink this, I won't be long."

She smiled at him, a very attractive smile. He sipped the coffee. It was quite bitter.

"You might need some sugar. I make it quite strong."

She passed him a bowl with white granules in it. He spooned some into his coffee and stirred. He sipped.

"Better?" she asked.

He nodded. She picked up her shoulder bag and left without another word. He heard the outer door close and the street door slam. He drank his coffee.

Outside Errol's team saw Dido hurry away from the office and hail a taxi. A bike followed it to Waterloo. Two of the team waited for Jamie Linmouth to emerge. Julia had said she wanted his participation evidenced. After ten minutes he hadn't appeared. Errol called Julia.

"Sykes has left. She's gone to Waterloo International and bought a ticket to Brussels. Linmouth hasn't come out of the office. Do you want us to go and get him?"

"Yes please, Errol. Be careful. I've no idea what Sykes might have done."

Errol gave his team the nod and two of them fiddled with the office door lock until they got in. They hadn't made a sound. Jamie Linmouth lay on the floor, gasping for breath. The team quickly sized up the situation and correctly assessed Linmouth must have been poisoned. The ambulance arrived in time to save his life, at least for now, and he was whisked off to the London Hospital in Whitechapel.

At Waterloo Alf, or rather Paulo Silva, slipped into the ticket office queue two people behind Dido Sykes. He heard her ask for a first class single to Brussels on the next available train. He did the same. There was an hour to wait. He watched her discreetly across the first class lounge. She was fidgety and although she appeared to be reading a magazine she wasn't concentrating.

Boarding was announced. His seat was across the isle and slightly behind Dido's, an ideal position. As they pulled out of Waterloo for the initial slow and bumpy slog across South London he saw Dido get a phone from her bag. He heard the call.

"Drew? It's me. I'm on the train. Meet me, we need to talk." She gave him the arrival time.

Silva relaxed and watched the cityscape roll by, then the open country, then the darkness of the tunnel. On the other side they emerged on to a smooth fast track and sped across the flat boring landscape of northern France and Belgium towards Brussels.

******

As the train thundered on Julia Kelso at last answered one of the many calls Raj had received from DAC Savernake. She went to his office.

He was standing in full uniform, his back to the door. She knocked and entered without waiting for his say-so.

"You wanted to see me, Colin?" she asked.

"Yes, I did…"

"Good, because I wanted to see you too," she interrupted him.

"How dare you!" he started.

"I'm interested in a certain flat in Bloomsbury, Colin," she gave him the address, "it's come up in an investigation. Care to tell me what you know about it?"

"You are impertinent, Kelso. I'm not going to be drawn into your point-scoring games."

"It's your flat, Colin. You rent it. I checked. Nothing wrong with that, of course. But it's who you meet and what you do there that *is* wrong. Am I getting warm, Colin? I'm asking because you're going red. Why don't we sit down?" She sat.

Instinctively he did the same, but winced as he did so. Julia noticed.

"A bit rough, was she Colin?" she was guessing.

"Get out of my office!"

"But you said you wanted to see me. You haven't said what for yet. Would it be about Dido Sykes - you might not know her by that name - who you met at your Bloomsbury flat yesterday morning around 11.15? I've photographs Colin, of you entering and both of you leaving. She left a good while before you, and she looked really pissed off. Do you want to see? You left an hour and a half later. You were limping. There was some blood on the seat of your trousers. Must have made a mess on the seat of your nice blue car."

"You had me followed? I'll see you out of the force for this Kelso."

"You're not asking why, Colin? You know I phoned Sykes on Sunday morning. She told you. Do you know her as Sykes or something different? Maybe her old working name, Debbi Saint."

Savernake paled. He was trembling with fury.

"She called your home number, a signal for you to turn on your secret phone. Am I right?" she didn't wait for an answer. "Then you spoke to her on your secret phone, or rather she spoke to you, I've seen the transcript. You addressed her in an interesting way. When she'd finished you drove to 'the place' as fast as the speed limit would allow. You're not a confident driver, Colin. You went straight to the Bloomsbury flat, 'the place' as she called it. She was already there so she has a key. You let yourself in. Twenty minutes later Dido Sykes or Debbi Saint or whatever she calls herself came out with a face like thunder. You still haven't asked why I know this Colin."

"You are conducting an unauthorised investigation into a superior officer! I am suspending you from duty this instant!"

"How do you know it's unauthorised? And why on earth do you think you can suspend me? You still haven't asked why. Well I'll tell you. Dido Sykes, your Debbi Saint or Mistress Whiplash has you by the balls, in more ways than one. She's telling you to manipulate and control policing activity that might impact on her criminal activities. She is actively engaged in trafficking young girls and using them as sex slaves and prostitutes. She knowingly procures young girls for rapists and paedophiles, and she then conspires to pimp them out. And you are helping her. Not for money, but for sexual services. In your case I'm guessing dominating services. That's why I know what you've been up to, Colin, because what you're doing is a corrupt betrayal of your service, your profession, and most of all the innocent girls who Dido Sykes preys on. I've checked and seen that you put yourself on the distribution list for all notifications of pre-planned territorial policing operations. She will have told you which ones she wants to know about, and you've been telling her, so that her money-making schemes continued undisturbed. You could have stopped her at any time, saved those young women from torture. That is so wrong, Colin. Now, what was it you wanted to see me about?"

Savernake sat behind his desk. His anger was dissolving into self-pity and despair. He shook his head. He looked at his watch.

"She gave me twenty-four hours, which is until now, to get rid of you. If not she said she'd do it herself. She said if that happened I'd be sorry."

"Well she's a bit preoccupied right now, in fact she's on a train to Brussels, so I wouldn't worry about deadlines too much. But I want you to do something, Colin, something honourable."

He looked up at her.

"Go to the boss. Tell him what you've been doing. Throw yourself on his mercy. Then tell your wife. After that Dido has no hold on you. She can only threaten to do you harm, and we're the police Colin. We can protect ourselves. Plus, if I can I'm going to put her in jail. Is that all?"

Savernake looked dejected. He nodded.

"Up to you now, Colin. If you decide not to be honourable I'm coming after you too. Just saying."

Julia stood and walked out, leaving his office door open behind her.

Chapter 44

The Eurostar pulled into the terminal just south of Brussels city centre. Paulo followed Dido as she walked briskly up the platform and out on to the concourse. A tall, well-bult and handsome man was waiting for her. She didn't kiss or greet him but kept walking. He fell in beside her. She was talking rapidly. The man pulled at her arm to stop her. He gripped both her shoulders and turned her towards him. Paulo watched as her face lost its composure and she started shouting at him. He couldn't hear the words but could imagine what was being said.

The man, presumably Drew Strathdon, put his arm around her shoulders and guided her towards the exit and the line of waiting taxis. Paulo picked up his pace and stood quietly in the taxi queue behind them. He heard the man say 'Aparthotel Montgomery'. Paulo got into the next taxi and said the same thing to the driver. The destination was a relatively new block of serviced apartments not far from the European Union complex. Paulo's taxi pulled up in time for him to watch Dido and Strathdon enter the building and walk to the elevators. Dido seemed familiar with the place.

Paulo paid off his taxi and found a seat in a café with a clear view of the entrance. He ordered a café crème and waited. As he watched he saw a window open on the third floor. Dido stepped out onto the balcony, despite the cool damp weather, and lit a cigarette. She was still talking animatedly. Strathdon joined her and tried to put his arms around her. She shrugged him off.

Paulo made his move. He used the phone Linmouth had been given to call her. He saw her turn her head and walk into the room. She emerged a second later with a phone in her hand. She was staring at it as if it were a snake. She answered.

"Looks like you're having a bad day, Dido. We'll be meeting soon, maybe in Brussels." Paulo disconnected the call.

He looked up at the balcony. All of Strathdon's calming effort was immediately undone. She was off again. Paulo ordered himself some *moules frites* and a glass of pale gold beer.

An hour later Dido emerged from the apartment building. A taxi pulled up and she got into it. He watched her mouth the word 'Eurostar'. He paid and followed. He was behind her in the ticket queue again. They both bought first class single tickets to London. This time his seat was at the opposite end of the carriage but he could see her clearly enough. He bided his time.

As the train descended into the gloom of the tunnel under the English Channel he slipped into a vacant seat opposite her. She started and looked up at him from her magazine.

"That seat's taken," she said.

"No it isn't, Dido," he replied, "Paulo Silva."

He extended his hand. She didn't take it. He didn't mind.

"I said we'd be meeting. How is Strathdon? He seemed concerned that you were so upset."

She took a deep breath.

"What do you want?" she asked.

"Jamie Linmouth told you what I want, didn't he? I hope he delivered my message clearly."

"Whatever he said made no sense to me. I don't know who you are or what you want, but I want you to go away and leave me alone."

"Wouldn't that be nice? I know about your trafficking business. I know what Luan Krasniqi's making out of it, and it seems like good easy money. I like that. So I'm taking over Krasniqi's business, the Sofia franchise if you like. I want the rest of it too, as Linmouth told you. Did you talk to Strathdon about it?"

Dido said nothing and sat tight-lipped.

"I can ask him myself. He provides the travel documents. Is he a partner or do you just pay him for each girl?"

Dido's head jerked up. She started to say something but clamped her lips tight shut again.

"What have you got on him, Dido? Or should I call you Christine?"

She said nothing, but he could see that her mind was in turmoil. He stopped speaking and sat opposite her for the remainder of the journey in silence. The train pulled into Waterloo International. She stood. He followed her. They descended to the platform and started walking towards the customs post and the exit. They didn't slow down as they walked through the crowds on the outside concourse.

Dido stopped. She turned to face him, looking up at his face. A smile slowly appeared and she looked as if she was about to speak. He bent towards her.

The pain was incredible. He could barely breathe. His face felt like it was on fire and he was completely blinded by the stinging liquid she had sprayed in his face. He fell to the floor, attracting nothing but irritated tutting from the evening commuters. He dragged himself out of their way and sat against a wall in an alcove, hoping that no good Samaritan would stop to help him or call the police. After half an hour his chest eased up and he could see blurry shapes. His face still burned. She had given him a massive dose of CS, concentrated tear gas. He cursed himself for letting complacency set in. Now she was on the loose and he doubted he would find her so easily again.

He stumbled to a washroom in the station and tried to bathe his stinging face, being sure to keep his eyes shut. After a while he tidied himself up and found a cab. He'd lost his overnight bag, which had in it the phones her had taken from Linmouth but nothing else of any significance. He didn't know if she'd taken it or if it had been picked up by a passer-by. He recalled it had a piece of notepaper from the Cannizaro Hotel with train times on it. He decided that it was best not to go back there for now. He told the cabbie to take him to New Malden, and from there he walked back to Raynes Park trying to purge the remaining gas from his painful lungs. It was late by the time he got to the flat.

Mel was not best pleased that he had turned up unannounced, but her tone softened when she saw the state he was in. She took him in, helped him shower the residue off his face and body. She had no clothing for him so she wrapped him in towels and put him to bed. He told her what had happened.

"You idiot!" she said and kissed him goodnight.

Chapter 45

The following morning Mel started to see signs of the impact of the respective interventions of Julia Kelso and Paulo Silva. Emails had been sent to the crime groups in Budapest, Bucharest, Skopje and Ljubljana all containing a single code word, which would presumably initiate some kind of emergency plan. Why Sofia hadn't been included was not immediately clear to her. The three remaining temporary phones belonging to Sykes, Strathdon and Shah all disappeared from their networks. She expected the permanent phones to follow shortly. The 'missing link' phone, now confirmed as belonging to DAC Colin Savernake hadn't been seen on the network that day, and probably never would be again. In short, the interventions had taken the intelligence gathering operation back to square one. Mel hoped her friends knew what they were doing.

******

In Sofia Luan Krasniqi was close to panic. He had heard nothing more from London since the visit on Friday by the scared looking boy with the idiotic talk about pineapples. She had sent him, Luan knew that, but he wasn't going to do business with the office boy. Not after his encounter with the madman Silva. He wanted to speak to her, but he had no way of doing so. The last phone number BB had given him for emergency contact with her wasn't working. There had been no response to the second email he had sent. He didn't even know if it had been delivered. The boy had said arrangements were being made for four new girls, 'conversions' as they were termed, and he had taken the descriptions with him. He had no idea where the descriptions had gone. To top it all off his phone had just beeped. Silva was calling him. He didn't pick up.

******

Dido Sykes, otherwise Christine Leclerc, was still fuming in her hotel room. She did not like things going wrong, and she really didn't like Julia Kelso messing with her business. But Kelso would have to wait. Dido had things to fix urgently. Her hotel was at Canary Wharf. She ventured out into the subterranean warren of shops and cafés that ran beneath the soaring towers. In an electronics outlet she bought a serviceable laptop and a few necessary accessories which she took back to the hotel. She plugged the machine in and set it up before connecting it to the hotel's data port in her room. She wasn't concerned about the hotel seeing what she was doing, it would mean nothing to them and no one would be able to follow any trail she left.

She connected to the internet and navigated her way through a complex network of gateways and firewalls until she was safely in her own server, which was located far away across the Atlantic. She saw the email sent by Jamie Linmouth from Sofia, as directed. It contained the descriptions of the four girls together with their photographs. She appraised each one dispassionately, quietly approving Luan's taste. She sent the descriptions to the secret email address for

Drew in Brussels. Business had to go on, at least for now. She gave instructions for him to source four documents and send them to Shah in the usual way. The only difference this time was that he was to hurry. The documents had to be with Shah by Thursday at the latest. Dido wanted the conversions underway by next weekend. Her London sojourn was coming to an early close, but she wanted to go out on her terms.

She read and ignored Luan Krasniqi's urgent pleading second email, and then set to work remotely cleansing the machines she had abandoned in the Clerkenwell office she could no longer use. Using a remote email address she terminated the lease on her Chelsea Harbour apartment and settled the outstanding account. She arranged for someone to go there and pack all her things up in a container and ship it to a genuine address in New Zealand, where it would be a surprise for whoever received it. She had no idea who lived there, but better an unknown person on the other side of the world than the interfering and forensically astute Julia Bloody Kelso. Dido didn't think there was anything incriminating in the apartment, but she was taking no chances.

Dido then hacked into the bank account of the hapless Jamie Linmouth, who was either dead or dying as far as she was concerned. She reinstated his overdraft with a much higher limit and promptly transferred sixty thousand pounds, the amount she had deposited the previous week, through a series of dead ends back to one of her own accounts. She had no need of the money, it was simply a matter of principle.

Before disconnecting from the internet Dido did two more things. Firstly, she emailed a bank in Toronto using appropriate security passwords asking them to remove a package from her deposit box and have it sent urgently to the bank's branch in the City of London for her collection in a two days time.

The final thing she did was to negotiate the tricky and sensitive pathway into the dark web, that part of the internet which had been adapted by savvy users to avoid prying eyes and authority. There she placed a contract, a hefty one, on the heads of Julia Kelso and Paulo Silva. One hundred thousand US each, with a 100 per cent bonus if one assassin could deal with both at more-or-less the same time.

Satisfied, Dido disconnected the machine and took a long bath.

******

Julia Kelso was at her desk. She had Errol's reports. Mel had called her with the news about the loss of intelligence coverage. She had asked Errol to send someone get a search warrant for the Clerkenwell office to retrieve any computers or records or toxic substances, and to arrest Dido Sykes in the unlikely event that she was actually there. Could he do the same with the Chelsea Harbour apartment? Sykes was well and truly in play for the attempted murder of Jamie Linmouth, who was still very seriously ill in hospital with some strange kind of poisoning. The magistrates court was crammed and it took Errol best part of the morning to get his warrants signed off. By the time his team got to the respective addresses the apartment was already stripped bare, having been re-let within minutes of Ms Leclerc giving up the lease and all of the previous resident's belongings had been shipped to an off-site location. The apartment was being deep cleaned ready for the new occupant, who was moving in that afternoon. The office was pretty much as they had left it the previous day. They bagged up and took away anything they could find, which amounted to two computers, a bowl of sugar and some tea-bags. When the IT people turned on the computers they had been completely reconfigured and the disks were irretrievably empty.

Julia called DAC Savernake's office. They told her he hadn't been seen so far today, nor had he contacted the office or responded to calls to his home phone or his official mobile. His staff officer had been despatched to Broxbourne to find out what was going on.

She sighed. All in all the weekend, and the week so far, had been a disaster. Her last hope of getting back on track was Jasmira Shah.

Julia decided to do two things, three even. Firstly she was going to go home to Dolphin Square and hit the gym for a long hard hour. Then she was going to get showered and changed and head out to Raynes Park to shout at Paulo Silva. After that she would need some food, and probably a reasonable amount of gin.

******

Paulo Silva was also reflecting on the weekend and his day trip to Brussels. He readily admitted he had screwed up. Dido Sykes was better than he had given her credit for, and now he had shown his hand to her he was unlikely to get a decent chance to have a go at Andrew Strathdon. That left Jasmira Shah, and it was unlikely that Dido would leave her in play for much longer unless she thought that the London trafficking operation could be salvaged.

He was concerned about the four girls being held by Luan Krasniqi. He had an idea of how to recover them, but a lot would depend on intelligence coming from Mel's sources. God only knew what was left of those.

He had thought of going out for a run, but the residual pain in his lungs erupted ferociously when he bent to put his shoes on so he gave up on the idea. Sykes had inflicted more damage than he'd thought. He lay back on the bed, deflated. All his stuff was at the Cannizaro hotel. He would rest for a while longer then make his way up there, carefully though, in case Dido Sykes had worked out where he was staying.

As it happened Dido Sykes had no idea where Paulo Silva was, but many other eyes were poring over hacked credit card transactions looking for mentions of anyone of that name checking into hotels, hiring cars or buying plane tickets. They were also looking for one Julia Kelso. She was a lot easier to find than Senhor P Silva, that being one of the most common names in Portuguese and therefore almost ubiquitous in Portugal, Brazil, Mozambique and a few other places besides where there are sizeable Portuguese populations. A small pack of wolves was on their trail, aroused and encouraged by the US dollars that Dido Sykes had laid out as bait.

Chapter 46

In Brussels Andrew Strathdon worked late into the evening. His colleagues had long since adjourned to the restaurants, bars and clubs that the once-boring Belgian city now boasted. The influx of well-heeled bureaucrats and the well-funded lobbyists who fed and watered them had created booming business. Anyone with any influence at all need never pay for a meal throughout their tenure in the city.

Once he was alone he logged into the missing persons database and started his searches. He quickly identified a handful of likely candidates. He eliminated two he had used before, but selected four girls of the right age and of similar appearance. He put in a request for the documents, which would be retrieved from the archive automatically and despatched to him overnight. He would have them with the first mail delivery in the morning. Once he submitted the request and it was acknowledged he moved the records from the missing persons database. They would disappear from all the border checking systems and the Schengen Information System when they updated themselves automatically every hour.

Strathdon closed down his computer and sat quietly in the semi-darkness of his office. He thought about Dido and the way she had been yesterday. He had never seen her lose her composure before, and it was a worry. She was undoubtedly a strange and enigmatic woman, she always had been. Remote, calculating, very clever, and uncannily able to read people. Drew was sure that Dido could persuade almost anyone to do almost anything and think it was their own idea. He never felt as good as he did when he was near her, except for yesterday when he had seen her shaken and vulnerable. Her email that afternoon was reassuringly assertive, she was back in control. He often asked himself why he was doing the things he did for her. In the end it came down to the fact that it made him feel good. She recognised and encouraged his need to get what he wanted in his own way. He had been brought up to think that selfish aims were bad. Dido showed him this was not so. He was allowed to please himself. She allowed him to please himself.

He let himself out of the building and despite the light rain he walked the kilometre or so back to his rented serviced apartment. Dido hadn't let him touch her yesterday. He didn't really mind. He knew that next time she would allow him to make up for it. He stopped for a whisky or two at the bar near his apartment, and he was in bed alone sleeping soundly an hour later.

The following morning he was in his office bright and early. The first mail delivery was already in and he collected the four envelopes addressed to him. He checked the contents and was satisfied. He went back to his apartment and spent the next hour making travel bookings in each of the four names, each girl using a different route but ending up in London within a day or two of each other. He collated all this and packed it in a large padded envelop with the passports. He composed a summary email for Dido and sent it on their secret system. He addressed the envelope to Jasmira's cover name at the convenience store in Kennington, and he left this with the receptionist downstairs to arrange for a courier to take care of it. His service account would be charged, of course. Jasmira could collect the documents and travel tickets the following evening.

He made his way back to the EU complex and his day job. Which he was really good at.

******

Julia Kelso was shaken by the news that DAC Colin Savernake had been found dead. He was at his home. The staff officer who had found him was an experienced detective and he quickly worked out that DAC Savernake had had a violent argument with his wife, which resulted in him bludgeoning her with a golf club, a driving wood, before hanging himself in the garage. There was no note, but also no other explanation. Julia could think of one: Dido Sykes.

******

As Julia sat reflectively in her room, Mel was reading a report that had just landed on her desk. She re-read it and picked up her phone.

"Jake, it's Mel," she began, "we haven't lost absolutely everything. I'm looking at an email sent by Strathdon, at least I'm guessing it's him, to one of Dido's addresses. It's written in gibberish, but if I'm interpreting it correctly he's sent four travel documents and details of travel arrangements by courier to be collected by Shah from the 'usual place'. There's a twenty-four hour time lag on emails, so I'm thinking the pickup must be today, hopefully it hasn't already happened."

Kelso was shaken out of her torpor and swung into action. She called Errol and told him to meet her in the lobby, the Back Hall as it had always been called. She had forgotten why. Errol was already there waiting. She smiled at him.

"Let's walk. We can talk as we go," she said.

Julia had never given Errol the full story, but she did now, except she omitted any mention of Alf. She outlined how she thought the conspirators operated, and admitted that precipitate action on her part had closed down very nearly all of the intelligence leads she had been relying on. Only one source was currently available, and that was slow and incomplete.

"There is a bit of good news, though," she said, "Jasmira Shah has been sent a package containing travel documents and tickets for four trafficking victims who are about to be sent to the UK. They've been groomed by someone who knows what he's doing and they're all being deceived. When they arrive they'll all be forced to work as prostitutes. If we can get our hands on Shah with those documents we can save those poor girls and hopefully break the conspiracy."

Errol listened, and without being asked to he phoned his team. They scrambled for a surveillance and possible arrest operation and headed for Whitehall. Julia and Errol were walking up Clive Steps towards the Foreign Office.

"You'll need to identify her for us, Julia, and we can't just hang around in Whitehall. Give me a few

302

minutes to find somewhere we can use. Wait here and call me if you see her."

Julia nodded. He went off into Whitehall and cast his eyes over possible observation posts that gave a view of the end of King Charles Street and Downing Street. He knew from his ministerial protection days that there were a variety entrances and exits to the Foreign Office, but that the majority of workers used the King Charles Street entrance. Few of them turned right and went down Clive Steps into St James Park, preferring to go to Westminster tube station and the bus stops in Whitehall, or to take the short walk to either Charing Cross or Waterloo stations. Errol went into a tourist gift shop and spoke with the owner. Five minutes later Julia joined him in a first-floor store room above the shop from where they had a good view of the street below, albeit through a very grimy window.

"Good spot, Errol. I like your style. How's Steven?"

"He's good. He's just finished night shift so he's at home sleeping. We need to concentrate now. You won't have much time to spot Shah and my guys will need as much time as you can give them to latch on to her."

Julia's admiration for this confident officer grew. Not many sergeants would have the balls to tell a Commander to shut up and concentrate, however politely. She smiled and did as she was told.

It was not yet lunchtime and there wasn't much traffic in or out of the Foreign Office. As the clock moved slowly towards noon and then one o'clock more people started coming and going. Lunchtime. She studied the crowds carefully.

Jasmira Shah was wearing a red overcoat, an unusual garment and a god-send for Errol's team. Julia pointed her out to Errol who spoke calmly and clearly into his covert radio set. He saw one of the girls on the team fall in a few paces behind Jasmira.

"Ok, Julia. We'll take it from here. What do you want me to do if we see her pick anything up?"

Julia had been thinking about this for a while. If she was to have any chance of getting to Sykes and Drew she would need to talk to Jasmira and make her an offer.

"Detain her, but stick her in a van and bring her to the underground car park at the Yard before taking her to a station. I want a word with her before it goes official."

Errol raised an eyebrow but didn't question Julia's instruction.

"OK. You go back to your office and wait. I'll call you as soon as anything happens." With that Errol left.

Julia gave him a few minutes then went downstairs herself. She thanked the shop owner for his help and made her way quickly back to her office.

Chapter 47

Julia made several calls, ending with a quick one to Mel to tell her what was happening.

"Where's Alf?" she asked.

"I haven't heard from him today," Mel said.

"I want him on standby. If I can get my hands on Shah I'll need him to go and get the girls to a safe place, out of Krasniqi's clutches. He'll need to move fast."

"I'll find him and get him to go to the flat." Mel hung up.

Alf didn't answer his phone. He was out running, or with his troubled lungs just walking, on the Common, but he returned the call as soon as he got back to his hotel. She said he'd to go to Raynes Park as soon as Mel told him to, and he waited in his room.

******

Errol's team followed Jasmira Shah to Waterloo Station. She walked right through the concourse and out the other side. She took a circuitous route along back alleys before emerging in Lower Marsh, a road jammed with cafés, restaurants and shops. Further on she found the shop she was heading for. She went in. The team watched and waited.

Jasmira was in the shop for less than a minute. When she came out she had a carrier bag in her hand. In it the team saw the corner of a brown padded envelope. Errol gave the order and called Julia.

Jasmira Shah didn't have time to call out or protest. She was surrounded by three people, one female and two male, who wordlessly penned her in as a white van pulled up. They bundled her into the back and piled in after her. Jasmira was in shock, which was quickly turning to outrage.

"How dare you!" she started to hiss, "I am a senior diplomat and you have no right to do…"

"You're a clerk, love, and you know it," the female person said. "Someone wants a word with you. Now shut it."

Jasmira was silenced. She started to cry quietly.

The ride to the underground carpark was swift and brief. The rear doors of the van opened but there was little light outside. The three people in the back with Jasmira got out and a single figure climbed in instead. Jasmira couldn't see her face as darkness returned to the back of the van.

"Well, Jas, what have we here?" Jasmira recognised Kelso's voice.

Julia flicked a switch and a light came on. Jasmira was half lying, half sitting on the floor of the van. Julia sat cross-legged with her back to the doors. She reached for the carrier bag. Jasmira struggled briefly. Julia slapped her cheek, just once and not very hard. It was enough to deflate Jasmira Shah.

Julia opened the envelope. She was wearing latex gloves and she pulled out the four passports, each in its own envelope together with a folder of travel tickets. The passports were from various European countries, and each belonged to a young female citizen.

"What are you doing with these, Jas?" Julia asked.

"You've no right to touch them. This is official government business!" Jasmira said, but not very confidently.

"We both know there's nothing official about it. What are you going to do with these?"

Jasmira said nothing.

"Drew Strathdon sent these, didn't he? What for?"

Jasmira said nothing.

"You do know you're going to go to jail, don't you Jas? For a very long time. If you're a bit helpful you might just do yourself some good. If you're not I don't really care. Have you ever been inside a jail, Jas? Even as a visitor it's no fun. You're what, thirty-seven, thirty-eight now? With the charges you're looking at I reckon you'll be almost eighty by the time you'll be eligible for parole. You'll get life, that's for sure, and it all depends on the tariff the judge sets. Abuse of trust and position, bribery and corruption, conspiracy to kidnap, rape and murder, that's forty years Jas. In anyone's book."

"What do you mean, conspiracy to kidnap and rape?"

"And murder. That's what you've been doing, Jas. Or didn't Dido and Drew tell you what it was all about?"

Jasmira was shaking her head.

"I don't know what you're talking about. Drew said it was just to get deserving people into the UK. People who could contribute, make a difference. He said that the UK's immigration laws were all wrong. They allow the wrong kind of person in, not good, decent people. In my position I could help, he said. Dido said that as someone from a migrant family I should see how decent people are disadvantaged by the rules."

"Did she say people like you, Jas?"

Jasmira nodded.

"Did she say good, decent people like you, migrants who got to Oxford and got a good job in government?"

Jasmira nodded again.

"So why did you take money for helping them, Jas? Dido and Drew paid you, didn't they? And you paid people to help you."

"Why shouldn't I get paid? The beneficiaries are paying, to cover all the costs and expenses. They can afford it."

"No, they can't Jas. The girls you're helping to traffic, they're nearly all girls aren't they, are young, innocent and usually poor. Most of them are, were, virgins, when they arrived here. The gangs behind the trafficking auction virgins off to rapists for a price. Once they're not virgins anymore the girls are forced to be prostitutes. They're sex slaves, Jas. And Drew and Dido get a big slice of all the money they make for the gangsters. That's where your money comes from, Jas.

"Now, let's start again. What are you intending to do with these passports and travel documents?"

"How do I know you're not lying?" Jasmira said.

"You don't. The only way you'll get to know for sure is when you go down for forty years. Now talk to me, Jas, not just for your own sake but for the sake of these four girls."

Jasmira started to cry.

"Let's go to my office. It's upstairs."

Julia helped Jasmira from the van and up the narrow staircase to the lift lobby. She walked Jasmira through the uninterested throng of police officers and visitors and up to her office. She silenced Raj with a glare and shut the door behind them. Julia passed Jasmira a box of tissues and a glass of water.

"From the beginning, Jas," she prompted.

Jasmira took a deep breath.

"I'd always admired Drew at Oxford. He was so dynamic and popular, but he never seemed to take any notice of me. Especially after you turned up. So I hung around on the periphery. After graduation I got a job in the FCO, that's when he showed up. He charmed me. I was engaged by then, it was an arranged marriage, but Drew made me feel so different. Valued. One day he brought Dido along. I thought it would just be me and him, as usual. We were meeting every week or two by then. In private."

Jasmira glanced up, embarrassed but also slightly smug. She was telling Julia that she'd been having an affair with Drew, who would have been Julia's fiancé at the time. Julia let it bounce off.

"So this time he brought Dido. The three of us were in a hotel bedroom," Jasmira continued. "It was bizarre. Dido flattered me. Said she'd always admired me and had watched as I progressed in the FCO. She said I deserved so much more, but as a woman and an Asian I was unlikely to get what I was entitled to. She said that as a woman she felt my pain and humiliation. She said we women must stick together and take what's rightfully ours.

"After this Dido left. She left me in the room with Drew, and we did what I thought we'd been planning to do. Afterwards we got dressed and went downstairs. Dido was waiting in the lobby. She had a laptop computer. She signalled for us to come over to her, and she showed me what she was looking at. It was a video of me and Drew, just a few minutes earlier. Dido had placed cameras and had filmed the whole thing from the moment she'd left the room. Drew was perfectly calm, but I was in pieces.

"Dido said everything would be fine. The video was just for her, no one else would ever see it or know about it. And I could still have everything I wanted and deserved, including my sessions with Drew. My husband and family would never know. All I had to do was help a few deserving people out.

"So that's how they dragged me in. For the last three, four years I've been going to that shop, collecting passports and tickets, making sure that they had the right stamps and permissions to work in the UK. If they needed London issued stamps I put them in. It's easy to do. If they needed local-issue stamps I had people in Embassies who owed me favours, or who took money from me. They would do it.

"I sent the passports and travel documents out to the Embassies in the Diplomatic Bag. Dido knew who my contacts were, and she would arrange for the documents to be handled in whichever country was involved. It's only been five countries, Bulgaria, Romania, Slovenia, Hungary or FYR Macedonia. A week or two after I sent the passports out they would come back to me, again in the diplomatic bag. Just like all the routine consular business. Even now I'm in HR no one takes any notice of the correspondence I send and receive. I'd put them in a padded envelop and

310

take them back to the shop where I'd collected them. That's the last I'd see of them.

"For each document I was paid a thousand pounds. I was paid another two thousand pounds every month to pay my people. They get, got, four hundred pounds each a month regardless of how many documents they handled. The money was always in cash, used notes, coming to me through the same shop. I sent the payments out in the diplomatic bag as well."

"What about your own payments, Jas? Where's the money you received?" Julia asked.

"It's all gone. It only ever amounted to four or five thousand a month. London's an expensive place. My husband has expensive tastes. My family expects me to have a certain lifestyle. The money just about covered my extra outgoings."

Julia was looking at the documents spread out on the table in front of her. She made a note of the names, passport numbers, and any other details. She also noted the travel details.

"Where are all these for, Jas?" she asked.

"All for Sofia. They have to be there this week."

"Who's your contact in Sofia?"

Jasmira told her. The contact was UK-based staff posted to Sofia, a junior officer in the consular section. Julia wrote down the contact's name and number.

"Right, Jas. I want you to do it, exactly as you normally would." Julia passed the documents back to Jasmira across the table. "But this is the last time. I need to warn you that if you tell Strathdon or Dido Sykes about this meeting or our conversation there is a very real possibility that they will kill you. Dido has

311

already killed Bijan Bukani and tried to kill his successor. I think she's also killed two other people in the last twenty-four hours. She's a very dangerous woman, and Strathdon is a very dangerous man. I'm not telling you this to scare you, Jasmira. I'm telling you because I have a duty to, and also because it is true.

"If you let me down in any way at all I'll be coming for you and you will go to jail for forty years. You might prefer a meeting with Dido to that, but at least with forty years there's a chance you might come through it alive. Am I making myself clear?"

"Yes," Jasmira said softly. "What about afterwards, when I've done as you've asked?"

"You'll be arrested. Your cooperation will be a mitigating factor. It's up to the Attorney General, but I won't be fighting it if your legal team put up a case for immunity. I can't make any promises, you know that."

"And my job?"

"Really, Jasmira? You need to ask? You'll be needing that family of yours once the dust settles. Now, I'm going to give you a number to contact me. It's my outer office number and whoever answers it can get a message to me wherever I am at any time. I want to know the minute you've sent the documents. Don't use any phone that Dido or Drew gave you. Call on an FCO phone through the switchboard to the Scotland Yard one, using the government phone network. Do you understand?"

Jasmira nodded.

"Right. I'll see you out. Don't mess me about, Jas, this is serious business."

Julia walked Jasmira out of the building. When she was done she called Mel.

"We need to talk, all of us and urgently."

"OK. My place, one hour," Mel said.

Chapter 48

Mel got there first. Julia was next, and Alf followed her in a few minutes later. He looked serious.

"I don't want to worry you, Jake," he started, "but I think you had a tail. Just one man on his own, and he's not one of the good guys."

"I didn't see anyone." Jake said.

"OK. You two stay here until I call or come back. I'll take a key, so don't let anyone in at all, do you understand?"

Julia nodded. Mel looked worried.

Alf let himself out. He was wearing his builder's clothes and presumably he had his van nearby. Alf took the long way back towards Raynes Park station. He saw the man he had noticed earlier. He was sitting in the very seat that Alf had used several times before in the pub from where he could watch the comings and goings around the station. He was relieved to find that the man hadn't managed to place Julia in Mel's building.

Alf sized the man up. He was well-built, slightly above average height, with a chiselled unsmiling face. He exuded a hostile air and people in the pub were leaving him well alone. He was sipping at a fizzy water and keeping watch out of the window. He was menacing, not subtle, and Alf didn't like the look of him at all. He didn't want to do it, but he'd have to use Julia as bait.

Alf went to his van, which was parked in a side street nearby. He started it and was able to pull up near the pub, on yellow lines with his hazard lights flashing. He busied himself at the back of the van. He called Julia. As instructed, she walked briskly towards the station. His van was facing her, close to the kerb. The man in the pub rose as he saw her and started to follow her, closing the gap. Alarm bells were ringing in Alf's head. The man didn't have any intention of following Jake; he meant to harm her.

Alf timed it well. As the man approached Alf swung the back door of the van open as fast and hard as he could. There was a resounding thud as the man walked straight into it. Alf closed the door and looked down. The man was dazed but furious. He was struggling to get up. Alf didn't wait. The trusty lump hammer pounded into the man's head, splitting it wide open. A second, equally hard blow, finished him off. He lay bleeding on the pavement. People were starting to gather. Any doubts Alf may have had were dispelled as he glimpsed the grip of a handgun in a holster under the man's shoulder. A long-bladed knife fell from his sleeve.

Alf mumbled something in Portuguese and leapt into the van. He sped off, knowing he had taken a massive but necessary risk. He could hear sirens. Alf had scouted the back streets and alleys in the area and he knew where he was going. He stopped by a block of run-down garages. He removed his outer overall and threw it into the van. He doused the rear of the van with white spirit and the remnants of a can of diesel fuel. A match was all it took and the van was well alight in a few minutes, by which time he was long gone.

An hour later he was back at Mel's. He had gone back to his hotel, showered and changed. Julia was sitting in a chair. Mel was at the table, red-eyed.

"I've no doubt at all he was hostile," Alf started.

"Me neither," said Jake, "I'll find out what I can about him later. Best not get involved for now. If he was a hit-man it's a worry."

"Let's not speculate for now," Alf said. "What was it you wanted to talk about?"

Julia told them about the events earlier that day, and about everything Jasmira Shah had said.

"So, we've got four passports on the way to Sofia. They should be there late tomorrow. We need to find the girls they relate to, which means letting the delivery of the passports take place. I think you need to be there, Alf. Use the name Jamie Linmouth with the Embassy contact and then hook up with Luan Krasniqi. It'll fit with the line you've taken about taking over his business. He'll be furious, and wary. I've spoken to Hugh Cavendish at Vauxhall. He's going to give you a bit of local support, trusted contacts who won't ask questions, especially about an Albanian gangster. Try to get hold of the girls and leave Krasniqi to them.

"There's an International Office for Migration team in Sofia. IOM will take care of the girls and get them to a place of safety. Once that's done you'll need to get the hell out of there."

"OK," said Alf, "how do I make contact with the local support?"

"You don't. They'll be keeping tabs on the Embassy official who'll be handling the passports. They'll pick you up. You shouldn't be aware that they're there."

"That's all a bit ad hoc, Jake," he said.

"It's all we've got. Sorry. I'm sure you'll manage."

316

"What will you be doing?"

"I need Drew Strathdon back in London. I want him and Sykes locked up. I've got Shah writing down everything she can remember about each and every person she helped facilitate into the UK. I'm putting a team together to track them all down, those who are left that is."

"What about me?" Mel asked.

Jake stood and went to her. She gave her a hug.

"You've done enough already. You've pulled all this together. It's time for the rough stuff now. But if you're really wanting something to do...."

"I know. I'll get the bloody drinks in!"

******

In her hotel room at Canary Wharf Christine Leclerc was furious. She had had a response to her contract. Someone who said they had a handle on Kelso and planned to deal with her that day. The person had taken a deposit and she hadn't heard from him since. The cheating bastard had better be dead already, she thought. She went on to the dark web again and took out another contract on the person who she believed had swindled her out of fifty thousand US. A message flashed up to say that a rumour was going round that the 'swindler' had been killed in an incident in south west London. No further details. Christine Leclerc decided that Kelso and Silva would have to wait. She had the conversions to finalise, and then she had to disappear.

******

Paulo Silva had decided not to use his own name to travel. He was disturbed by the presence of a professional killer on Julia Kelso's tail, and if his current assessment of Dido Sykes was anything like correct she was a clever and resourceful enemy. He didn't want to advertise his movements. He was loitering on the tube station platform at Heathrow. He saw what he was looking for. A man on his own. Clearly tired and distracted, equally clearly just off a plane. He had British Airways tags on his shoulder bag, several of them. He was a frequent traveller. More importantly he was around the same height, age and build of Paulo Silva himself. Facially he was close enough too.

Paulo sat in the same train carriage as the man, who had fallen asleep. His bag was on the floor between his feet. Paulo could see the corner of a red passport sticking out. Paulo stood to let a woman take his seat. The train was pulling away from Hammersmith and was filling up with people. The train lurched. Paulo fell forward slightly, apologising to the people nearby who he had inadvertently jostled. He got off the train at the next stop, Baron's Court, and hopped on to a waiting District Line service. The stolen passport was safely tucked in his jacket pocket.

Paulo, or Stewart Ellis as he temporarily was, went to a travel agent in Earls' Court and bought a business class ticket to Sofia for the following morning. He paid cash but used the stolen passport as identification. He was hoping that the tired man wouldn't notice it was missing until he was on the ground in Bulgaria.

On the flight he feigned sleep and didn't speak to anyone. He passed through immigration and braced himself for the hazardous cab ride into town. He had chosen a different hotel this time but didn't plan to stay the night if he could avoid it.

As soon as he was clear of the taxi he made a call to a local mobile number from a phone booth. The Embassy official answered.

"This is Jamie. You've got something for me." It was a statement, not a question.

"Yes."

"I'll be on a park bench by the art gallery in twenty minutes exactly. I'm wearing a blue raincoat." He hung up.

Exactly twenty minutes later a young man approached him nervously. He had a package under his jacket, barely concealed.

"Jamie?"

Paulo nodded and held his hand out. The young man handed the package over and turned away. He walked off. Paulo noticed two men who had appeared in the park shortly after the young man, presumably they were his 'local support'. They were leather jacketed, of course, and reassuringly lumpy.

Paulo walked to the Radisson. He made sure Krasniqi wasn't there, and then he called his mobile from a payphone.

"Luan. It's Paulo. I've got what you need for the conversions. You know where to find me." He hung up and waited.

Ten minutes later Krasniqi's BMW pulled up. He was in the back, with two gorillas in the front. He approached Paulo.

"First things first, Luan. Get rid of the staff and get in the driving seat. If you don't do what I say you're not getting the conversions. Oh, and you won't be alive tonight."

Krasniqi glowered. Reluctantly he complied and the gorillas stepped down from the vehicle.

"Tell them to wait for you here. You won't be long," Paulo instructed.

Luan Krasniqi said something in Albanian. The two thugs shrugged and sat down, ordering coffees as they did so.

Paulo and Luan got into the car.

"I need to see the girls. I want to know what I'm investing in. You said two were in your apartment. Get the other two there as well. I've not got long so get on with it," Paulo said.

Luan made a phone call.

"Fifteen minutes," he said.

"That's about right. Let's drive."

The car made its way through the city and started the climb up the slopes of Vitosha. After almost exactly fifteen minutes they pulled up at Krasniqi's apartment building. A second BMW was parked outside it.

Paulo followed Luan in and rode with him in the lift to his floor. Luan looked jumpy and anxious. He unlocked the door to his apartment. Paulo followed him inside.

There was no sign of any girls. Two more large men sat on sofas in the sitting room.

"Where are they?" Paulo asked.

"In their rooms," Luan said.

"Show me."

Luan led the way. Behind one door was a pretty blonde girl, no more than seventeen, who turned and smiled nervously at Luan. Three more girls were in other rooms. One on her own, the other two together.

"Very good, Luan. I like your taste. I'll go and get the things you need for the conversion. I wasn't going to bring them with me. All the arrangements are made. One girl leaves this evening, two tomorrow and the last one on Saturday. Different routes of course. You'll be in London with me to meet them."

"I'm not going to London," Krasniqi said.

"Suit yourself. I'll meet them on my own then, but I'll need some information from you. I'll probably come back for another chat, or maybe I won't need to. You see, Luan, apart from your sweet talk with the girls I'm not sure what it is you bring to this operation."

Krasniqi was stunned. He started shouting. The two thugs in the sitting room rose and started coming towards them. Paulo really hoped his 'local support' was up to the mark. He darted past Krasniqi and opened the apartment door.

The two men from the park burst in. With silenced pistols they took out the two thugs. One of them then shot Luan Krasniqi between the eyes. Paulo nodded. The whole thing had taken just a few seconds.

Paulo went back to the bedrooms and gathered the girls. The 'local support' had thoughtfully dragged the bodies into another room.

Paulo spoke to the girls slowly and in English.

"Luan is not what he says he is. He is a criminal who tricks girls into going to London where they are forced to be sex slaves, prostitutes. That is what he had planned for you. Do you understand?"

They all nodded.

"I was thinking it was not right," the young blonde one said. "Now I see I am not the only one here it makes sense, what you say."

"I'm going to get you to a safe place. Nothing bad will happen to you now. People will help you, either to go back to your families or to make a new start."

One of the girls was crying quietly. The blonde nodded. She said a few words to the others.

Paulo picked up Luan's car keys and led the girls down to the vehicle. The 'local support' got into their own car.

"Follow us," one of them said to Paulo, "we show you where the IOM is."

Half an hour later the four girls were in the caring hands of IOM staffers and on their way to a new life.

Paulo decided to hang on to Krasniqi's car. He headed south out of the city on the E79 towards Greece. By evening he was at the border post at Kulata. Rather than try to cross into Greece in Krasniqi's BMW he found a hotel for the night. The following morning he bought a ticket for the train to Thessaloniki. By early afternoon he was on a plane to Paris, and being within the Schengen travel area he had no need to use his passport. He got the last Eurostar of the day back to London, treating himself to a few drinks to celebrate. His shoulder bag had the envelope with the passports and travel documents for the four girls. If the 'local support' hadn't have

322

worked out Paulo had no doubt that by now he would be dead, and the girls would be on their way to a life of slavery. He ordered another drink from the stewardess as the train entered the tunnel under the English Channel.

Chapter 49

Alf eventually arrived back in Raynes Park. He had called Mel and taken some extravagant precautions to make sure he wasn't being followed. As far as he could see he wasn't, and nor was there any obvious surveillance activity anywhere near Mel's building. She let him in. As expected, Jake was also there. Jake hugged him.

"All done. Krasniqi is no more, the girls are safe. Here are all the documents you got from Shah. Now I need a shower." He placed a large envelope on the table.

"Hugh's friends turned up, I take it," Jake said.

"Thankfully yes. If they hadn't I wouldn't be here. Krasniqi wasn't at all happy to see me. If he'd got his hands on the passports it would have been all over."

Mel handed him a large tumbler of whisky and a bath towel. He disappeared with both and came back ten minutes later. The whisky had gone and he had the towel wrapped around his waist.

"Sorry, no clean clothes," he said.

"You said that last time. I think you're just a secret flasher," Mel said. "So, what next?"

"I need to get Drew Strathdon to London. I want him to call a crash meet with Dido. I want to get them both together," Jake said.

"How are you going to do that?" Mel asked.

"I've got a couple of ideas. I'm going to sleep on it and decide tomorrow."

"How about I go and get him?" Alf asked. "I know what he looks like and where he lives. I think if he got a visit from Paulo Silva he might run back to Dido, don't you?"

"He might, but he might just vanish. I don't want to fuck this up again, not now." Jake was distracted. "I should go. I need to think."

"I'm not sure you should, Jake," Mel said, "after that business yesterday you've no idea who might be looking for you. If someone picked you up and followed you here they could well have found your apartment."

"I'm with Mel," Alf said, "until we've finished this you shouldn't go home, at least not alone. And before you even think it that doesn't mean you can go there with Mel. You know I can't be seen with you. So you're here for now, or in a hotel."

"It's too late to get a hotel," Mel added.

"Talking of which, I should get back to mine," Alf said.

"I put your shirt in the washing machine while you were in the shower," Mel said, "sorry."

Alf laughed.

"I'll get the duvet," he said.

Mel looked at Jake, quite content with the outcome.

******

The following morning Jake had relaxed, thanks in no small part to Mel's nocturnal ministrations. She had decided what she wanted to do.

"You go to Brussels, Alf," she said, "get Strathdon back here to meet with Dido. Just don't tell me how you're going to do it."

"Sure," Alf said.

He finished his toast and coffee, put his clean shirt on and got a minicab to Gatwick. There he hired a mid-range saloon car and headed off towards the Channel Tunnel and the car shuttle. He paused in Belgium only to buy a sandwich, a bottle of water, two pocket-sized canisters of mace spray, and a very realistic replica Walther PPK, just in case. He was in Brussels less than two hours after leaving Calais. He parked near Strathdon's apartment block and sent Jake a text. She acknowledged. He waited.

Back in London Mel and Jake had spent the morning deep in thought and discussion. As ever, Mel's organised mind helped Jake put her action plan in order. Mel had been quietly working on analysis of communications and whatever historic emails she had been able to recover. Piecing them all together she had narrowed down likely geographical locations for the brothels run by the various crime groups using Dido Sykes' services. They were all in or near London. Mel had also been able to estimate the number of gangsters and girls involved and had even found names for a few of the hired helpers. She found lots of references to the 'director', the seedy pornographer Bernard Croxley, and had discussed his activities with the encyclopaedic Barbara in the NCIS porn unit. Her view was that some of Croxley's recent offerings overstepped the bounds of legality and he was now in play for multiple charges of assault and rape.

Mel had been in contact with an old friend at Europol whose wife's brother was something high-up in the EU's technology department. Mel asked if he could check out the names on the four passports they had to see if they were on the missing persons database. If not, could they have a look at archived back-up tapes for the past week or so to see if they had been on the database and if they had been why they weren't there now.

The contact came back and said the four names had been removed out of hours on a terminal in the legal affairs department of the Migration Directorate. No reason could be found.

"That's great," Mel had said, "it's what we thought. Now, could you get your brother-in-law to see if he can find other names that have been removed from or restored to the database in the same way, going back as far as possible?"

"What is it with you Brits?" her contact grumbled, "whenever we Europeans give you an inch you demand another bloody mile?"

"Just ask yourself why you're moaning at me about this in English," Mel said.

"Fair point," the contact said.

"I'll make it up to you. Bye now." Mel hung up.

Julia Kelso mapped out an arrest and search plan designed to locate and rescue as many trafficking victims as possible and take into custody everyone involved in their incarceration and exploitation. But the people she really wanted were Sykes and Strathdon.

She called Errol. She asked him to tail Jasmira Shah and be ready to take her into custody when Julia gave him the nod. She didn't want Shah on the loose when she brought Strathdon and Sykes into play. It wouldn't be safe for her. Dido would have no compunction about killing Shah to silence her, and

Julia was sure that Jasmira would give evidence in exchange for leniency, if not immunity.

Once she was satisfied and she had her teams lined up she sent a short text message to Silva.

"Go" it said.

******

Silva waited a while longer. He hadn't seen Strathdon enter or leave the building. Then he saw a movement at the third-floor window, the window of Drew's apartment. He was inside. Paulo walked swiftly into the lobby and ignored the reception desk. He went straight to the elevators and rode up to the third floor. He knocked briskly on Strathdon's door, or the door he assumed was Strathdon's on account of the floor layout. Strathdon opened it. He wasn't looking his best.

Drew Strathdon hadn't shaved and he looked tired and drawn. He looked at Paulo blankly.

"Hello Drew," Paulo said, "late night?"

Silva leant on the door as Strathdon tried to slam it. He forced it open.

"We haven't met. My name is Paulo Silva. No doubt Dido has told you about me."

Strathdon couldn't hide his shock.

"It's time the three of us had a sensible discussion about our business arrangements. There have been some changes. Luan Krasniqi is dead. I have the four girls, the 'conversions' as you call them. I am the Sofia operation now, and pretty soon I'll have the other four operations as well. I'm not seeing what it is you do exactly to earn your thirty percent after costs, which works out nearer sixty percent of the profits. It's time we renegotiated.

"I want you to call Dido now and set up a meeting this evening in London. Then we'll go and see her. Use your phone and do it now."

"And if I don't?"

Paulo sighed and produced the Walther pistol.

"Is she really worth it, Drew?" he asked.

"You don't know her."

"I know enough. Now do as you're told and call her. If you know anything at all about incentives you'll know that it's better to think something bad might happen to you in future than to know something bad will definitely happen to you right now. Your choice."

Strathdon picked up his phone and pressed a speed dial button. As he did so Silva also pressed a speed dial button on his own phone.

"Put her on speaker," he told Strathdon.

Dido's voice was tinny but clear enough. Mel and Julia could hear her relayed through Silva's phone to a mobile phone in Julia's office.

"Why are you calling me?" Sykes asked without any greeting or preamble.

"It's urgent. We need to meet. Silva is here in my apartment."

"Silva? What does he want?"

"He says Sofia is finished, dead, and he has the conversions and the papers. He wants to discuss the business arrangement."

"What have you told him?" Dido hissed.

"Nothing. He knows everything anyway."

There was a pause.

"OK. We'll meet this evening."

"In a public place," Silva interjected.

"In front of the London Eye at 8pm this evening." Dido's phone went dead.

"OK," Paulo said to Strathdon, "let's go. You're driving."

Chapter 50

Dido Sykes was alarmed. Drew would never call her like that unless he was under extreme duress. The whole enterprise was crumbling. Time for her to go.

She set up her laptop and got to work. First, she booked a private charter flight in the name of Christine Leclerc from Luton Airport to Le Bourget in Paris. Then she booked a busines class seat on an Air France flight from Charles de Gaulle to Frankfurt, this time in the name shown on her Canadian passport which had arrived via her bank a day earlier. Her final flight booking was on Lufthansa, a first-class seat to Boston's Logan Airport departing the following day.

She transferred her connection to the dark web. She rescinded her contract on Kelso and Silva. Instead, she sent an instant message to an established contact with an exclusive line in short-notice assassinations, at a very high price. The contact was a former US Special Forces veteran who lived in the back of beyond in the far west of the United States. Dido had no idea who he was, and she didn't want to. She had used his service a few times, most recently to terminate Bijan Bukani and then Colin Savernake and his wife. She felt a momentary pang of sadness, even regret, but then asked the person to dispose of Drew Strathdon and Paulo Silva in just a few hours time in Central London. It was a tall order, but the contact said an arrangement could be made. The fee was astronomical, but Dido agreed. She added Julia Kelso to the contract, at a time and place of the contact's choosing, as long as it was within four weeks. A further large amount of money was transferred to an offshore account. Dido disconnected.

She left her hotel room wearing the clothes she stood up in and carrying only a shoulder bag containing her new identity, clean underwear and a few credit cards. There was also a large amount of cash. Another flat bag held her existing mobile phones and the laptop she had been using.

Dido, or rather Christine Leclerc, boarded a river bus at Canary Wharf. The flat bag slipped quietly from her hand into the brown waters of the Thames as the river bus docked. She alighted at Embankment Pier and took the underground to Kings Cross. There she got a taxi to Luton Airport's general aviation terminal. She was in Paris two hours later. Another taxi took her to Charles de Gaulle airport. In the toilets of the business class lounge her Christine Leclerc passport was torn to shreds and flushed down the pan. She spent the night in an airport hotel at Frankfurt and at lunchtime the following day, East Coast time, she was in a rental car heading for her substantial house north of Boston in the foothills of the White Mountains. Dido Sykes and Christine Leclerc were no more.

******

While Dido was preparing to disappear Drew Strathdon and Paulo Silva were passing a tense but uneventful journey from Brussels to London. They didn't speak. They drove through the business class lane to the shuttle. They stayed in the car. Silva made Strathdon drive all the way to Central London, ordering him to pull up near the Imperial War Museum. It was already dark. The clock moved slowly towards 8pm. When it was time Paulo drove them towards Waterloo and the London Eye, the massive Ferris wheel installed for the millennium and seemingly destined to remain in place forever. There weren't many people around.

Paulo spotted the Special Branch team, but there was no sign of Dido Sykes. A few large teenagers were messing around on BMX bikes and skateboards. Paulo's attention was drawn to a pair of them who seemed not to be enjoying themselves much. They were circling slowly but scanning the faces in the crowd ceaselessly. Paulo sensed the hand of Dido Sykes. He stopped the car.

"Out you get, Strathdon," he said.

"What about you? Aren't you coming?" Strathdon asked.

"I wouldn't be that stupid!" Paulo said.

Strathdon had opened the door. Paulo gave him a hard push and he half tumbled out on to the pavement. As soon as Strathdon was clear Paulo gunned the engine and drove away. One of the BMX bikes tried to intercept him but wasn't quick enough. The other BMX bike was involved in a race against Errol Spelman and one of his team, both of whom had drawn their weapons and were sprinting toward Drew Strathdon.

The BMX biker saw sense and pulled back. He disappeared rapidly along the embankment towards the cover of the crowds going into the National Film Theatre and the many bars and cafés surrounding it.

Errol let him go. Handcuffs locked on Andrew Strathdon's wrists.

Errol called Julia. She was already at Belgravia Police Station with the sobbing Jasmira Shah.

"Looks like Sykes has done a runner. We got Strathdon. There were a couple of hoods who looked like they'd been hired to either spring him or top him. They got away. You say the meet was only set up a few hours ago?"

"That's what I heard," Julia said.

"Well," said Errol, "to get any kind of hit team in place in that time frame is almost impossible. I'm not surprised it didn't work. Anyway, we're bringing Strathdon to you now. We let the car he arrived in go, as you said. It looked like a minicab. We can follow it up later if you want."

"Thanks Errol. Nice one. It's a shame about Dido Sykes, but I'll get her one day. See you in a bit."

And so it started to get wrapped up. Jasmira Shah couldn't say enough to help, even going so far as to draw up a list of all the names and nationalities she could remember. The list grew long, and Julia shuddered to think of all the young people who had been duped and sentenced to an unthinkable life of pain and torture, just to make a few people obscenely rich.

Strathdon almost fainted when Julia Kelso walked into the interview room where he was being held. She showed him the four passports she had and told him exactly when, where and how he had obtained them.

"Dido's dumped you, Drew," she said, "according to the guys who brought you in there was a hit team looking to take you out. It could only have been Dido who set that up, Drew. She wanted you dead." Julia said this calmly.

Strathdon sat quietly, his legal brain assessing his options.

"What am I looking at, Julia?" he asked.

"Conspiracy to rape, kidnap and murder. Misconduct in a public office. Numerous offences in Belgium. I've got enough, Drew, to prove all the UK stuff. Jasmira's been very helpful. We've got the EU's IT people doing a forensic search of your missing persons database, the one you set up ostensibly to make recovery of missing people easier but in fact the idea was always to facilitate trafficking of young girls as sex slaves. You're going away, Drew. For a very long time."

He sat quietly.

"It was all Dido's idea. I'll talk, tell you everything, but I want a lawyer. Have you arrested Paulo Silva?"

"Who's Paulo Silva?" Julia asked. "I've never heard of him."

Chapter 51

Julia and Mel collected Kim from hospital. Kim was weak and needed a wheelchair. Her skin was even more yellow than when Julia had last seen her. Nevertheless she smiled happily as she was pushed to a waiting taxi. It wasn't a long ride to the airport, nor a long flight to Cork. Kim and Julia sat together in the front row of the plane with Mel in the row behind.

Julia filled Kim in on events.

"So who was it tipping off the scumbags every time we were going to raid them?" Kim asked.

"Colin Savernake," Julia said, "he made sure he had all the advance notices of planned operations. He knew where all the houses serviced by Dido Sykes's gang were."

"So the fucker could have stopped it?"

"Yes. Any time he wanted."

"I'll kill the bastard!"

"Too late, Kim. Someone beat you and me to it."

Mel and Julia helped Kim off the plane to the waiting wheelchair and a few minutes later they were in the arrivals hall.

Ben and Sarah, Kim's twins, ran across the concourse in a very un-adolescent way. They bent to hug their mother, Sarah crying with joy. Flora stood quietly and shyly a few feet away beside a dark-haired woman with a friendly smile and lively intelligent eyes. Julia walked to Flora and hugged her. The dark haired woman extended her hand.

"Roisin," she said, "Flora's been teaching me to cook."

"I'm Julia, and this is Mel. The twins' mum is a friend, we've brought her to see them." Julia smiled.

"Thomas told me some of the background. The kids are settling in well and will be starting school next term. Flora's grand and good company. We've loads of room for Kim too. It is Kim, isn't it?

"Yes. She's not well and she'll need a lot of looking after. It's good to know she can stay on for a while. It'll help settle her for the road ahead." Julia was looking at Kim and her kids, who were so thrilled to see each other.

"Shall we go?" Roisin asked.

Roisin led them to the car park where the old blue VW camper van was parked. It had bright red L plates front and back. Flora beamed with pride.

"I will drive us," she said.

Roisin sat in front alongside Flora. Kim was planted on one of the bench seats in the back with the kids squeezed in either side of her. Mel and Julia sat on the other bench. Flora drove carefully, coping with the VW's idiosyncratic gearbox very well.

"Home is about half an hour. I've put the children and Flora in the big guest cottage. There's a downstairs bedroom with its own bathroom in there, so I thought Kim might want to bunk down there too. We've plenty of room in the house for you two if you're staying over, which you're very welcome to do." Roisin was chatting away to Mel and Julia, pointing out sights. Kim and the twins were deeply engrossed in their own conversation. They pulled into the drive of the old manor house and Flora brought the van to a halt. She grinned.

"Not too scary, I hope." She leapt out and went to help Kim.

"Flora's doing really well, Julia," Roisin said. "When she arrived she would hardly speak and was scared of everything and everyone. She's great with the children, half mother and half sister. They've borne up well, been very brave without their mum. I'm so glad she's here now."

"You're being very kind to them." Julia stated.

"Not a bit of it. Thomas asked a favour of us. We're always more than happy to help him, after what he did for us. My uncle would be dead these many years without Thomas. He's as good as family now."

"I'm sure he'd be very happy to know that." Julia said. Mel was watching the exchange closely.

"He's close to you then?" Roisin asked.

"To both of us," Julia nodded towards Mel, "he's special to both of us."

Roisin's eyes flicked between the two women, but she said nothing.

"Let's get everyone inside. I thought we'd all have dinner in the house this evening then leave Kim and the gruesome twosome to their own devices."

The twins grinned at the description. The evening was welcoming and warm. Kim stated at the outset that she wasn't well and the bloody doctors had put her on the waggon, so just water and soft drinks for her. She was sure Julia and Mel could manage her share of the wine.

After dinner Roisin showed Mel and Julia to their rooms.

"You're sharing a bathroom, and there's a small sitting room you can use too. Treat it as home. Thomas said you're a gin-monster, Julia. It was very rude of him, I know, but we've put a bottle in the sitting room. There's a fridge in there too with ice and tonic."

"I'll be having words with Thomas about impugning my reputation when I see him! Mel's actually worse than me."

Roisin left them to it.

"You're quiet Mel. Everything alright?" Julia gave Mel's hand a squeeze.

"I'm fine. It's just these last few weeks have been a strain. I've found it hard. Let's have a drink and talk rubbish for a bit, shall we?"

******

As Julia and Mel started on the gin 'Thomas', otherwise Alf, Declan, Paulo and god knows who else, was in a drawing room in Donnybrook, Dublin. Eugene Flynn sat on the opposite side of the chessboard. He looked distracted.

"Can we pause for a while, Thomas, we need to talk."

"Is everything alright, Eugene?" 'Thomas asked.

"Yes and no. I think there's danger for you, and for your friends. I asked the lads to keep an eye on things for me, down in Cork. Roisin knows. She doesn't question me. There was some unhealthy interest in your friends when they arrived. The lads are impressed, by the way, with your taste. They said one was a 'blonde bombshell' and the other 'drop-dead gorgeous'. Too conspicuous for Cork in the winter, I'm afraid.

"The lads noticed someone trying to tail them from the airport. They had a word. It seems that a couple of gombeen gobshites from up near Dundalk are out to make a name for themselves. During their chat with my lads they let slip that there's some crazy American trying to organise a mishap for your blonde friend, as well as for some man called Paulo Silva. I don't know anyone of that name, but I do know someone who fits his description. The gobshites said the American has put in place a contract, a big one, but because there's very little notice of the blonde's movements everything's a bit haphazard.

"As it happens, I know of this crazy American. He's a veteran who lives in an old shack somewhere in the mountains of Colorado or some such place. He runs an assassination agency. Realistically it sometimes helps to know people like that, but this is too close to home. I've had a word in certain quarters and Grizzly Adams will be getting a visit from the Feds in the next day or two. Meanwhile, the gobshites had a nasty accident on the road back up to Dundalk. They'll be sorely missed."

"When was this accident, Eugene? My friends only arrived a few hours ago."

"It happened any minute now. Seriously, Thomas. The crazy American doesn't come cheap. Whoever hired him will be seriously out of pocket, so is unlikely to simply give up. I don't want to seem inhospitable, but I think your friends should leave Cork first thing in the morning. My lads aren't resourced for round the clock active service for more than a day or two. I think you need to go too. You know what you've been involved in, and who you've upset. Go and sort it all out, then come back and we'll finish the game. I'd like to meet your friends too. I want to find out what attracts beautiful women to bad chess players who can't stop singing after just one bottle of Bushmills."

"Thank you, Eugene. Can Roisin get them to the airport in the morning?"

"She can and will. I'll call her to book flights for them."

"It's a long story, Eugene, and I'll tell you when we've a few days to spare. For now, can I ask a favour?"

"You can always ask. It doesn't mean I'll do it." Eugene was smiling.

"Kim, the mother of the twins staying with Roisin, is very ill. To be frank she needs a lot of medical care and will do so for the rest of her life. She's all the kids have, and I want to make sure they'll all be alright financially. Can we do a fund for them, like we did for Etienne McMorrow?"

"Of course. That's no problem."

"There's Flora too. She's got no papers. Kim and the children are all she has."

"Roisin's already raised the matter of Flora. In a few days she'll be getting an EU passport from somewhere or other. She'll need to get used to a new name. Once she has it she's as good as Irish and we can get her 'regularised'. I'll put some money her way too, of course. Let's face it, Thomas, it's not like you're short of it, now."

341

******

Two weeks later Julia was driving herself and Mel along the M5 in Devon. The motorway petered out and they progressed along the A38 for a while before slowing on to smaller roads leading towards the coast. It had been a long drive from London. Mel hadn't said much, but only because Julia had been on the car phone pretty much all the way. The investigation following the arrest of Drew Strathdon and Jasmira Shah was progressing rapidly. All of Jasmira's minions had been recalled to London and arrested.

Julia had given Mel's communication mapping data to one of her teams and they had identified and closed down six brothels so far. More than thirty girls had been recovered and the same number of foreign and British gangsters had been nabbed. The slimy pornographer Bernard Croxley had been arrested mid-shoot during the making of a very violent video. All the active participants had been charged with rape and GBH and were remanded in custody getting to know their fellow inmates.

Eventually the phone signal died and Julia disconnected the phone.

"Sorry about that. So many loose ends. Now we can have a few days off." Julia turned to smile at Mel.

"Are you sure you don't want some time on your own with him?" Mel asked. " It's going to feel a bit strange, the three of us together again."

Given the threat against Julia she and Mel had decided to move into a serviced apartment in Central London until they could get something more individual and permanent fixed up. They had effectively been living together.

"I mean, don't get me wrong, Jake, the last week or so's been great. I've really liked being with you, but I'm not good at sharing so much. I'm a day or two away from screaming, and not in a good way. I could happily just go off and read a book somewhere."

"He'd be disappointed not to have some time with you. I've been very happy at the flat, happier than I've been in a long time. Spending evenings with you, and nights, has been wonderful. I really like making love with you, too."

"You know I don't do that, Jake. I have sex at most."

"Tomayto / tomato, call it what you want. All I know is I enjoy it, and unless you're a very good faker you do too. It's been different, sleeping with you every night after work and everything, not like the odd weekend and night here and there. It feels good. I enjoy making love with Alf too. So do you, you told me, and he likes it as well. It's nice to be enfolded in big strong hairy arms from time to time. Not that yours aren't strong and hairy. Ow! That really hurt!"

Mel chuckled.

"This is all a bit bonkers. I did ask Alf once, not long after I'd bounced you two into bed together. I asked him if he liked the thought of you and me having sex. He said he did. He also said he liked having sex with you and with me. Then I asked him if he liked fucking you more than he liked fucking me."

"What did he say?"

"He told me to shut up."

"Quite right too. We're nearly there. Let's just see how it goes. We follow your rules, you know. No one does anything they don't want to do."

Julia pulled up in the drive of a large, secluded house overlooking the Dart estuary. It was an out-of-season holiday let that Declan had rented for two months so he could 'write'. He opened the door when he heard the car.

He was delighted to see them both and carried their compact luggage into the house. The sitting room had a large terrace which gave on to the river, and even in the failing light the view was stunning.

"I've got dinner," he said, "and before you start panicking it's frozen. I've just got to stick it in the oven. Drinks?"

They sat on the terrace huddled together under a blanket and beneath a patio heater. Mel and Jake were either side of Alf. They didn't feel especially talkative, which suited them all nicely. After an un-disastrous meal they started to unwind and talk, mostly about the case at first but later about their respective plans for and thoughts about the year ahead.

When the time came Mel excused herself and went up to bed. She lay in the room she had chosen and waited for the sounds of Jake and Alf to subside, then she got up and went to their room. She slipped into the massive bed beside them, snuggled up close against Jake's naked back and fell into a deep sleep.

They awoke as the weak winter sun lit the bedroom. It was directly above the sitting room and had a similar but slightly smaller terrace overlooking the river. Mel picked Jake's robe off the floor, put it on and went down to get some coffee. When she returned with a tray laden with coffee and toast Jake was standing at the window looking down on the river. Alf was behind her, his arms wrapped around her. He kissed her neck. Mel put down the tray and stood next to them enjoying their contentment. It was a perfect morning.

Far away, across the river, a camera shutter clicked rapidly as a long lens focused on the three figures standing close together in the house on the opposite bank.

******

Across the deep cold Atlantic the woman who used to be Dido Sykes looked at the images as she sipped her green tea. It was early in New Hampshire. She studied them closely. She could see Kelso's face clearly. She was standing with her back leaning into Paulo Silva, whose arms rested protectively on her bare shoulders. The one with the light brown hair was slightly to one side looking at both of them, smiling. Dido re-read the message which came with the pictures. She typed her reply, just three words: "All of them!"

Other books in this series by Jo Calman

Book 1 : A Transfer of Power

Calman writes with the authority of someone who has worked across law enforcement. Characters with depth and accurate locations brought the book to life. It's a long time since I read a book in one sitting, but once I started, I wanted more – reader NW

Book 2: A Price for Mercy

Thoroughly enjoyed Jo Calman's latest book and can highly recommend it. There's no waffle, just action, excitement and a chance to re-connect with Kelso, Dunn and Ferdinand. Awaiting the next one with bated breath. Thank you Jo!- reader Donna

Available now on Amazon

or through

www.jo-calman.com

Printed in Great Britain
by Amazon